OE'

D0980948

San Funea Sena (X2)

Simen Oe

MORE PRAISE FOR DARA JOY!

REJAR

"Dara Joy . . . sets our hearts ablaze with a romance of in-candescent brilliance. An electrifying talent, Ms. Joy delivers a knockout love story in which the romance is red-hot and the adventure out of this world. In a word, wow!"

—*Romantic Times*

HIGH ENERGY

"The bright, shining star of fabulous new author Dara Joy gains added luster with this scintillating romance. . . . One of the most delightful courtship romances of the year, sparkling with intelligence and wit to please the most discriminating of readers. A joy indeed!"

—*Romantic Times*

KNIGHT OF A TRILLION STARS

"Dara Joy . . . writes with a wit, warmth and intelligence that will have readers flocking. . . . A full-bodied love story brimming with fiery sensuality and emotional intensity."

—*Romantic Times*

Tyberius Augustus Evans
and
Zanita Masterson
Cordially invite you
To join them
In a
Ghostly Mystery
To be solved
At
The Florencia Inn
On
Martha's Vineyard.

R.S.V.P.
BLACK JEANS OPTIONAL

HIGH INTENSITY

DARA JOY

LEISURE BOOKS NEW YORK CITY

A LEISURE BOOK®

August 2000

Published by

Dorchester Publishing Co., Inc.
276 Fifth Avenue
New York, NY 10001

ISBN 0-8439-4747-0

The name "Leisure Books" and the stylized "L" with design are trademarks of Dorchester Publishing Co., Inc.

Printed in the United States of America.

To Elegant Edward,

You are riding that Orient Express in heaven, drinking fine champagne and lychees, surrounded by cats and Steuben glass, saying in that droll voice with a big theatrical sigh, "Dara, darling, will it ever end?"

You brought magic and dance and such wonderful wit to my door—a guardian angel in the guise of a friend. I can still hear your laugh. You were kindness, Ed, and I will miss you always.

HIGH INTENSITY

"Yield to temptation; it may not pass your way again."
—Robert A. Heinlein *(The Notebooks of Lazarus Long)*

Introducing this episode's guest cat:

Hippolito . . .

Chapter One

"I'll have the steak bomb."

Tyberius Augustus Evans, renowned theoretical physicist, sat back in his seat with an expression that said his universe was about to display a fascinating exposition on the principle of Chaos.

This expression was directed at the love of his life, Zanita Masterson, with whom he associated the very foundation of modern physics. From his experience in the field of Mastersonmatics, he was positive he was about to witness a wondrous spectacle.

He leaned further back in his seat to patiently observe the "event."

Blithely unaware of her paramour's absorbed visage, Zanita gazed up at the waiter and asked sweetly, "It comes with cheese, onion, peppers, and mushrooms, doesn't it?"

The waiter smiled back, completely unaware of the fate that was about to befall him. The corners of Tyber's sensuous lips curved. *We have ignition, Houston.*

"Yes, ma'am," the young man chirped.

"I don't want any peppers." She smiled up at him.

"All right." The waiter smiled back as he wrote down "no peppers" on the order. Tyber snorted and waited tolerantly. He was not to be disappointed.

"And . . . instead of regular onions, can I have caramelized ones?"

"Sure." He scratched on his pad and started to turn to Tyber for his order. Tyber did not even glance at his menu. He knew they were not even close to entering a trajectory to planet Zanita. Touchdown was nowhere in sight.

As if on cue, Zanita said, "You know what—I think I'll have mashed potatoes instead of the fries!"

The waiter paused ever so slightly before he began to write. "Uh-huh."

Tyber began his countdown. *Ten . . . nine . . . eight . . .*

Zanita bit her lip as she scrutinized the menu. "Ummm . . . put some avocado on that, too."

"Avocado?" The waiter's eyes popped out.

Zanita nodded. He scribbled "avocado." Tyber

16

snorted and continued counting. *Three . . . two . . . one . . .*

"Oh, and forget the roll."

The waiter stopped and stared at her, dumbstruck. "B-but it—it's a sandwich!"

Lift offffff! Tyber's ice blue eyes flashed in silent appreciation of the fabulous display of entropy. With Zanita, disorder had a certain order to it.

Zanita waved her hand to indicate that such details were unimportant in her scheme of reality. Tyber grinned, displaying two curved dimples, as he turned to the dazed waiter.

"I'll have the chicken salad sandwich."

The waiter swallowed, pen poised over the tablet, ready for the Euclidian translation. "And . . . ?"

"That's it."

The young man gratefully took their menus and beat a hasty retreat.

"I'm starving." Zanita smiled at Tyber as she ran the toe of her shoe over his jean-clad ankle.

Tyber cocked his eyebrow at her, then picked up a glass of water and slowly sipped it. "And here I thought this was just a ruse to make me leave the symposium."

"God, Tyber, that was so boring."

"Boring. Marcus Schlammerthimmer happens to be one of the foremost minds in nanotechnology; he—"

17

Zanita slipped off her shoe and strummed her foot up the inside seam of his jean-clad leg. "—is boring."

Tyber sucked in his breath and gave her a firm look that said he was not going to be distracted. At least not until they finished lunch. "Okay, I admit he is a bit on the long-winded side but he—"

Zanita wiggled her toes against his muscular thigh. Tyber had spectacular thighs. And that was but one in a line of many spectacular attributes in the extraordinary Evans package.

Zanita's thoughts went to what the man had done to her that morning when she had awakened in his bed, completely tangled up with him. His long chestnut hair, tousled from sleep, had swung forward as he leaned over her. He had used the tips of his hair to torture her mercilessly as he brought her to peak several times.

As usual, he had taken her thoroughly, displaying that innate pirate streak in him. Mischievous devil.

Unlike any other man she had ever met, Tyberius Augustus Evans, renowned eccentric, constantly made her crazy for him. More than once she wondered about the sensational level of excitement in their relationship. The passion didn't seem to be lessening at all. In fact, against all odds, it seemed to be increasing.

After many such incredible mornings with

him—as well as afternoons, evenings, and middle of the nights—Zanita had come to the decision that she was not going to do anything to tamper with the status quo of their relationship. She wanted them to stay just as they were—wild for each other.

Why take a chance and mess with perfection? she reasoned.

And it was perfection . . .

Zanita took a dainty little breath in an attempt to disguise her rapidly escalating pulse.

She suspected her ruse didn't work when those bedroom blue eyes gleamed at her.

She knew positively that it hadn't worked when the "dimple of hidden knowledge" appeared next to the curve of his well-formed lips.

Zanita was very familiar with the dimple of hidden knowledge. After all, the man was not simply a genius. He was an aware genius.

Which made it very difficult for her to get away with anything.

She frowned in annoyance. The sexy scientist was too sharp for his own good! Or rather, her own good. "You should be thanking me for rescuing us."

Tyber's eyebrows arched in amusement. "Really."

She nodded. "Instead of hearing about polywogs and nurks, you get to enjoy a simple lunch and an afternoon of shopping."

"That's polygons and nurbs." His lips twitched.

"Whatever. This is so much more relaxing."

Behind Zanita's back, the door to the kitchen suddenly banged open. An irate chef stood in the doorway, hands on hips, white hat crushed in one fist. He glared at the waiter beside him, who sheepishly pointed in Zanita's direction.

Tyber had no trouble reading his lips. "I might have known it was her!" He rolled his eyes and stormed back into his culinary sanctuary.

Tyber noted the observation with his customary enjoyment. Simple lunch? With Zanita? Like a guided missile, his unforgettable "Curls" struck fast and without warning. Often the exact target was a total enigma to all except she who controlled the inertial guidance system.

Once, she had rewritten the recipe for chicken marsala and had ended up with a whole new color combination for food. The striped effect was still a mystery to him.

There were all kinds of things flying around Zanita's head. Sometimes they landed. Tyber adored her.

Oblivious to the scene that had just taken place behind her, Zanita continued on with what she considered to be excellent plans for their afternoon in the city. While Cambridge had its academic interests, it also had some very unique shops. ". . . so I thought we could check out that new boutique that specializes in porcelain . . ."

Boutique? Tyber sat still in his seat. Where had that topic come from? "Baby, there is a lecture on hybrid radiosity at three o'clock that I want to—"

". . . dragons," she finished.

Tyber hesitated a beat. "Dragons?"

"Uh-huh." She took a sip of her coffee. "All the stuff you like, too, from what I hear. When I called for directions, they told me they just got a shipment in from England; you know, that artist you love?"

"Hmmm."

Zanita smiled prettily at him.

Tyber narrowed his eyes. "And just when did you call for directions?"

"About ten minutes after the lecture started. Remember when I went to the restroom?"

Tyber watched her with guarded fascination, saying nothing.

"Well, as soon as Schlimmerdimmer opened his mouth, I could tell this was going to be a real waste of time, so I decided to change our plans." She took another sip of coffee.

He couldn't suppress the smile that curved his mouth. "The man's name is Schlammerhimmer . . . I think."

Zanita waved her hand, erasing the man's

21

name from their frame of reality, not to mention the rest of their afternoon. The memory of the lecture gave her a twinge of pain. The man barely spoke above a whisper, only used the obscure terms spoken behind locked labs, and, worse, had the annoying habit of making weird honking noises in his throat whenever he paused in his speech. Which was every three minutes.

"Tell the truth, Tyber, you'd much rather go to that shop than listen to him get lost in his own importance. Besides, who knew what he was talking about?"

Tyber gave her a look. "You know, I am a theoretical physicist, sweetheart. Occasionally we like to indulge our wild side and listen to such lectures."

Zanita popped a piece of buttered roll into her mouth. "Speaking of wild side, Tyber, when are we going to investigate that ghost sighting you told me about at that tavern on Martha's Vineyard?"

The ghost sighting on Martha's Vineyard . . . he had told her about that when he had been trying to come up with something—anything—that would make her stay with him after they had finished their first investigation of the phony psychic healer, Xavier LaLeche. The two of them had joined forces and hearts on that case.

Initially, Tyber had simply agreed to help her investigation as a way of starting up a relationship with her—when she wasn't looking. Zanita had been opposed to any kind of relationship, so he had to tread very carefully, letting her think that he was not her boyfriend. While all the time, he was exactly that.

It had been a brilliant plan. If a bit bizarre.

But then he was known for his brilliance.

He was also known for his unique solutions. Pirate solutions.

This solution, however, was about to jump back and bite him on his parameter ram, so to speak. It appeared his Curls was not going to forget about the next investigation.

Not that he'd thought for one minute she would.

Zanita was a reporter with their small-town newspaper, *The Patriot Sun*. She was also a woman who liked to explore the unknown. Hell, she was with him, which was the "unknown" at its finest!

Tyber was very aware that he was considered an eccentric. He was also aware that his lady love was just enough of an oddball to make what they had together perfect. Or nearly perfect.

The waiter arrived with their plates, placing Tyber's in front of him. "A chicken salad sandwich," he announced loudly.

Then he turned to Zanita and gingerly placed her dish down, mumbling quietly, "And a . . . steak bomb."

Zanita looked down at the jumbled plate of food, and her eyes glittered like a predator's just before it strikes its prey.

"Anything else with that?" the waiter asked apprehensively.

"Worcestershire sauce."

Tyber choked on his water.

"Worcestershire . . . Right away, ma'am." The waiter sped off and immediately returned with a bottle of the sauce. He quickly placed it in front of her before another wacky request issued forth from those soft, full lips.

Zanita happily slathered sauce over the mess, slapping the back of the bottle with a prize-fighter's determination.

"I think Blooey is spoiling you," Tyber murmured.

Blooey was Tyber's all-around man and cook. He was also an ex-mathematician named Arthur Bloomberg who had gone slightly over the edge during his research with imaginary numbers. In Arthur's case, the study of imaginary numbers had the unfortunate tendency to illuminate the existential spirit. He couldn't find the "point" anymore.

So he left the building.

Now, the man was convinced he was on a pirate ship and Tyber was his captain.

Which was surprisingly close to a certain reality.

Tyberius Augustus Evans often looked like one, spoke like one, acted like one, and made love like one. In other words, once the rogue boarded, he gave no quarter. The man was ruthlessly sensual.

Zanita finished dousing her concoction with the Worcestershire sauce. "Don't be silly, Doc, Blooey hates when I add anything to his 'grub,' and you didn't answer my question."

Tyber put down his sandwich and regarded her intently. "Then we're even."

Zanita paused, hand in the air, holding the upside-down bottle. "What do you mean?"

"Our wedding," was all he said.

"Wh-what about it?" Zanita had been dreading this topic.

Tyber exhaled noisily. He spaced each word with the pause of importance. "When—are—we—getting—married?"

She swallowed. "Ummm, this looks great, don't you think?"

"Stop trying to change the subject. May I remind you that you asked me? I am going to hold you to this, Zanita—when is it going to be?"

Zanita's shoulders sank.

"Why are you suddenly so skittish?" He had already figured out the answer to that but he was setting a nice Evans trap. His love was hedging a wee bit too much. He recognized the signs. Parabolic Maelstrom was approaching. He intended to do everything he could to subvert it.

Zanita reached across the table and placed her hand over his. "Tyber, everything is going so great between us."

"And . . . ?" he prodded.

"Well, I'm afraid if we change anything, we'll lose what we have."

"You mean if we get married."

She bowed her head. "Yes."

Tyber looked down at the top of the short, black, curly mop and shook his head. She was nonlinear thinking at its finest.

"Baby, it will only get better once we are married."

She shook her head in tiny negation.

Tyber leaned forward. This was the one part he hadn't been able to figure out—exactly what was motivating her. "Why do you think that?"

"Because once we are married the romance will die," she said in a knowledgeable voice.

Tyber's lips parted in astonishment. "Where did you ever get that idea?"

She raised her enormous violet eyes to his. "I just read it somewhere—maybe in *TV Guide*."

"The ...

"Yes, be...

Now there...

logic.

Not.

Even though he ... ea-
son, he had expected ... these
lines. Not only expected ... ared for
it. He reached into the back ... of his jeans
and slapped several folded ...ers onto the
table.

"What are those?"

"Take a look at them."

Gingerly, Zanita picked them up. Her mouth
fell open when she saw what they were. A marriage license and several computer readouts
which clearly stated that they were married on
today's date at five p.m.!

There was a computer copy of the same
license, which stated that their marriage had
been witnessed by Judge Jockey and his assistant, Ms. Skootch. There were other sheets
which confirmed their marital status; even a

. . . onight," he said softly.

. . . ould have had a conniption

. . . ng Zanita, reacted true to her . . . y. In other words, she failed to see the . . . because she was fascinated by the pat- . . . ns of the leaves.

A tingle washed over her. She shivered with a reporter's delight at having made a discovery. She gazed up at him, eyes gleaming with awe, and reverently said the very last thing he expected. "You're a hacker!"

He rubbed his ear in embarrassment. "Ahhh . . . no, no, I'm not."

Zanita raised a skeptical brow, not even deigning to give the denial a whiff of belief. "This is incredible! You know, I suspected when you got those LaLeche files from the FBI, but this! How did you get the marriage license and the other documents? It all looks genuine."

"It is."

Now she frowned at him.

"Well . . . in one sense. I did this as an experiment, baby."

"What kind of experiment?" she asked warily. Zanita was very familiar with the Doc's experiments.

He held up his hand to forestall her objection.

28

"Don't worry, I put in an executable code which will go into effect in five days. It undoes all this."

"*What?*"

"I have five days to prove to you that you are wrong."

"What if I'm not?"

"We go back to the way we are now, and only you and I will know about our marriage. All proof will be wiped clean. But I am positive I can convince you to stay married."

As ideas went, this was a lulu. Zanita was not amused. "So if I win, there is no proof that we are married and we go on as we are?"

"Exactly." He grinned outrageously at her. "Fits your requirements to a tee, baby. Don't you love it?"

Her nostrils flared in rising temper. "Brilliant as usual." She stirred her coffee briskly. "Now tell me why you did such an outrageous thing before I bash your skewed head in!"

His square jaw dropped. "I told you, I can make it all disappear with a few keystrokes. I simply want to prove to you that nothing will change between us. I want to give you a test opportunity to show you that your theory of romance is wrong. That was all I wanted to do."

"But don't you see, Tyber, if I know that we are not really married, it won't work. The excitement will still be there."

He tried not to cross his eyes. He knew from experience how to deal with his love. "But we will be married, baby. For the next five days, actually four and a half, you will be Mrs. Evans."

"What happens after the five days go by?"

"I put a delete code into the executable . . ." He stopped suddenly before he revealed too much. He wasn't called a pirate for nothing. "Let's just say it all goes to the way it should be."

Zanita thought about the strange plan, wondering if it could work. It sounded interesting . . . maybe it would work.

Pressing his advantage, Tyber lowered his voice to a sexy purr. "I'll be sure to live up to my part." He smiled lazily at her. "Every chance I get."

Zanita gulped. A Tyber who was even more motivated was sure to be trouble. And she knew for whom. It was a radical experiment; she shouldn't even consider it.

On the other hand, Tyber had been dragging his feet on their next investigation. It was almost as if the man didn't want to investigate the ghost! Since she couldn't imagine anyone not being as excited as she was by the prospect, she brushed the silly thought away.

For whatever reason, Evans was procrastinating.

She drummed her fingertips on the table top.

This might be a good way to get him involved.

His observations were always right on the mark, and his keen mind was quick to put forward alternative explanations for events that seemed to have no logical explanation. His input was invaluable on these investigations, and she was not about to let him off the hook!

Besides, he was too damn sexy to leave at home.

A girl knew what to pack when she traveled, and stunning, sensual male was at the top of the list.

She narrowed her eyes at him.

Damn. Not the violet slits! Tyber inwardly steeled himself. The violet slits were always trouble. He waited patiently for the other foot to fall. She was up to something.

"What about our investigation of the ghost on Martha's Vineyard?"

Now Tyber's blues narrowed to icy sparks. The adversaries faced each other like two cutthroats on the bounding main. He called her bluff across the sea of food. "What about it?"

She hitched her shoulders preparing to fire at will. "Well, what's it going to be, Captain?"

He slowly gazed up at the ceiling, examining the painted cloud formations. He watched the wind catch at the billowing curtains—which began to look like sails. A pulse ticked in his maurader's jaw as he weighed the advantages.

31

"Very well. We'll investigate the 'ghost' and you'll be my wench . . . ah, wife." He raised his brows at her in challenge.

Zanita's eyes gleamed in satisfaction. "For five days."

"We'll see."

With those ominous words, he lifted his goblet of milk, saluted her with it, and chugged it down.

Zanita acknowledged the agreement by ramming her steak slice with her fork. It wasn't easy living with a pirate, but she was learning how to deal with him when he set a course to Kooksville. *Temporary marriage.* She hid her smile by taking a big bite of meat.

Seemed apropos.

Tyber rolled his red pickup truck to a stop in front of the iron gates that barred his Victorian mansion from the overly inquisitive.

According to the clock, they were now married.

She frowned. *How had she let him talk her into this?*

The sign on the gate read "My Father's Mansion."

Zanita remembered the first time she had ridden up to these gates, the distinct impression she'd had that her life was about to change forever. And it had.

She had been invited by Dr. Evans to what she had thought was a pool party. Tyberius Augustus

Evans was a renowned recluse, an eccentric genius who valued his privacy above all else.

Back then, she had been interested in obtaining an interview with the elusive physicist.

Back then, he had been interested strictly in her.

She had soon found out that the "pool party" was in actuality a private party for two engineered by the playful Doctor. Not that she had minded.

She never did get the interview.

But she did get the Doctor. Since that very first night, he had taken her into his world.

Tyber rolled down the window and pressed the button under the intercom panel by the gate.

"Did you leave the remote in the house, Tyber?"

"Nope. You might say this is an Easter egg in the Evans video game of life."

"An Easter egg? What does that have to do with—"

His features took on a mysterious, gleeful cast. "Never mind, baby. Just want to keep that old scalawag on his toes."

Static burst through the grill along with a squawk. A raspy voice fraught with irritation boomed through the intercom. "Blast and damnation!"

Zanita's lips curled. They were the exact same words Blooey had used the first time she had pressed that button.

"Who be ye, friend or foe? And ye better be friend for ye pulled me away from swabbing the kitchen decks and now that rapscallion Hambone is skidding across the floor like a bloody ice dancer! Speak up, I say, or I'll blast ye where ye stand!"

Tyber chuckled. Blooey, his all-around "man," gave idiosyncrasy a whole new definition.

"Stand to, sailor," Tyber's deep voice drawled. "We're coming aboard."

"Blast, Captain! I knows ye got that thigga-jig what opens the plank!"

"Of course."

"Then why did ye go bothering me?" the voice boomed, getting louder as it reached the end.

"Because I could." Tyber grinned outright.

A snort came over the intercom. "That ye can. C'mon wit ye then."

The gate squeaked open.

Zanita shook her head. She often wondered who was nuttier—the two eccentrics she lived with or herself for enjoying them so.

Tyber pulled through the gates.

A topiary dragon winked at them as they rolled over the cobblestone drive that snaked through the woods. The dragon was followed by other mythological creatures, all ensconced in the tree-lined glade that opened before them. Gnomes, winged cats, dragons galore, a three-headed beastie, and a mysterious wizard who seemed to be presiding over them all.

For some unknown reason, Tyber had claimed the wizard's name was Yaniff. Zanita had shrugged her shoulders. It would not be the first odd thing associated with this man.

After they passed the mazes, the gardens came into view. Though not in bloom during the dead of winter, they still echoed the magnificence that would be theirs in a few months.

The smaller ponds were frozen over.

Zanita grinned as she remembered that she had looked out of an upstairs window a few days ago and caught the cat, Hambone, sliding across the surface on his ample belly. The one-eyed pirate cat seemed to be enjoying it tremendously, for he repeated the antic countless times while she watched.

Tyber had heard her laughing and had come over to the window behind her. His strong arms had embraced her as he pulled her back to him and nuzzled her short curls. "Mmmm, what's so funny out there?"

"Hambone. He's belly flopping across the ice."

She could feel his smile against her hair. "He does that every winter, the bandit."

Now, at night, the ponds were empty of gleefully sinister belly-surfing cats.

A gaggle of Canada-geese flew overhead,

honking in syncopated gripe as the house came into view. Zanita always wondered why they bothered to fly anywhere if all they did was continually bitch about it. *Geesh*.

They passed the white gazebo. Once, before the snows had come, Tyber had made love to her there. She shivered at the luscious memory. He had been so incredibly passionate that day. So unbound.

Whatever his state, her physicist lover was always a force to be reckoned with. In the beginning, Tyber had made it his personal mission to "instruct" her on the mystery of physics; or more specifically, the practical applications.

And, oh, what practical applications he invented!

His technique seemed to be working, for damned if she wasn't learning the eggheaded subject. Although she seriously doubted that Newton or Einstein had been referring to what Tyber did when he "illustrated" the priciples.

One thing she knew for certain: when Tyber got that special gleam in his eye, he was preparing to give her one of his "exclusive" lessons. Torrid. Shameless. And with a concept, too. What girl could ask for anything more?

As they rounded the last bend in the cobblestone drive, the house came into view. Like the man, it was unique in every way. A Victorian mansion with seven turrets, it was decorated like a true painted lady in multiple shades of pastel colors.

Gingerbread trim bedecked the framework along with intricately carved original woodwork of flowers, ropes, and bows. Decorated garlands, which had been lovingly carved over a century ago, had been lovingly restored by the present owner.

For all his wildness, there was something about Tyber that conveyed a sense of permanence. Even with his maverick ways, the man was someone you could depend on. He had proved that to her during their investigation of Xavier LaLeche. The slick con man had proved no match for Dr. Evans. Tyber had outmatched him both in brains and brawn.

The wraparound porch had been decorated for the winter season with tiny lights strung through the intricate fretwork banisters. Ambient light shone through the beautiful stained-glass windows to dance across the snow-covered ground. It looked charming and warm.

It looked like home.

The car had not even come to a complete stop before the wide wooden front doors were thrown open and an incensed Blooey glared at Tyber from the doorway.

Tyber did not even bat an eye. "Something bothering you, seaman?"

Tyber always took great care to address

Blooey in the language he preferred. Namely, pirate-speak. That Tyber enjoyed their idiosyncratic exchanges was a moot point. Sometimes lately, Zanita suspected that the strange gleam in the little ex-mathematician's eye was delighted whimsy.

Yep, she was living in a nuthouse.

"We got to do something about that scurvy Hambone, Captain! He being nothing but a common brethren, not like meself, who has been elevated in importance by way of me fine cookin—"

"Excellent cooking," Tyber agreed amiably as he helped Zanita from the truck and winked at her.

"Just so, sir." Blooey nodded, causing his cap to list over his right ear. "What are ye going to do wit him, Captain?"

"Do?" They all walked into the hallway. Zanita removed her coat and hung it on the hall tree, her glance going to the inviting fire Blooey had lit in the parlor. Tyber strode over to the hall table to check the mail.

"Aye! *Do*. The bilge rat needs to be brought to heel, Captain."

Tyber's lips curled slightly at the corners as he continued to peruse his mail, throwing the letters into different to-do stacks. Zanita glanced over at the table and wondered how the man stayed so organized. She had one-hundredth of

38

the correspondence he did, and her desk was the leaning tower of Pisa.

"What did he do this time, Blooey, besides belly flop across the just-washed floor?"

Blooey closed one eye and glared at him with the other. It was an expression the little pirate had perfected. Zanita admitted it did make him look as if he were ready to swing a grappling hook, knife clutched between his differentially equationed teeth as he prepared to attack.

"Why, the varmint snatched me potted balls!"

Tyber almost choked. *"Your what?"*

"Me potted balls, Captain. And right big ones they are, too."

"No doubt," Tyber agreed warily, giving his cook an odd look.

Zanita snickered as she stretched her hands out to the fire, letting the flames warm the chill out of them.

"Not a right thing for a fellow member of the brotherhood to do. What do the articles say about such things, Captain?"

"Hmmm, the articles . . ."

The only articles Tyber was aware that the former Arthur Bloomberg read were the ones that appeared in scientific journals. Then he saw that Blooey was referring to the articles of the Brethren, which all self-respecting pirates and marauders abided by.

Tyber stroked his jaw. "The articles say that if

he's quick enough to get away with it, then the booty is his."

Blooey glowered darkly, almost looking as if he were about to pull out a cutlass.

His captain stared him down. "The key phrase is: if he's quick enough. Are you saying you are not fast enough to stop him?"

Blooey's mouth pursed. "But, Captain, he ain't no ordinary seaman! He's a sneaky bilge rat when he's in a certain mood!"

"Show him the error of his ways. I'll warrant that'll cure the problem."

Blooey narrowed his eyes. "And how am I to do that?"

Tyber gave the cook a knowing smirk as he reached over to the mail table and opened a small drawer. He pulled out a large pistol.

Blooey's eyes gleamed. "A pistol, Captain?"

"Aye. Shoot the bugger if he gets near the countertops. Like so . . ." Tyber demonstrated by pulling the trigger. A spray of water spewed across the room, hitting Zanita squarely on the back of the neck.

"Hey!"

Zanita glared at them over her shoulder. Blooey and Tyber chuckled, looking like co-conspirators in some nefarious plot.

She stuck her tongue out at them and gave them her back.

Tyber shook his head, his focus now on the

nicely curved backside presented to him. And when Tyberius Augustus Evans was focused, he was focused.

"Almost forgot to tell you, Captain, there is a message for ye."

"Hmmm?" Tyber slanted his head to the side to observe Zanita's derriere as it wiggled in front of the flames. She had always been a sucker for a roaring fire.

Which was why he had instructed Blooey to always make sure one was lit in the parlor and their bedroom during the fall and winter.

He smiled. Aye, he was a dastardly rogue. The derriere wiggled some more.

"A man by the name of Hubble called. Said that there is one other investigator besides him coming to the tavern this weekend and he just wanted to let you know. Mentioned something about the other side; didn't get that one, Captain."

"That's okay, Blooey. I think I know what he meant."

Zanita looked up from the flames and blinked. "A man named Hubble is investigating the ghost, too? Hubble like the astronomer? That is too funny."

"I suppose that sums up the whole tone of the investigation right there, baby, doesn't it?" Tyber grinned.

Her shoulders scrunched. "Tyber, you promised to be objective!"

"And so I shall."

Zanita crossed her arms over her chest. "I don't mean physicist objective—that's not the same."

His blue eyes twinkled. "Would you care to explain that?"

"Not just yet."

"Mmmm."

"Who is this Hubble anyway?"

"He's a skeptical observer. Comes from the Society for Cognitive Reasoning. They have some kind of catchy nickname, but I can't think of it right now."

"Why is he getting involved? Did you call him?"

"Of course I did," he said evenly. "I want everyone to know I'm investigating a ghost. So just to be sure, I also called Princeton, *Omni* magazine, and the National Science Foundation."

She decided to call that one dry wit. "So who called him?"

"The inn's owner. Guess he wanted to cover all the bases. I don't even want to know who the other investigator is; it might be someone with snakes and rattles."

Zanita was not happy with the Hubble addition. "Great. This is just what we need! The Grand Inquisitor breathing down our necks."

Tyber crossed his arms languidly over his chest. "He won't get near your neck, baby. I promise."

"Hmf."

"Or any other of your pretty parts."

"Hmf."

"Especially this chilly little . . ." He ran his palm over her backside.

"Tyber!"

Chapter Two

"Synthetic flesh! Synthetic flesh!"

Tyber and Zanita were sitting in the den, watching a really bad horror flick. They both sighed in bliss.

Each had assumed his or her usual favorite position. Zanita was stretched across the couch and Tyber was sitting on the floor in front of her, using the couch as a backrest. The position afforded the physicist the perfect vantage point to tickle Zanita whenever the mood struck him. Which was often. Yet in a random, unpredictable pattern.

Zanita would then retaliate by lifting the heavy fall of his gold-streaked chestnut hair to blow lightly on the back of his neck. Even though she was not a physicist, she knew the

44

exact pressure and force to use to cause tingles to skitter down his back.

He was still shivering from the last "attack" and trying to hide it.

Each took great delight in torturing the other with this game of hit-and-run seduction. It was a subtle yet devastating way to drive each other crazy.

During the next commercial, Tyber reached back over his head and lightly brushed the side of her left breast, then pretended he was reaching for the *TV Guide* to see what else was on.

He grinned when he heard her low gasp.

"What have you uncovered so far about this 'ghost,' Curls? And I hope you realize how much I love you. Hunting ghosts is not exactly a proper pastime for a respected physicist."

Zanita looked down at the top of his head, incredulous. "Tyber, everyone knows you're a kook."

Tyber threw her a look over his shoulder. Which was wasted, because Zanita was thinking about their investigation and her agile mind was already working on possibilities.

"Perhaps, but I am a *respected* kook," he grumbled to the TV picture. "I mean, eccentric."

Zanita ignored that. "The problem is that the spirit seems to be munching on the guests food—top gourmet kind only. He leaves the meat-and-potatoes fare behind for the plebeians. This spook is strictly after the gateaus and the ganaches."

For the second time that evening, Tyber almost choked. He turned and spaced his words with precision. "Tell me you are joking?"

He frowned at her when she smiled sweetly at him. "I don't suppose anyone has bothered to check for mice?" he added.

"Don't be silly, Tyber, of course they did, and everything else as well. You asked me what the spirit did, and that's what he does. Along with the usual spooky stuff . . . objects flying through the air, things going bump in the night, fog rolling in the living room . . ."

"Fog rolling in the living room." He stared at her silently through spiky lashes. The picture of disbelief.

"I'm surprised you don't know more about the case, since you were the one who suggested it."

He had the grace to look away guiltily at the reminder. Yes, he had presented it to her in the hope that she would hang around long enough for him to snag her. It was a typical pirate ploy and had worked reasonably well.

Until it backfired.

Actually, he hadn't done any in-depth research on the case. One of his colleagues, who had just come back from the Vineyard, had mentioned it to him in passing. As he recalled, Stan Mazurski had been snickering in the superior way scientists often have when they know they have the inside handle on the workings of the universe, and all lesser beings who think they see things that go bump in the night are to be treated like naughty children.

Despite his own scientific background, the attitude annoyed Tyber.

Tyberius Augustus Evans was his own man, plain and simple. In short, Tyber would never join any club that would have him as a member. He was a rebel, an individualist, a no-holds-barred rogue, and the only person he answered to was himself.

And . . . a petite, five-foot-something woman who had managed to abscond with his heart.

He glanced again at Zanita, the expression on his enigmatic face a cross between wary resignation and disgruntled interest. He knew he was love's tramp.

Zanita was once more struck by the sheer handsomeness and strength of his masculine features. There were times when the light fell on him in a certain way . . . it always caused her heart to skip a beat. Oh, how she loved Tyberius Augustus Evans! She knew without a doubt that there was no one else in the universe like him.

"What?" she whispered softly to him.

His lids lowered and the icy hot eyes gazed up at her. It was an unconsciously sexy male stare that always made Zanita's toes zing. It had something to do with those eyes . . . those pale blue eyes that had so much fire and intelligence.

Underneath her curiosity, he had felt her passion rising. Like a true brigand, he decided to let it smolder awhile. "Are you telling me that this supposed ghost haunts this inn by gobbling up the haute cuisine?" He burst out laughing. A deep, rich laugh of sheer disbelief.

"Tyber, this is very serious! The ghost is purported to continually mess up the innkeeper's best efforts. He nibbles on the salad nicoise, he polishes off the galantine, and he uncurls the spiral pears!"

"Spiral pears?"

"Not only that, he switches the place settings! Forcing boring people to sit next to each other. It's a dining disaster!"

Tyber clutched his stomach and roared.

"Stop that! It's not funny. I've read about similar cases, only not with . . . food. In Tasmania, there's this dreaded spirit called the Poopoobeedoo—"

"Please, you're killing me here."

Zanita stuck her chin in the air. "It's an ancient legend."

"Uh-huh. Is it related to the dreaded Scooby Doobeedoo?"

"Tyber, if you can't be serious—"

He tried to give her an affronted look. It

wasn't even close. "What do you mean? The Scooby Doobeedoo is a terrible nemesis."

"Oh, really? What does it do?"

"It hums Sinatra off key till it haunts you." A dimple curved his cheek. He pretended to shiver. "Horrible."

Zanita tried not to smile. "For your information, the Poopoobeedoo comes at night and has sex with you."

That made him grin. Broadly. "Well, baby, if I ever have to haunt someone—that's the job I want!"

Zanita threw a sofa pillow at his head. It bounced off the solid Evans IQ and careened into the wall.

"But all our ghost seems to be concerned with is food—"

"*Our* ghost?" He rested his chin in his palm as he leaned on the edge of the couch.

"Ahuh. When people are eating, the haunt changes the aroma of the foods to something awful, he curdles the clotted cream, and then makes rapping noises in the hanging copper pots—especially when the chef is trying to bake a soufflé. They all fall flat!"

Tyber tried to be appropriately serious. "Maybe the chef didn't use enough eggs?"

Zanita snorted. "I don't think so—Todd Sparkling is classically trained. Before this place on the Vineyard, he worked at some of the finest restaurants in Boston. He is a renowned chef. Or he used to be . . . with all of the culinary problems, I'm afraid his reputation is suffering."

"Tsk-tsk." Blooey walked into the room and plopped down in the oversized club chair. "I couldn't help overhearin' Captain. This dastardly devil has got to be stopped! Ain't no worse crime than destroying the artistic creations of a Man of the Ladle."

"Man of the Ladle." Tyber shook his head in an attempt to clear the fiber optics.

"Aye, Captain. 'Tis a serious thing. Next to the oath of the Brethren, I hold it in the highest esteem."

Hambone looked up from licking his fat paw and gave one huge, bored yawn.

"Me and Hambone will have to go wit ye on this one."

Tyber inwardly groaned. This was just what he needed to complete the Tyber flow chart of rational living: a wife who wasn't sure romance and marriage could combine, a whacked-out mathematician who was convinced he was on a pirate ship, and a CAT.

All going to Martha's Vineyard to hunt down a gluttonous ghost.

This time he truly groaned. Fortunately, the sepulchral howl of *"synthetic flesh!"* from the TV drowned out the cry for help.

"When are we leaving, Your Ladyship?" Blooey asked Zanita.

"Tomorrow afternoon. I want to get an early start so we don't miss anything."

Tyber glanced back and forth between the two of them and narrowed his eyes. "Who said all of us are going?"

Five eyes gave him startled looks. That, was if you counted Hambone's one-eyed, mildly interested look as startled. "Slightly intrigued" was a better description. Hambone had a certain threshold of dignity that was never lowered— except for the occasional giblet.

"Don't be silly, Tyber, we already agreed. Remember?" Zanita gave him a meaningful look. "Of course, if you don't think you are up to the challenge . . ."

He gritted his teeth. Oh, he was up to the challenge all right. His wife had no idea what he was up to. A slow piratical grin spread across his gorgeous face. "We go tomorrow. Blooey, call the Florencia Inn and confirm our arrival."

"Aye, aye, Captain!" Blooey hustled off to do his champion's bidding, his step chipper. By contrast, Hambone sagged onto the rug and let out a huge snore.

"Some investigator you're going to be," Tyber muttered to the chubby feline. "All the ghost has

51

to do is offer to share his booty with you and you'll be signing his articles."

The bandit cat opened his one eye to give Tyber a smug look that said, "In the scheme of things, who cares?"

Tyber crossed his arms over his broad chest, raised one eyebrow, and pierced the cat with a knowing stare.

Zanita recognized when the subject was getting away from them. "Tyber, I really think we need to—"

A loud pounding noise sounded at the front door.

"Who could that be at this hour?" Zanita stood up and started toward the door.

Tyber effortlessly rose from the floor, quickly overtaking her. "I'll open the door. We don't know who it might be at this hour."

"But Blooey must have let whoever it is in through the gate, so it stands to reason it must be a friend or a relative."

"That's exactly what I'm concerned about."

Zanita stuck her tongue out at his back as he went to open the door.

Tyber stopped and wagged his finger at her. "Shame on you, baby. You know I'm going to catch that tongue later." He gave her a slow smile. "No telling what I'll do with it."

Zanita could feel the flush rise on her face. Tyber had already opened the door, and her best friend Mills was standing there with her mouth gaping. She had obviously heard him.

Mills was packing. Caught by the scruff of his collar was a squirming, black-haired, green-eyed wolf-child. There was only one little boy that Zanita knew who was that beautiful and that defiant.

Cody Mazurski.

The boy looked and behaved exactly like his wild father.

And neither of them apologized for the imposition.

Zanita found her voice first while Mills was recovering from Tyber's outrageousness. "Mills, what are you doing here at this hour? And why do you have Cody with you?"

The name of the wolf-child was enough to snap Mills back to herself.

"Here!" She thrust Cody through the door. "Take him before that god-awful excuse for a father shows up."

Tyber caught Cody, who grinned up at him smugly.

"I swear the two of them have something cooked up between them! The kid keeps showing up at my shop, then claims he has to wait for Gregor to pick him up. Well, not this time!"

Tyber glanced down at Cody, who wagged his eyebrows up and down à la Groucho. At least the kid tried to contain his snicker.

Mills ran a shaky hand through her hair. "I've got to go—he's liable to show up at any minute, and I'm not in the mood to spar with—"

The sound of a motorcycle zooming down the drive came closer and closer.

"Ah, too late, Mills." Zanita commiserated with her friend as Gregor Mazurski, black-sheep brother of staid physicist Stan Mazurski, turned his cycle around in the drive with a spray of gravel. He was off the bike before it had stopped rumbling.

"Hey, Tyber." He strolled up to the porch and rested against the portico.

"Gregor." The men had become good friends since their initial meeting back when Tyber was helping Zanita go after Xavier LaLeche. Both were outlaws in their own way, and they loved Harleys. For men, this was a basis for a blood-brother friendship.

Gregor glanced over at Mills, his startling green eyes flashing with ill-concealed humor. "Why, if it isn't Miss Priss."

It was obvious that Mills was fuming. Zanita had to admit that when Mills fumed, she did look kind of . . . prissy.

"Why, if it isn't the modern-day answer to the village idiot," Mills shot back.

Tyber gave the thumbs up on that one to Mills.

"Mills, Mills, Mills. Can't believe you absconded with my kid again. What are we going to do with you?" Gregor shook his head and made low clucking sounds with his tongue.

Mills threw him a venomous look.

"You know very well that *you* left him at my shop. Don't even try and deny it. One of my girls saw your motorcycle turn the corner." Mills didn't think it necessary to add the girl's description of Gregor. Something about him being a real babe . . . She exhaled noisily. "Why you two persist in tormenting me, I'll never know."

Cody's lower lip jutted out as if on cue. "You don't like me, Mills?"

Mills was instantly contrite. She adored Cody, but that was beside the point. "Of course I like you, Cody! This has nothing to do with whether or not I like you."

"What exactly does it have to do with?" Gregor leaned against the door frame and purposely baited Zanita's friend.

Zanita snickered. Mills's family roots went back to pre-revolutionary days. She was not going to be flustered by one tall, gorgeous, green-eyed man.

Zanita was not disappointed. Mills put her hands on her hips and stared the miscreant down. "I am not talking to you. The only thing you've ever done in your life worth anything as far as I can see was producing this boy!"

"Really." Gregor bent closer over the porch railing, resting his chin on his arm. He smiled wickedly up at her. "That's good, because I can make a bunch more just like him." He gave her a "wanna see?" expression.

Mills shared a disgusted look with Zanita and stormed past him, heading to her car.

Gregor and Cody watched her every move until she was out of sight, far down the drive; then as one they turned and gave each other the high five.

"Why do you torment her like this, Gregor?" Zanita was smiling.

"Because she's tormentable." He grinned back at her, gave Tyber a half wave, took his son, and left.

Tyber closed the front door. "You know, it would make things a lot easier on us if those two just got together."

"Not going to happen."

"Why not? They seem to be always sniffing around each other."

Zanita grinned. "Did you say sniffing or snipping?"

"Well, either."

"Gregor is sniffing, Mills is snipping."

Tyber shrugged as they went back into the parlor. "Yep. They are complete opposites."

Zanita gave him an incredulous look. "Well, so are we."

"What are you talking about? We are exactly alike."

Zanita's mouth dropped open. "How can you say that? We are nothing alike!"

Tyber sprawled across the couch and pretended to focus on the B movie in front of him. A mad scientist—*probably a physicist*—was attempting to befriend an alien that had the improbable appearance of a set of false teeth with little fluttering wings attached to it. Zanita was already entranced, glued to the set, agog.

"What kind of movies do you like?" he purred.

Zanita's gaze reluctantly flicked to the hunk sprawled next to her on the couch. "That doesn't prove anything."

He never took his eyes from the TV set. "Restaurants?"

"Coincidence."

"Travel?"

"Who doesn't?"

He rolled over on the couch and crooked his finger at her. She bent toward him. He whispered something in her ear.

Zanita blushed. "That has nothing to do with it."

"All right. What about . . ." He murmured something so erotic and so sensual that it was probably illegal in some states.

Zanita gasped. "Quit that!" She jumped up and backed away from the couch a few steps. He winked at her and patted the seat next to him.

"Tyber, you are a scientist. I am a reporter—we are poles apart."

"Nope."

"How do you figure that?"

"We both 'investigate,' you with your reporting, me with my science. We're two peas in a pod, baby. Speaking of pods, let's cuddle while we watch the movie . . ."

She pointed her finger at him. "You have tunnel vision!"

He grinned.

"I'm going to the kitchen to get a snack; want anything?" At the magic word "snack," Hambone lifted his head off the floor, showing sudden interest. "And don't say 'nope,' because whenever you do, you end up eating most of mine."

His smile was pure deviltry. "Nope." He crossed his hands behind his head. "I'm fine."

Zanita rolled her eyes and headed off to the kitchen. He was after her snack!

Tyber chuckled as his focus shifted back to the fickle-hearted alien, which was now delightedly munching on the scientist who had tried to befriend him. "Take a lesson from this, Gregor," he murmured dryly. "You must begin to think of Mills as a set of teeth with wings."

He relaxed back into the couch and fell into that trancelike state most appropriate for watching such a movie.

A few minutes later, Zanita burst into the room, flinging the pocket doors open with a snap. "Tyber! Tyber!"

He raised one brow lazily. "Hmmm?"

"Come quickly! I want to show you something unbelievable!" She grabbed his hand in an attempt to pull him off the couch.

"What is it?" He tried to pull her onto his lap.

"I found a popcorn kernel that looks just like a brain!!! It's got two hemispheres and a convoluted surface and everything! I put it in a ziploc bag so no one would—"

At that moment Blooey walked in munching on a bag of popcorn. A *ziploc* bag of popcorn.

Both Zanita and Tyber stared at him. Zanita's face crumpled into the picture of horror. Tyber's was vastly amused.

"Blooey, that isn't the bag I just left on the counter, is it?"

"Aye, Yer Ladyship. I figured ye changed yer mind the way ye took off, so I availed meself of the bag for the popcorn."

"Stop eating! It could still be in there!"

"Iffen you mean that one kernel ye left, I'm afraid I popped that in me mouth before I poured the rest in. It be lying in Davy Jones' locker now." He patted his potbelly.

Zanita let out a wail.

Chuckling, Tyber refused to let go of her hand when she tugged at it. "A popcorn brain," he murmured, his sensual voice laced with teasing amusement. "What a loss to the world of science."

She yanked her hand free and stormed off to the kitchen to get something else.

Blooey and Tyber stared after her.

"Wimen be strange creatures, Captain."

"Aye, Blooey. That they are. Only some are a mite stranger than others."

"We're a lucky ship, aren't we, sir?"

Tyber laced his hands behind his head. "That we are, sailor. That we are."

Zanita came back a few minutes later with a plate bearing a huge slice of cake. Apparently, losing a scientific find required recompense on a grand scale.

Hambone's nose lifted, testing the worthiness of the possible offering as the plate zoomed by. Quarry tested, he lumbered to his feet, and belly swaying, tried to unobtrusively follow Zanita to the couch.

Cake was prime cat-catch.

The marauder cat swiveled his one eye, like a cannon turret, and tracked the booty.

Meanwhile, as Zanita licked the fork of gooey frosting, Tyber was watching her with a growing . . . desire. This was his wedding night. Even though he was doing his best not to make it seem that it was, like any groom he was more than anticipating it.

"What do you have there, hmmm?" he purred, snuggling in close to her.

Zanita wasn't fooled for a minute. His voice had a real husky edge to it. The Captain was setting a course. He was after the cake! "It's a chocolate chocolate die! die! by chocolate fantasy double blitz cocoa fudge cake."

"Mmmmm . . . Looks good." He seared her with a smoldering look. "Can I have a taste?"

Zanita moved the plate slightly away from him. She had expected this. The snack-stealing rogue! She tried a stalling tactic first. "I got the recipe for Blooey from the Sentinels of Rejar."

That stopped him. "The *who*?"

"The Sentinels of Rejar. They adore chocolate. Once they even made a chocolate . . ." Her cheeks flamed. Her eyes shifted back to the television screen.

"Yes?" The dimples in his cheeks deepened.

Zanita swallowed. "Let's not go there."

"Let's go there," he whispered seductively, letting his hot breath feather against her earlobe . . .

"My God, what is that set of teeth doing to the dog?" Zanita was outraged. The cake almost slid off her lap as she sat forward. It was okay for aliens to munch on scientists, but she drew the line at dogs. Apparently, so did Hollywood, because a flame thrower appeared just in the nick of time to save Spot.

"There's always a flame thrower around somewhere."

"Yep. Aliens never prepare for attack by fire. Wonder why."

"Speaking of fire . . ." His foot slid sexily over her calf.

Zanita turned her head and looked at him knowingly. "How far are you willing to go with the seduction to get the rest of this cake?"

He rubbed his jaw. "Pretty far."

She wagged her finger at him. "I asked you."

"So you did." His arms went around her and he pulled her to him.

Zanita's brow furrowed. "Are you using the cake as an excuse?"

"Ahuh."

"Oh."

His warm lips nibbled the corner of her mouth, where he licked a bit of chocolate frosting. "Mmmm very tasty."

"Umm, let's watch the end of the movie." They had just begun the challenge and Tyber was nowhere near the finish line.

He paused, giving her a thoughtful look. "I'll tell you how it ends. There are these electrical high wires—"

She put her hand on his mouth. "Don't spoil it for me."

"Are you serious?"

"Yes. I want to watch this. It's a prime example of—of cinema orthodontia."

"Uh-huh." He settled back on the couch next to her. After a few minutes, his hand strayed to her lap. With a few misleading strokes, he diverted her attention, nabbing the plate of chocolate cake.

"Tyber!"

"And you fell for it." He grinned the grin of victory as he lifted the fork to his mouth. "Luscious," he whispered as he slowly tasted the sinful desert.

"You—!"

He viewed her out of the corner of his eye. "I wasn't talking about the cake."

"Watch—the—movie."

"I can't."

"Why not?" They were lying in their shell bed and Tyber was of an amorous mind. Perhaps "mind" wasn't the right word.

"Because it's *expected*, Tyber. I don't know if this was such a good idea."

Tyberius Augustus Evans gazed down at his new bride and significantly paled. This was a new glitch. "What are you talking about?"

"I don't know, it's just that . . . I feel different since the program engaged."

This was trouble. He tried a sympathetic

stance with a dash of hurt. "You don't love me anymore, baby?"

"Of course I do! What has that got to do with this?"

He gave her a carefully guarded look—one he had learned to perfect around her when she was in her obscure mode. "Well, what is it then?"

"It's as if we're expected to do this."

He gave her the Mysterious Face of Mars look. "I don't know about anybody else, but I certainly expected it."

"Don't you think it takes away the spontaneity?" She had the nerve to look serious.

A muscle in his jaw began to tick. "Sweetheart, originally it was *you* who asked me to marry you."

Zanita's violet eyes filled with tears. "You—you didn't want to?"

"Yes, dammit! I wanted to!"

Her lower lip quivered. "But you never mentioned it . . ."

Tyber looked up at the ceiling, seeking divine help. At the moment none seemed to be forthcoming. He took a deep breath. "It was on the tip of my tongue." To show her how sincere he was, he showed her his tongue, pointing to the tip.

"But did you really *want* to?"

Tyber sighed. A big, from-his-toes sigh. "Zanita, I wanted to marry you right from the beginning and I had every intention of making sure it happened."

Zanita beamed up at him.

Tyber noted the pleasure in her eyes; he breathed a sigh of relief. With Zanita, his non-linear-thinking love, he could never be sure where the conversation was headed. This was just one of the many reasons why he loved her.

The trait was a continual source of intriguing exasperation. The genius in him loved exasperation. It was the whipped cream to his hot cocoa.

So, he wouldn't have it any other way. Except, on their wedding night, he would have liked to hit the home run before he had to run the bases.

It appeared his response had calmed whatever momentary glitch had hiccuped her system.

He rubbed her nose with his own. "There, now, c'mere, baby, I—"

Two small hands pressed against his broad chest, holding him off as effectively as if they were a human bench press. "No. I just can't."

The Captain narrowed his eyes and glared down at her for a full minute.

Then he rolled over onto his back and groaned. It was not unlike the sound a dog makes when it knows it's dinner time and there is no bowl forthcoming.

Before Tyber realized what was happening, Zanita took the opportunity to scoot off the bed and run across the hall into another bedroom. By the time he was up and in pursuit, the door bolt was already sliding into place.

"Come out."

"No."

Tyber swore, a thing he rarely did.

"I'm sorry, Tyber. I—I just can't."

"I have a key, Curls."

"Don't you dare use it!"

"Zanita, come out of there!"

A door opened down the hallway, and Blooey stuck his stocking-capped head out, followed by Hambone. "Trouble on the mainland, Captain?"

"Promise me you won't come through that door, Tyber!"

Blooey and Hambone gave Tyber expectant looks. After all, Tyber was their Captain, and a hell-born pirate to boot! Would he lose face now before his men?

Tyber put his mouth close to the door and spoke low. "Let me get this straight—you can't because you feel you're supposed to?"

"Exactly."

The Captain knocked his forehead against the wooden door. Twice. He had never seen the broadside coming.

"We need spontaneity!" she called out through the panel.

"I'll give you spontaneity," he warned in a low

voice just before he turned and strode back into the their bedroom.

Zanita bit her lower lip. What did he mean by that?

An Evans storm was coming.

Perhaps she shouldn't have goaded him quite so much. Then again, there was no telling how creative a thwarted pirate could get with only four days to prove his point.

A small smile played about her mouth.

Chapter Three

The trip to the vineyard was torturous.

Blooey was seasick on the ferry, claiming he had to get his sea legs back because he had been "landlocked" for so long. Hambone, true pirate that he was, perched on the very edge of the bow of the boat, the sea spray misting his orange fur. Zanita swore that the cat had a diabolical grin plastered on his mug as he constantly scanned the horizon. She wondered if he was scouring the ocean for fishing boats to attack and board for booty.

Tyber had given her one searing look from under his lashes that morning and never once mentioned last night. She was not fooled. The battle lines had been drawn. Somehow she had awakened in their bed with him wrapped around her. He must have gotten the key to the room while she was sleeping and brought her back. Pirates.

Since it was the beginning of winter, they had probably caught one of the last ferries of the season. If a snowstorm hit during their stay, they would have to see about getting a plane back. As it was, the island was already snowed-kissed; although everyone agreed it was enchanting.

Everyone except Hambone, who issued one of his yawns.

Hambone's yawns could be interpreted in a wealth of ways. There was the "hmm?" yawn. The "so what?" yawn. The "get lost" yawn. The "this is actually interesting sort of" yawn. And the ever popular "I'm yawning" yawn. Zanita wasn't exactly sure which yawn this was but opted for the "this is actually interesting, sort of" yawn.

When they arrived at the inn, Todd Sparkling, the chef/owner of the Florencia Inn, met them at the door. He was one of the younger breed of chefs who enjoyed mixing regions and styles in his cooking; he was very much into "concept cuisine." Everything he produced looked like a miniature work of art—with a fig attached to it.

Chefs had a strange obsession with figs.

"Come in! Come in! Did you have a good trip over?" The dark-haired chef escorted them into the parlor, helping them with their bags and equipment.

Built over 150 years ago, the Florencia Inn was surrounded on all sides by a lovely wrap-around porch. The place was an odd combination of beckoning warmth and pockets of eeriness. Set apart from the seasonally busy Edgartown, the inn was located in Menemsha, a quiet section with gently rolling scrub land

Of course, all of the Vineyard was quiet at this time of year . . . if one didn't count the stray ghost or two kicking it up on the rustic side of the island. Zanita had noted in her research that many ghost sightings seemed to occur around bodies of water, or in places surrounded by water—such as islands.

So this seemed the perfect location for an investigation. Even the name of the place conjured up images of supernatural goings-on.

As they entered the house, she whispered to Tyber, "You know, Menemsha sounds like the ideal location for all kinds of spooky, unearthly things."

He stared at her as if he were checking her sanity.

"Menemmmmmmsha . . . *ooooo* . . ." she moaned.

Tyber placed his hand on the back of her neck and shoved her through the door.

She was undaunted. To add to her theory about the sea and spirits, Zanita had discovered that the water at Menemsha beach was colder than at any other location on the island.

Besides, it was one of the few places in all New England where one could watch the sun set over the water. There was a connection there . . . somewhere. In her mind, this was a perfect place for bananafish and things that go bump in the night.

When she mentioned her findings, Tyber immediately countered her hypothesis.

"You do realize that many of these sightings could simply be electrical disturbances caused by the surrounding water—much like what occurs on the moors in England?" he gave her a Tyberific grin.

She snorted. "Will you give this a chance!"

"And which chance would that be," he murmured before bending down to brush his warm lips across her earlobe. "I am here to investigate"—his hot tongue flicked quickly at the small lobe—"*everything* that goes bump in the night. And I know just where I'm going to start."

Zanita shivered at the spine-tingling touch. "Tyber! Stop that!"

He chuckled low in his throat as he carried the rest of the bags through the door and dropped them in the parlor.

Blooey, still wheezy from the trip, reeled in behind them. Hambone, on a leash, trotted with a lively step beside the little pirate. Zanita had been frankly stunned when Blooey put the leash on the despotic feline and he didn't squawk. Tyber had quickly explained to her the Law of Hambone Motion: Appear to go along with anything that seemed in a cat's best interest, no matter how bizarre.

Feline philosophy—gotta love it!

"Would you like a mini-tour before I show you to your rooms?" Todd asked.

"We'd love it!" Zanita answered for everyone. "It's so lovely here."

"A quick tour would be great. The more we're familiar with the layout, the easier it will be for us to delve into this problem you're having." Zanita noted that Tyber had said "problem," not "ghost." There were some notions that were beyond the scope of even a free-thinking physicist—and it appeared that this was one of them.

The chef beamed with pride at their enthusiasm. From what they had seen of the inn so far, he had every right to be proud. The parlor was a cozy room dominated by a large stone fireplace, flanked on both sides with wooden built-in bookshelves. The decor and style of the house seemed to be reflective of the owner's eclectic taste in cooking. Many different periods were melded together, but rather than being discordant, the decor was homey . . . with a splash of weirdness. Tyber and Zanita loved it.

Todd began showing them around the first level, taking them through the dining room, then the attached greenhouse—fragrant with the many fresh herbs he used in his cooking—and then to the large, professionally equipped kitchen.

Blooey stopped along the way to pick a few lids off the steaming pots. He inhaled appreciatively. " 'Tis a fine concoction yer brewing here, mate."

"Thanks, Blooey. Somehow, after we spoke on the phone, I had feeling you'd be a kindred spirit." Tyber and Zanita covertly glanced at each other. *Kindred spirit?* They doubted Todd had ever put one toe on a pirate ship, especially while solving a set sequence. As far as they knew, neither involved figs.

"I'll show you to your room" Todd went on. "We'll all be gathering in the parlor at seven for drinks. That way everyone can get acquainted before dinner."

"All?" Tyber asked as he glanced out the window facing the back of the inn. Rolling land, lightly dusted with snow, led to a pine forest in the distance. A hundred-year-old stone wall separated the meadow from the woods and seemed to delineate the far perimeter of the land. It was already becoming dark outside. He noted a taller hill some distance from the house, partially hidden by a copse of trees.

"Nice, isn't it?" Todd came up behind him. "It's not an ocean view but I love it."

"I was thinking it's very similar to the property around my house."

"Good old New England vistas. By the way, Gramercy Hubble arrived earlier this afternoon, and Calendula Brite came in just before you. They're freshening up now."

Todd opened a narrow door in the kitchen which led to a well-stocked pantry. Another door at the other end of the pantry led to a fruit cellar.

"So is your mother down there?" Tyber had the nerve to grin.

Todd chuckled. "No, but something else is. On occasion all of the fruits are scattered about. And some of them have gone from pre-peak to rot in just a few hours, for no reason I can tell. The air turns foul, too."

"No other entrances down there, I presume?"

Todd shook his head. "None. And I lock the door when I go up at night. Can't figure it out."

"That's why we're here." Tyber spoke softly.

"Yeah, and I appreciate it, believe me. My business is starting to suffer, and I've worked very hard to make this place a success."

Zanita put her hand on his arm. "We'll straighten it out; don't worry."

Todd patted her hand. "C'mon, let me show you to your rooms. I heard you were newlyweds so I saved the best suite for you. Its got a sunken whirlpool tub and a private veranda overlooking the backyard." He winked at them.

"You're my new best friend, buddy."

Zanita punched Tyber's arm.

The room was a testament to sybaritic pleasure.

A mahogany canopy tester bed—not too large, Zanita noticed—faced a free-standing stone fireplace. It was a bed made for close cuddling on cool winter nights.

"Now, don't you go hogging the bed tonight, baby," Tyber drawled.

Zanita smiled. They both knew who it was that sprawled unchecked across a bed. Like a pirate captain.

They walked around the fireplace, noticing that the other side of the grate faced the sunken tub. The outside wall facing the whirlpool was almost all glass and overlooked the back end of the veranda—complete with ornate hammock. It was already dark outside; pale moonlight glanced off the thin blanket of snow on the meadows.

As they both watched, several new flakes began to fall. Along with the temperature.

Zanita knew what that meant. "Oh-oh."

Tyber ran his hand down the back of her neck to massage the tender skin there. "Uh-huh. The channel might ice up. We might have to fly back, but don't tell Hambone."

"He hates flying, huh?"

"Hell, no. The rogue loves it. Last time, he

75

snuck into the cockpit when the stewardess opened the door and jumped right onto the pilot's lap."

"My God. What happened?"

"Well, Hambone, being Hambone, thought it would be immensely amusing to sharpen his nails on the pilot's . . . landing gear."

Zanita started laughing. "You're making this up!"

He grinned, shaking his head. "Wish I were. When we finally landed, and it was not a smooth landing, believe me, we were told in no uncertain terms that we were no longer welcome to fly the friendly skies."

Zanita giggled.

Tyber bent down and nuzzled the back of her neck. "Would it surprise you if I told you I want to make love to you before we go down to dinner?"

"No."

"Oh."

"I know you too well, Tyberius Augustus Evans. Remember the Marble Manor Inn? We no sooner got into the room and saw that golden marble floor in the bathroom . . ."

"True." His breath feathered down the side of her neck, sending tingles along the sensitive skin.

His hand brushed down the front of her body, just grazing the tips of her breasts as he leaned into her with his hips and *rocked*. There was no

mistaking the swelling in the front of his jeans—
nor the pressure of it—as he rubbed against her,
all the while nibbling tiny kisses on her throat.

Zanita was wearing one of the long Indian
dresses she preferred lately. The soft, gauzy
material traveled well.

Apparently it crushed well, too, as Tyber gathered a handful of the material in his fist and easily lifted the back of her loose dress. His other
hand skillfully slipped her panties down her
legs. After that she heard the distinct rasp of his
zipper.

"What do you think you are doing?" she asked
dryly.

"Tai chi," was the flippant response. He bit the
back of her neck.

"You can't! We're facing the window! Someone will see us!"

"Maybe. Maybe not." A very hot tongue licked
the side of her throat in a slow tasting. "It is dark
out there and we are facing the back, but I suppose if someone was walking out there . . ."

His tongue dipped under the back neckline of
her dress as his hands came around to her front.
Under cover of the fabric, he cupped her
breasts. The pads of his thumbs scraped across
her nipples, flicking them instantly into two
swollen nubs.

Zanita swallowed. The Captain was taking the
helm. Part one of the attack. But what if some-

one saw them? "Tyber, are you crazy? We—" The hard length of him slid coaxingly over her bottom like a brush of satin-coated steel. "*Ohhhh . . .*"

Instinctively she stood on tiptoe.

Then blushed when she realized what she was doing.

The man was turning her into a textbook case of Pavlovian response! A brush of his lips and she opened her mouth. A low growl from him and she was purring. This was not good. Pirates never have inhibitions. She started to squirm.

"Shhh . . . just keep the front of your dress down and no one will be the wiser." He smiled wickedly against the skin of her throat. "Lean forward for me, baby,"

"Wh-what?" He positioned her forward himself. She sucked in her breath as she felt him slide between the backs of her thighs.

He captured her small hand in his and brought it down to the front of her dress where he let it skim across the juncture of her thighs. The supple material rustled over her and him. The velvet tip of him was between her legs. Zanita sucked in her breath.

"Did you say you wanted spontaneity, baby?" His white teeth nipped her shoulder. Then the rogue teased her by flexing snugly against her curls. Spontaneously.

"I'm sure no one will be expecting us to do *this*."

It took a moment for Zanita to digest what he was saying. "Doc, you can't be serious—"

"Mmmm-hmmm. Think of it as cause and affect."

"Isn't that cause and effect?"

"Nope. I cause. . . ." He sank solidly into her from behind. Zanita cried out. Something between surprise and ecstasy. ". . . You affect."

"I can't believe you're doing this!" She wiggled on him.

"Why not?" He flexed firmly inside her.

"Because . . ." She stopped for a moment. Was that a light flickering in the distance? Her nose pressed against the glass pane. "Is someone out there?" What if it was one of the guests or Todd? "Oh, god, Tyber, you have to stop!"

"Uh-uh." His hand dropped between her legs. Soon he was teasing her nether lips with feather-light strokes of his fingers. Meanwhile, the tip of his manhood withdrew to pulse lightly against her feminine core, just barely teasing at the portal. He was so hot.

Hot and ready.

Her dewy moisture immediately covered him, and he used the liquid silk to lubricate his entire shaft by continuing to slide forward against her but not in her. Zanita could feel the cold rasp of his metal zipper as it scraped against her buttocks. The combination of his burning heat and those cold metal teeth, his stroking fingers and biting lips, was enough to send her right into a sharp, swift release.

Tyber felt the rapid flutters against his finger and around his shaft. The sweet quivers almost undid him. "Yes, yes, yes . . ." he breathed raggedly into her ear. *"C,mon, baby . . ."*

"Tyber!" Zanita cried out the name of the person responsible for her state before she sagged back into his strength.

The Captain captured her delicate earlobe with his teeth. His low, passion-rough voice vibrated along her neck in a prolonged, deep growl.

Even after all this time with Doc Evans, it still amazed Zanita how passionate he could be. She had come to realize that Tyber's passion was an intrinsic part of his makeup. The man was alive.

And she loved him for it.

There was no one else like Tyber. There never would be.

Life with him was a constant adventure. Even the simplest act of reading in bed together or watching an old B movie in the middle of the night carried with it a surge of excitement. That was what it was like to be with Dr. Evans. The man was unconventional and unpredictable.

And when it came to sex, Tyber Evans was high intensity wrapped in a lethal package.

She had agreed to this trial-by-computer marriage. So far, he was more than living up to his end of the challenge. As she recalled what he had just done to her, her lips curved upward in an utterly satisfied way.

Seeing her dreamy reflection in the glass, Tyber's ice blue eyes gleamed provocatively. He slid his slick, firm member over her derriere. *"See how wet you've made me, baby . . ."* he whispered hoarsely.

Zanita shivered as she felt a droplet of his own dampness combine with hers.

Then that strong body slanted over hers. Strands of chestnut hair skimmed over her shoulder in a long, silken swath. He captured her lips with a rough, deep kiss, his tongue flowing wholly into her mouth. Tyber didn't just taste her—he devoured her.

In contrast, his manhood barely dipped into her. Zanita cried out in pleasure while he swallowed the sounds he was causing her to make. Slowly, he surged into her, inch by inch—letting her feel every ripple, every nuance of his fullness.

"My god." Zanita had trouble catching her breath.

Tyber smiled against her swollen lips. "Why, thank you, Curls."

Despite the intense situation, Zanita couldn't stop a snort. "As if—" She sucked in her breath as he pulled her back taut against him, the flat of his hand riding low on her belly. He was in to the hilt.

That was when he began moving with a clockwise, circular motion of his hips. Zanita stopped breathing altogether. "Ohhhh . . ."

But Tyberius Augustus Evans was just starting. Placing his palms on the curve of her hipbones, he guided her into a *counterclockwise* motion.

The effect was stellar.

On both of them.

"Damn, that feels incredible," Tyber whispered. He groaned as Zanita ground back into him while rotating on his shaft. Her derriere brushed against his own curls causing his breath to skitter across the back of her neck and shoulders like a sultry windstorm.

Her fiery actions caused the man to become incendiary. He tried to thrust even deeper into her, his powerful movements raising her slightly off the carpet.

Zanita inhaled sharply. "Tyber, if someone is out there, they will know what—"

"No one can see us," he breathed raggedly. "The hammock blocks the view from the yard." This disclosure came as he delved yet more vigorously.

"*What?*" Zanita stopped moving. "Why did you let me think . . . ?"

Tyber's fingers pressed into the curve of her hips, trying to get her to resume her exquisite movements. They were driving him wild. "It added to your sense of excitement and spontaneity. C'mon, baby . . ." His coaxing voice was husky.

Zanita's heel ground into the top of his foot.

"Ow!" He almost released her. Almost.

"I can't believe I fell for that!" She tried to squiggle away from him. He held her tight.

A dimple curved his cheek before he swiftly planted a short kiss on the curve of her shoulder. "Me either." He withdrew partway, only to thrust back very solidly.

Zanita moaned raggedly. "Tyber! This is not what we agreed! You created a false tension!"

"Uh-huh." He surged sharply once more.

"You're cheating! You can't cheat!" His next movement was so powerful that it caused her to invent a totally new pleasure sound.

"I'm not cheating, baby. I'm showing you that it's still great between us—even though it is *expected* of us." He bit her lip with a sexy, short tug.

Zanita's brow furrowed. It was really hard to think at the moment—but she was sure he was befuddling her again. Tyber was a premier befuddler. Since that first time he had shown her what true pleasure was, he had been befuddling her on a regular basis.

"Just because you have me at a disadvantage, don't think—"

"*Disadvantage?*" He placed the heel of his hand over her pubic bone and pressed in sharply. Every muscle in her body drew up in rapture.

He seized her mouth in a devastating kiss as his talent took them both to Nirvana. He poured into her, moaning against her lips.

Sagging weakly against him, Zanita tried to regain her breath. Tyber gently lowered her dress. Bending down, he rested his damp forehead against the back of her head.

"That was beautiful, Mrs. Evans." He watched her reflection in the glass as he carefully rearranged her dress.

Zanita stuck her tongue out at him.

He laughed; one of those slow, sexy pirate laughs of his.

She was not going to let him get away with this! There was a lot at stake here. Sure, he'd won the first round by shifting her focus—but that didn't prove anything. Geniuses were very tricky. "There are still four days left to the contest. I'm not Mrs. Evans yet."

He stroked his chin. "Four days, hmmmm? Well, I have more than four hundred years' worth of excitement . . . just for you. Mrs. Evans." He smacked her lips.

Zanita wondered if she should worry.

"I can't wait to indulge myself in your savory buns, Todd!"

Tyber nearly choked on the pistachio-truffle puff he had just popped into his mouth.

Zanita obligingly patted his back as everyone stared with various degrees of interest at Todd's neighbor and guest, Mark Kevins. He was a handsome young man, in a surgically perfect way. They had all joined up in the parlor for pre-dinner hors d'oeuvres and drinks as the chef/owner had suggested. From what Zanita could gather, the two young men had known each other most of their lives. They both had grown up on the island. Recently, Todd had returned to the family home, continuing the Sparkling tradition of innkeeping.

Blooey was the first to speak after such an *outré* comment. "I've heard about them saucy buns. They're a bit famous hereabouts, Captain. Why, there's a rumor a big outfit wants a bite out of them."

This time Tyber did choke.

Mark put his hands on his hips. Indignantly. "They can just get in line!"

"Yes, we all can't wait, Todd." Calendula Brite

smiled at Mark. He had been her assistant for a number of years, and she treated him like a fair-haired child. Mark, in turn, idolized her. When he'd heard that Todd was having problems at the inn, he'd called in his friend and mentor, Calendula Brite.

Tyber glanced over at the parapsychologist. At first inspection, she was not what he expected. A medium of some renown and a self-proclaimed paranormal expert, Calendula Brite was a woman of modest height and build, who dressed with the bland conservatism of the Beacon Hill over-fifty set.

One would never guess by looking at her that this woman claimed to have catalogued no fewer than sixty "living" specters and was the current president of the Society for Fantastical Research.

A society that Tyber had always had severe doubts about.

What bothered him most about the group was that they constantly claimed to be doing "scientific" research, yet they did not adhere to any scientific method he could discern, and their results, as far as he could tell, were dubious at best. They never produced any actual data, even though they claimed they had it in their files. That annoyed Dr. Evans.

"What about you, Dr. Evans? Are you in the mood for savory buns?"

Calendula tilted her pale blond head in his direction, smiling slightly.

Tyber had to admit she was charming.

"I'm always up for savory buns." He looked at Zanita out of the corner of his eye and winked.

There was a wealth of suggestive meaning behind that wink. Zanita tried not to think of glass windows and heated kisses. She squirmed in her seat.

Tyber chuckled knowingly.

"Do you think the ghost will make an appearance tonight, Todd?" Mark changed the subject away from buns, savory or otherwise.

"Good Lord, I hope not." Todd sighed. "Last time I made a lobster bisque, he toppled a bottle of lemon juice into the mix—right after he ate almost half the pot. Curdled the whole thing."

" 'Tis a bloody crime!" Blooey jumped out of his seat, ready to do battle with the cuisine-wrecking ghost. Nothing upset the little pirate more than fine dining gone amuck.

Calm as always, Tyber took a slow sip of his drink. "How do you know someone didn't sneak into the kitchen and do it? Why do you think it was the, as you say, ghost?"

"Because I was out of fresh lemons and I would never use bottled juice." He grimaced in distaste.

Not understanding the vagaries of chefs, Tyber shrugged. "So whoever it was brought his own."

"Also, a strange, thick mist covered the kitchen floor."

Tyber raised an eyebrow.

"What was the mist like?" Zanita got excited. She leaned forward in her seat.

"Thick, wafting. That's when the pots and pans began to hum."

"Hum?"

"Yes. It was very eerie." Todd shivered at the memory.

As Tyber leaned back into his chair, mind ever working, Hambone's stomach growled, reminding everyone about dinner.

Zanita grinned. "Just in case—I hope you cooked something else besides the bisque tonight."

Everyone laughed.

Todd chuckled. "Once I found a stack of waffles right here in the parlor—stuck to the top of the chandelier." He pointed to the very spot.

Everyone gazed upward. The Florencia Inn was an old house and the ceilings were exceptionally high. Almost ten feet. Presumably, one would have to be an extremely tall person or have a ladder handy to do the deed.

"That's damn odd, Todd." Mark still stared at the light fixture as if he were looking for clues.

"Once, when I was doing an investigation of the Hollow House in Louisiana, we found a plate of beignets balanced on the limb of an old oak tree," said Calendula Brite. "It was the very limb that a cook was hanged from 144 years ago."

"Blimey!" Blooey's eyes bulged out. It was obvious to Tyber that his cook's rationality had already been shanghaied by the spooky tale.

"You see, the poor thing loved beignets. Unfortunately, she was a slave who also liked to snoop, and one day she inadvertently found a very incriminating letter that had been sent to her master. She had no idea what was on the paper—not being able to read." Calendula crossed her legs and waved her hand. "But they cut out her tongue, just in case."

Zanita shivered. "That's horrible."

"It gets worse. The master then sent her out into the fields. Well, naturally, she wanted to get back into the house, where conditions were somewhat better. She came up with the idea of poisoning the master; they say she had some skill in doctoring and knew they would call her to the big house to come and heal him. Her plan was that she would cure him, and he would be so grateful that he would let her back into the house."

"What happened then?" Blooey was captivated by the grisly story.

Tyber looked over at Zanita. His lady-love was just as captivated. He smiled to himself. His baby always loved anything that smacked of weirdness. He laughed to himself. *Including me.*

"So," Calendula continued, "she baked some beignets. Only problem was that she laced them with something that made him a wee bit too sick. He died."

Hambone's eyes closed halfway and he began to purr in a low tone.

Damned if the cat isn't enjoying the lurid story, too! Tyber shook his head. *Bloodthirsty heathens, the lot of them. Oh, what the hell, they're my heathens.* "So that's when they hanged her?" he asked in spite of himself.

"Yes. But before they did, she put the sign of the curse on them. To this day, a decent beignet cannot be fried at Hollow House. We found the sugar-dusted plate on the anniversary of her death, crawling with ants. Later that day we spotted ants in the slave quarters."

Everyone in the room was suitably awed.

Everyone except a certain physicist.

Tyber stared at her stone-faced. "And you don't think it possible that the establishment, which I am sure runs a healthy tourist trade, may have placed the beignets in the tree to add to the legend?" He didn't even bother to comment on the ants.

"Absolutely not. Mark and I thoroughly checked it out, didn't we, Mark?" She didn't wait for his answer. "Do you know, there is an indentation of a beignet on the master-bedroom ceiling? No matter how many times they paint over it, it comes back. It's uncanny."

A curved line of amusement grooved Tyber's cheek as he tried to imagine the terrifying image of a depressed pastry having a tenacious hold on the ceiling. He quickly sipped his drink to hide his expression.

"Maybe we have a similar phenomenon here with the waffles, Calendula?" Mark's face was alight with the possibility.

"Manifestation of a breakfast item is very rare." Calendula almost dismissed the connection, then reconsidered. "Although it might explain some of the other occurrences."

Tyber set his drink down on a side table. "Before you all run away with this scintillating supposition, might I dare to suggest that there has to be a rational explanation for all of this?"

"Bravo, Doctor! Bravo!"

Everyone turned in the direction of the basso profundo voice that boomed from the doorway like the blast of a foghorn.

Blooey took one look at the dark, burning eyes, the flyaway grayishblack hair, and the blacker than night suit, and immediately came to a conclusion.

" 'Tis the blackguard hisself! Attack, I say! Attack!"

Hambone, as gullible as his sidekick in matters of superstition, immediately launched himself into kitty attack mode. He hurled through the air in a streaking blur of orange fur.

And hightailed it directly out the door.

"Come back here, ye yellow-bellied scalawag!" Blooey hightailed it after Hambone.

Zanita and Tyber looked at each other and shook their heads.

"Gramercy Hubble, I presume," Tyber calmly stated.

"At your service, Dr. Evans."

At that, the dark specter of Cognitive Reasoning floated into the room like a cloud of gloom.

Chapter Four

"Nonsense! It's all nonsense!"

Gramercy Hubble had been repeating that phrase every five minutes since he entered the parlor. Unfortunately, he carried it right into the dining room with him and continued to dish it out at regular intervals as if it were part of the menu.

To say it caused some irritation with Calendula and Mark was a severe understatement. Every time the proclamation issued forth, Calendula pursed her lips and Mark looked ready to hurl a punch.

Zanita had to admit that the man was truly annoying. It was especially abrasive to her that he seemed to immediately align himself with Tyber. So far, her temporary husband had done nothing to dissuade Hubble of the notion that they were in agreement.

Her mouth firmed. Tyber had promised to be objective! Sure, the beignet/waffle stories had their holes in the batter, but that didn't mean they weren't dealing with the genuine article now. There was a lot of unexplained phenomena going on in this place. Besides, the house had a certain creepy feel to it that bespoke supernatural happenings.

She wondered why weird things always seemed to occur at places like this, then reasoned that the atmosphere just lent itself to it. Sort of a feng shui for ghosts.

As a matter of fact, she couldn't recall any instances of ghosts in sleek new high-rise penthouse apartments.

Zanita made a mental note to ask Calendula if she knew anything about feng shui and, if so, whether it had played a part in any of her past investigations. The energy of this house, along with the layout, was very convoluted. Lots of places for spirits to get "stuck."

Reluctantly, Zanita turned to Gramercy Hubble. "Mr. Hubble, how does your society explain the photograph that Mark took?"

Just before they had gone in to dinner, Mark had shown them a Kirlian photograph in which he had captured a spirit hovering in front of the fridge over a platter of Long Island duckling. It was a rather large, fat blob of white smoke. In the center of the top portion of the picture was a bright red circle. Mark had explained that this was where the spirit's energy was strongest. Near its mouth.

Which made sense, since the haunt seemed to be so enamored of fine dining.

"Nonsense! It's all nonsense!"

Zanita gritted her teeth. Gramercy Hubble was going to make this a long weekend.

"The Society for Cognitive Reasoning has long known that Kirlian photography is a sham. It proves nothing and shows nothing." He swallowed a huge bite of Todd's Nine Pepper Pork and began coughing. Calendula smiled like a sorceress.

Patting him on the back, Tyber handed the man his glass of wine. When he had stopped coughing, he turned to Calendula and said, "Suppose you're going to say the ghost did that, Ms. Brite?"

"Wouldn't think of it, Mr. Hubble."

Her remark was an insult either way it was interpreted. Mentally, Zanita gave the lady medium the "okay" sign. At this point she didn't care if Gramercy Hubble made sense or not. Nobody ever likes a smartass.

"Hey, what's all this Mr. and Ms. stuff? C'mon, everybody, we can be more informal than that." Todd stepped in as host to lighten the atmosphere.

Mark put his fork down. "I don't understand how you can say that, Hubble, when it has been shown that we can illustrate electromagnetic radiation coming directly from a nebulous source."

Well, at least Mark's down to calling him Hubble, Zanita thought.

"Rubbish! What do you say, Dr. Evans? Or should I say Tyber?"

"Tyber is fine." He glanced over at Zanita. His love was staring at him with the tiny violet slits. In the interest of his own survival, he paused, twirling his glass thoughtfully, before he responded diplomatically, "Kirlian photography has its supporters and detractors. What I'm interested in is how you got that picture, Mark, and what it shows."

Mark seemed flustered. "Well, I was visiting Todd one night"—he hesitated briefly before continuing—"and I happened to go into the kitchen for a late-night snack. The refrigerator door was wide open, and there he was! I knew what had been happening here from Todd, so I always kept a camera close by. It was a good thing, too, because as soon as I snapped the picture, he vanished."

"How convenient," Hubble sneered.

"Are you saying I doctored that picture?" Mark was getting hot.

"It's not a difficult thing to do. In fact, photographs are the easiest medium to tamper with—which is why they are not allowed as evidence in courtrooms anymore. Unless, that is, they are Polaroids. We psi-cogs won't even look at regular photos."

Psi-cogs? Zanita blinked.

Mark started to rise out of his seat. "I never touched—"

"It's okay, Mark. I know you didn't," Todd said, trying to appease his friend.

"Just because a picture can be tampered with doesn't mean it was, Hubble." Now everyone was talking to the man using his surname.

"True, true. But in this case—"

"The picture was not tampered with," Tyber proclaimed, stunning them all. He threw the photo in question on the table. "I can discern no under or overexposure, no double exposure, no light leaks, no reflections, no refractions, and it appears his equipment was not faulty."

"No, he has the best equipment," Todd agreed.

Everyone paused for a moment. Todd, realizing what he had said, blushed. "I mean . . . never mind."

"So it is genuine!" Zanita brightened at the discovery.

"As far as I can tell, yes."

"Which means—" Zanita began.

"Only one thing," Tyber finished for her.

"The ghost is real," she whispered.

Tyber winced. "Well, the *other* only thing."

Zanita frowned, looking up at him. "Which is?"

"That the scene had been purposely staged for the photo to be taken."

Dead silence followed that remark.

Tyber had just introduced the possibility of foul play.

"Bravo, doctor! Bravo." Gramercy Hubble gave them all a look of supreme righteousness, making him appear rather like a grand inquisitor of medieval times who has just proven his point over his tortured victim.

Zanita kicked her loving husband under the table.

"What did I do, baby?" he mouthed.

"Absolutely nothing." She turned away from him.

Of all the mysteries in the universe, Tyber surmised that women had to be the most complex.

"There are many ways of seeing ghosts."

They had all retired once again to the parlor, replete from Todd's fabulous meal. Apparently the ghost wasn't partial to Nine Pepper Pork. As they left the dining room, Tyber quipped that was a shame since they could surely snag the spook by following the trail of his sneezes.

Zanita winced. What was she going to do with the rogue? Ghost investigations required a modicum of seriousness. She turned to the Captain, set her sights, and hurled a fulminating glare his way.

The shot didn't even bounce off the target.

He simply smiled slowly at her. The Captain always knew exactly what she was thinking! It was uncanny. Tyber's unique color contrast of chestnut/gold hair and light blue eyes rimmed with jet lashes never failed to take her breath away. *He is a sexy devil*.

The sensual smile broadened.

Zanita's lips parted in surprise. She bit her lip and peeked at him again.

A dimple curved his cheek! Twinkling blue eyes observed from beneath lowered lids; ice blue glittering under long black lashes. She covertly stuck her tongue out at him.

"It's not uncanny, baby," he bent down to whisper in her ear. "I just know *you*."

Zanita's expression squinched up.

Tyber chuckled. "You almost look like Hambone when you do that."

Zanita ignored his baiting. Besides being a genius and a rogue, the man was also a premier baiter. And he took so much pleasure in baiting her that she decided she wasn't going to give him the satisfaction of it!

A low laugh teased her ear.

She sighed dramatically and brought her attention back to Calendula and Mark.

Turning in her chair, Calendula continued to

respond to the question Zanita had asked regarding the methods of recording and sighting spirits.

"Nonsense. All of it nonsense," Hubble barked on cue.

"Mr. Hubble, please." Zanita gave him an annoyed look. The older man flushed and looked away.

"Please go on, Calendula."

Calendula smiled at her. "Despite what our esteemed *'psi-cog'* believes"—she gestured in Hubble's direction—"we are very exacting in our research. For instance, one time Mark and I were on an investigation in England—near the Cotswolds. There are lots of ghosts in England, you know. I think they must prefer the damp climate there . . . but anyway, a report came into our center about a couple who had been driving down the road that night past this house where all sorts of strange happenings had been reported in the past. Footsteps in the dark, blinking lights—that sort of thing. They claimed they had stopped the car near the side of the house. Apparently they were in an amorous mood and, well, you can imagine."

Tyber blinked twice at Zanita, who fidgeted in her seat.

"Since the inside of the mini was getting a bit, ah, steamy, they rolled down the windows. That's when they heard the footsteps. They quickly sat up but could see no one—even though the steps seemed to be all around the automobile. Of course, the house had a history of such things, which added to their terror and suggestibility. They quickly rolled up the windows and immediately left the place."

"Ghostus interruptus?" A-not-so-innocent dimple appeared in Tyber's cheek.

Everyone chuckled at that one—even Calendula.

"When Mark and I went back to investigate, we did not discover the spirit we had hoped for. You see, if they had only driven back and investigated a little further, they would have realized that a group of the neighbor's pigs had gotten loose. The footsteps they heard were nothing more than some hogs rooting around behind the hedge."

Tyber's masculine lips parted in feigned astonishment. "Zanita, they must be from the English branch of the Hogs."

She threw him a dirty look. Tyber never overlooked an opportunity to tease her about the Hogs.

"The hogs?" Mark asked her, puzzled.

"Never mind," she gritted out, making a mental note to make Tyber pay for that one later.

"And just how do you conduct these so-called scientific investigations?" Hubble sneered. "What clinical criteria do you use?"

"Mark and I have brought with us most of the standard equipment used in these investigations: lights, mics, digital voice-activated audio recorders, high eight cameras, TV cameras, magnometers, thermal graph cameras, and other similar tools of the trade."

Calundula turned to address Todd and Zanita. "The problem with relying on equipment is that we have found that at locations with real activity, equipment often mysteriously fails at key times. Many parapsychologists have reported this perplexing phenomenon."

"What kind of failures are we talking about?" Tyber asked.

"New or recharged batteries suddenly go dead, or the equipment inexplicably stops working. We have no explanation except to note that it is a very common occurrence on these expeditions."

"And a very convenient one, at that," Hubble jeered.

Tyber had to agree with the psi-cog on that one. Like Hubble, he had a hard time accepting mysterious equipment failure. He would want an answer, preferably one rooted in the scientific method.

"Do you have any possible theories as to why these failures occur so often?" he inquired seriously.

Calendula studied him. "None that you would

be inclined to accept, Doctor. We just know what we have experienced."

"Would you say that these failures most often happen at peak occurrence?"

"As a matter of fact, yes."

"That is too coincidental for my taste," Tyber stated. Hubble nodded in curt agreement with him.

"We also agree, Dr. Evans. The Society for Fantastical Research believes that these two factors are linked in a very definite way."

"You're saying that the more energy is manifested during an occurrence, the greater the chance that—whatever it is—knocks out the equipment." It seemed reasonable to Zanita.

"That's what we think happens, yes."

"Nonsense! It's all nonsense. If the equipment always fails at the optimum time, it is so that there will be no tangible evidence! The Society for Cognitive Reasoning has posted a ten-thousand-dollar prize for the first person who can prove a genuine ghost exists! Do I need to tell you that not one subject—living or dead—has come forward to collect this money? Not one." Hubble gestured with his hand in the air. "You'd think with all this hullabaloo over seeing spirits in every relative's attic, we would have at least *one* incident authenticated!"

Calendula straightened the back of her hair,

Dara Joy

her only outward gesture of irritation. "The reason no one will come forward, as you say, Hubble, is that your group sets out to make a mockery of believers. Proof can be subject to interpretation. What's more, there is always a way to *disprove* something, if one is so inclined. And your group does this with a glee bordering on the maniacal."

"How so, Calendula?" Zanita took out her pad and pen and began jotting down notes.

"Let's say someone comes to his group, the psi-cogs, and says they have experienced genuine poltergeist activity—dishes flying about, doors slamming on their own, that sort of thing. The next thing you know, the psi-cogs are out there showing *scientifically* that the house was built in such a way that when a truck—which is over a certain weight limit—passes by the road when the temperature is eighty-six degrees, it will cause a vibration to occur in the wood struts that support the foundation of this so-called haunted house, which in turn will cause the door to slam and make the dishes leap off the shelves."

Tyber stretched out his legs and crossed his arms behind his head. "So what's wrong with that?" he said. "It's real. It's a fact. It's proven. And it certainly seems more logical an explanation than spirits doing the rumba in your living room."

"It's *one* explanation, but it might not be the *right* explanation. Those types of solutions can always be found if one wants to search hard enough for them . . . and stretch credulity far enough."

"Whoa!" Tyber sat up. "You're saying that believing in poltergeist activity is not stretching credulity?"

"I'm saying that mysteries can be explained away by any number of remedies in this life, Dr. Evans. That doesn't mean they have been truly solved."

Tyber thought about it, choosing not to respond. Calendula had a point. He always kept an open mind. Governed by reason.

"We also know what some of us have seen with our own eyes," Calendula added softly. "For some, that is all the proof we need."

"The eye is easy to fool. Seeing is often not believing, as has been shown countless times."

"Perhaps. But the eye of the heart is not easily fooled. And that is why when someone has what I believe to be a genuine experience, it is undeniable. The truth is seen with the heart." She turned and stared straight at Zanita.

Zanita looked at her, lips parting slightly. *Does the woman know of my experience?* Zanita wondered. Calendula was a famous medium. What talents did she truly possess?

Hubble's guffaws of ridicule drew her attention away from that line of thought. "So we will let our hearts govern our reason? Ms. Brite, what can you be thinking?" He snickered. "Are you telling us that what *you* personally have witnessed has led you to believe in ghosts?" His wily question was designed to discredit her before Tyber.

Calendula did not even flinch. "Unequivocally. Of course, what a 'ghost' is, is a matter of speculation as well."

"What do you mean?" Puzzled, Zanita stopped jotting notes.

"Some say they are living entities from another dimension. Others believe them to be spirits bound to the earth after death for various reasons, or they may be an echo of a strong event, emotion, or memory that occurred in the past—like an imprint—that only certain people can see. Still others subscribe to the theory that ghosts actually are manifestations from the living."

"From the living?" Zanita tapped her pencil against her lips.

"Yes. Especially in the case of poltergeist activity. Such manifestations could be occurrences of psi-activity from an adept living in the house. Studies have shown that there are often children present in the home that experiences poltergeist activity."

"That kind of narrows your experimental field, doesn't it?" Tyber joked.

"Well, experiments in the paranormal are, by their very nature, difficult. How do we know what tools to use to 'observe' an unknown entity? And what inferences can we attach to the data we do obtain? Many students of parapsychology believe that we cannot measure these things using standard experimental techniques."

"That makes sense," Zanita agreed.

"I have to disagree." Tyber contradicted his wife, earning him a glare and—he was sure—a cold patch in the bed that night.

"Why is that, Dr. Evans?"

"Because the laws of physics must be valid in all realms to be valid in any realm. And because we are experiencing this phenomenon in *this* realm of being. Therefore, the same laws of cause and effect must apply to the frames of reference, namely the observer, and the apparition in question within the spatial coordinates of our plane."

"Excellently put, Doctor." Hubble nodded concisely once.

"Not necessarily, Tyber. There have been many case studies where an apparition appeared but not everyone present observed it. If what you say is true, how do you explain that?"

"If this was a *physical* manifestation, and by that I mean an entity capable of reflecting light, then all those capable of seeing it would see it. Period."

"Unless the apparition is *selectively* choosing who sees it and who doesn't," Zanita put in.

"Exactly!" Calendula readily agreed. "That is one reason we think it is so difficult to photograph a spirit. It aligns itself to certain psychic energies."

A small groan escaped Tyber's lips. "The physics," he muttered mournfully.

"The physics must be wrong." Zanita raised her brow at her husband.

Tyber's brows lowered. "I don't think so, baby."

"Or . . ." Blooey suddenly spoke, surprising every one. "A new theory is needed to explain these quantum states!"

Everyone gaped at the little pirate. Occasionally, the old Arthur Bloomberg came shining through in spades.

"Quantum states, Blooey?" Tyber barked as he leaned toward him.

Blooey rubbed his bristly chin. "Aye. Might be from such an alternate state, don't ya think, Captain? Depending on the subatomic levels, perhaps. In which case the physics to explain the phenomenon would fit neatly with the physics we already know. . . ."

Tyber's eyes squinted. "Anything is possible. But then so is a Unified Field Theory, and we have yet to see it raise its eventful head."

Blooey guffawed. "They're waiting for you, Captain, hey?"

Tyber grinned.

A sudden loud clanging from the other room made everyone jump.

Blooey spoke in a hushed whisper. "There 'tis now, I'll wager . . . dragging itself about the house like some misbegotten beastie." Clearly all traces of the old Arthur Bloomberg were gone.

They all were utterly silent until the strange noises stopped.

"D-does that happen often, Todd?" Zanita's face was slightly pale from the experience.

"Very often."

"How creepy."

"Damn, did anyone think to record that?" Calendula snapped her fingers.

"I did." Tyber pulled a small recorder out of his pocket and replayed the sounds in all their laggardly, rumbling glory.

He clicked off the player. "All this proves is that these sounds did occur. In no way does it prove a paranormal event . . . unless a wave analysis shows differently, which I doubt."

"That is right, Doctor." Hubble walked over to the sideboard and poured himself a hefty glass of Todd's finest cognac.

"But what else could be causing them?" Zanita wondered.

"Any number of things, baby."

"Doctor, may I ask what else you brought for experimental equipment?" Hubble sat down with his drink and nonchalantly pulled out a pipe. He lit the bowl, puffing small clouds of smoke into the air. The blend was not the most aromatic Zanita had sniffed.

"Just this small tape recorder, some night vision scopes, and a Possineg 55."

"*A Possineg 55?*" Zanita had never heard of it.

"Yep."

Calendula's brows rose. "I'm impressed, Tyber. A Possineg 55 is a professional photographer's instant camera. It takes black-and-white positives. Impossible to tamper with."

Zanita glanced her husband's way. She was always impressed by him, but when he surprised her with some little brilliance like this, in an area she had no idea he knew anything about, he absolutely turned her on.

He returned her interested stare with a steady, simmering look that clearly said "Later baby."

"But do we really need all this?" Todd shrugged. "All I'm interested in is getting rid of the blighter."

"It's important because we have to be sure who your 'blighter' is, Todd, and we have to know what is going on here."

"Tyber's right. Because of Mark, I have a great respect for you, Todd. We owe you the truth." Calendula patted his hand.

Todd sighed. "Does this kind of—of haunting happen often?"

"You'd be surprised. As has been pointed out, physical proof is very hard to obtain; and even if it is, it is always in question. Many of us feel that it will never be obtained in such a manner. I, myself, feel that if someone is inclined to depend on gauges and dials for answers, then maybe the paranormal is just not for them. The founder of our organization said, 'You either believe it or you don't'—which is not a very scientific approach, but makes perfect sense to those of us who do believe and *know*."

Tyber looked distressed, and Zanita knew that Calendula's statement did not sit well with him. She, on the other hand, understood very well what Calendula was saying. Once, when she was about ten, she saw her Aunt Louise walk across the front lawn of her grandmother's house and wave to her as she sat on the porch swing. The fact that Aunt Louise had been dead for seven years at the time made the event a bit of a shock.

Zanita had waved back rather stuporously, blinked, and come to her senses—only to discover that Aunt Louise was gone. The remnants of her presence seemed to be everywhere, though.

As Maurice Chevalier was fond of singing, every little breeze seemed to whisper Louise.

Zanita never forgot the experience, but she never told anyone. Yet it was that incident that made her want to explore the paranormal and write about it.

Gramercy Hubble, however, was not inclined to let Calendula off the hook. "It seems to me too convenient that you people always have some ambiguous answer when asked a direct question."

"You people?" Mark started to get up again when a great thudding noise shook the house.

Zanita gasped and clutched the arms of her chair. The chandelier began to sway as the pounding noises got louder, vibrating through the entire parlor and causing several crystal glasses on the sideboard to tinkle.

Calendula jumped up. "My god, Mark, quick! We have activity! Get the seismo—"

"Ah, that won't be necessary." Todd scratched his ear. The pounding got louder and louder as it approached the side door to the parlor.

"Why not?" gasped Zanita.

Hambone's head lifted and he sniffed the air. His ragged ears flattened to the back of his head. Like all animals, he seemed to be sensitive to the paranormal.

A huge black shadow drifted across the parlor carpet from the doorway.

Zanita squeaked in alarm.

Then the room began shaking again as the unknown entity lumbered forward. It eyeballed each person present with a dull brown stare.

Then it sat down right in the middle of the floor with a loud *thump*.

It was a massive thing. Grossly obese. And it carried with it the laconic look of the dangerously dull-witted.

"By Captain's Morgan's rum chest! Wot in the name of the Brethern is that?" Blooey's eyes bugged out.

Todd frowned sheepishly. "Allow me to introduce Hippolito. My, ah, cat."

Hippolito. Large, ungainly Hippolito, whose weight far exceeded his IQ lifted a massive, Godzilla-like paw. He stretched it out in the air, toes extended, and struck a pose not unlike Marlon Brando in *On the Waterfront*.

It had pathos.

It spoke of the human condition.

It beseeched but a crumb of the pistachio-truffle pâté.

"That was the lamest evening I have ever spent," Tyber continued to grouse as they walked through the woods.

The moon was almost full, its beams glittering off the light dusting of snow. Zanita loved the crunchy sounds their boots made as they traversed the field along the stone wall and then doubed back along the edge of the pine forest.

Their breaths created moisture trails in the night air.

"It wasn't that bad, Tyber. In fact, I thought it was kind of interesting. And the food was superb."

"Mmmm." He squinted, looking at the house in the distance. They had circled around and were facing the back of the property.

"You have to admit that some of the things that have happened seem strange, and Todd doesn't strike me as the type to make up stories. Neither does Mark."

"Mmmm." He continued gazing at the house.

"You know, I think Calendula is fascinating. The stories she told gave me the heebie-jeebies. I just bet—" She slipped on an icy patch.

Without taking his eyes off the house, Tyber grabbed her arm to steady her. Then he took her hand in his as they continued walking along.

"Thanks. I just think what she does is so fascinating. Do you think we'll experience any of the events that Todd spoke of during our stay?"

"I'd bet on it." He scanned the back of the house.

"That's good, because—what are you looking at?"

"Someone's in our room," he murmured in a low voice.

"What?" Zanita's head whipped around to scan the back facade. It seemed so far away, she wondered how he could tell. "How do you know?"

"I just saw a flashlight beam glance off the top of the Palladian window. There." He stood behind her and, putting his hands on her shoulders, pointed her in the right direction.

"Do you think it's Todd, leaving a good night chocolate on our bed?"

Tyber glanced down at her and shook his head. "Nope."

"Why would someone be in our room?"

"Oh, I can think of several reasons."

Zanita turned halfway around and crossed her arms over her chest. "Well, name a few!"

"For one, I'd say someone was very interested in the type of equipment I brought."

"But you mentioned what you brought earlier in the parlor."

"Someone's not very trusting."

"But why? We're just here to help Todd investigate the ghost."

"Bingo."

Zanita glanced back at the room. There was no flicker of light now. Whoever had been in there was gone. She bit her lip. "Are you sure it was a flashlight? Not a candle? Or something else?"

Tyber ran his index finger over her cool cheek. "It was a flashlight, baby. Whoever was in that room was of this realm. Sorry to disappoint you."

"I still don't see what possible interest our

room could hold for anyone . . . and why not turn on the light? Everyone knew we were going out for a walk. You said it loudly enough after Hippolito let out that god-awful sound."

Tyber winced at the memory. Even Hambone had heard enough and exited the room with grand feline dignity. "Whoever came into the room did not want to risk anyone else seeing the light on under the door, and that includes us. Come to think of it, if we had come back sooner than expected, they must have known. . . . Remind me to check the room for other exits when we get back, baby."

"Secret passages?" Zanita laughed. "Really, Tyber."

"I'm serious. Something is going on here, and it may not be . . ."

"What?" She held her breath and gazed up at him with the look that always turned him to mush. He didn't have the heart to dash her hopes for this ghost story, even though he had been skeptical from the start.

"It may not be all supernatural, baby."

Zanita's mouth opened, but nothing came out for a minute as she thought it over. "Why do you say that?"

"I don't know what's going on here—but it just feels *odd*—in a lot of ways. That's all I can tell you."

When Tyber got that feeling, he was usually

right. He almost sounded like a psychic, but she knew from experience it was pure cognitive process. It was as if his subconscious brain had already seen something and he was starting to store the data for later computation.

"I know, I've felt it too, but thought it was simply because the place is purportedly haunted."

"Just in case, let's be careful here. Until I get more info, consider everyone a suspect, including that wit-challenged cat. I'll advise Blooey and . . ." He was about to say Hambone.

Zanita looked at him and arched her brow.

"Ah, I'll alert the *crew* to watch their backs and keep an eye on the suspects."

"Suspects? Suspects in what?"

"I don't know yet."

"Tyber, try to remember that this is supposed to be a simple ghost-hunting investigation. You really don't need to liven it up any more than that."

He took her hand again and resumed the walk. "If that's all it is, well and good. But if it isn't, then—"

"Someone is making it *seem* as if it is," Zanita finished for him.

"Yes. And that is what we really need to find out."

She bit her lip. "You act as if the ghost is not even in the picture! I don't think I like that. You promised me—"

"He's in the picture, all right—but only as a footnote, right now."

Zanita looked back at the house one more time and froze in her tracks. She yanked on Tyber's arm.

"What is it, baby?" Concerned, Tyber turned quickly toward her.

"You can see our room from out here!" she gasped. "You told me that no one could see us!"

Tyber's brow furrowed. "That's curious."

"I'm going to kill you! How could you let us— What's curious?"

"Someone moved the hammock on the veranda."

Zanita followed his gaze. "Where was it before?"

"Right in front of that juniper bush to the left of the window."

"Maybe the secret passageway is on the veranda," she quipped sarcastically.

Tyber didn't react to her jibe. He just looked pensive.

"Well, I think I've had enough walking for tonight. It's getting cold. Why don't we go in?"

"Uh-uh. We need to go around to the other side the house." Before she could say anything, he took her arm and half dragged, half led her.

"How come?"

"I'm memorizing the outside layout, including any possible entrances or exits."

Zanita viewed the sexy genius askance and took a shivery little breath.

Tyberius Augustus Evans was her kind of man.

Chapter Five

"Stop going through my underwear!"

Zanita was indignant.

Tyber's lips twitched. "I'm just making sure nothing was tampered with, baby. Besides, I thought you liked me going through your underwear."

"Will you be serious? You've checked this room thoroughly three times! Nothing has been changed, left, or altered. And just what do you think anyone would be doing in my underwear?"

Tyber chose not to answer that. He held up a skimpy pair of pink lace panties, letting them dangle from his forefinger. "They could have planted something in . . . when did you get these?" A dimple popped into his left cheek.

Zanita grabbed the bit of lacy frill from his hand and stuffed it back into the drawer. "Never mind that."

"Someone was in this room. They were here for a reason. I want to know why."

"Are you going to examine my nighties, too?" she flung at him, exasperated.

"What nighties would those be?" he drawled, giving her one of his special looks. The kind that had a tendency to turn a woman into Jell-O. The kind that said, " 'You don't ever wear night-gowns around me."

She flushed. "When are you going to check out the veranda?"

"Not now. It's too dark to see anything, and I don't want to put the light on out there; it will only draw attention to the fact that we're search-ing for something. I'll check tomorrow in the daylight. In the meantime, I'll place the ham-mock back in its original position. That way, if there is some hidden trapdoor out there, no one will be able to use it without us knowing about it." He walked over to the French doors and, after checking the locks, opened them and stepped out onto their private porch.

Zanita leaned against the door frame as Tyber dragged the hammock back in place. "What would be the purpose of having a trapdoor on a porch? I never heard of that. Do you think there is something stored under there? Perhaps a hidden room of some sort?"

"Could be. But my guess is that it's a passageway under the main part of the house. Probably built when the house was constructed—maybe as an emergency exit or for some other reason we aren't aware of yet. What do you know about the history of the house?"

"Not much. Just that it's been in Todd's family since it was built in 1835. Apparently it's been an inn for most of its history. The family has added a few rooms along the way and modernized both the plumbing and kitchen over the years, but basically the house has retained most of its original characteristics."

"Hmm." Tyber came back inside, securely locking the French doors behind him.

"Since this has been an inn all this time, and so many people have been in residence here throughout the years, theoretically our ghost could be just about anyone from the past with an axe to grind."

Tyber had different ideas. "Or anyone from the present with an axe to grind."

Zanita stuffed her hands in the pockets of her sweater. "Possibly. We'll just have to wait and see what happens. I don't think anyone was ever murdered here, but it's very possible a guest might have died while in residence . . . although Todd told me it had never been mentioned to him in any family lore. Depending on what happens tonight, Calendula said she may try channeling the spirit."

Tyber stared at his wife with a deadpan expression. "Channeling."

In that moment, it was painfully obvious to him how much he loved her. He could be at home right now, playing the fourth level of Nukestar on his computer. Then there was that awesome new hybrid action-adventure game, Quest for Killing, in which the player shot every single living and nonliving thing in existence in a manly rampage while solving Mensa puzzles between kill-fests. At the end of the game, the winner even got to play solitaire (since he would be the only one left alive).

Now, *that* was quality entertainment.

Instead he was about to watch a woman go into a self-induced wig-out so she could speak to a dead guest. *True love, baby. True love.*

Zanita lifted her chin in challenge. "Yes, channeling. And I don't want to hear one word."

"Mmmm-mmmm-mmmmm. I just go crazy when you get rough with me."

On this first night of observation, they had agreed to set up shop in the library. After the dinner hour, the ghost most often caused mischief in the library, focusing on Todd's extensive cookbook collection. Calendula and Mark hoped

123

to capture the poltergeist activity that had been observed by Todd and some of his guests.

Tyber glanced at his watch. "We did say we would meet back in the library at midnight. It's show time, baby."

Mark had already set up most of his equipment in the library. Wires and cameras were strung everywhere across the floor, and they had to carefully pick their way through the complex network. It was a warm room, with deep tones of red on the walls and furnishings. A lovely wrought-iron circular staircase faced the oak bookshelves.

Gramercy Hubble was standing by a large marble fireplace, a supercilious smirk on his face as he watched the setup with obvious contempt. "The trappings of science without the substance," he muttered to Tyber.

"At least give them a chance, Hubble." Tyber spoke in a low voice to the psi-cog and nodded a greeting to Calendula.

Hubble snorted. "Do you really think we're going to experience anything here that can't be explained in rational terms?"

"I don't know what we're going to experience, and neither do you. We need to be unbiased to objectively observe the experiment. *Then* we'll take it from there . . . as scientists from a scientific prospective."

Hubble liked that. "Right," he agreed. "We remain logical men, true to our rationality."

That was not exactly what Tyber had said, but he rationally let it go. For Hubble, this ghostly horseman was never going to ride. There was no sense in beating a dead horse.

Zanita took a small brownie square from the refreshment cart. It was almost like a piece of fudge, it was so rich. "Mmmm. No wonder the ghost hangs out here, Todd. This is delicious!"

"Smile, Curls!"

Zanita looked up and Tyber snapped her picture, brownie in hand with a chocolate fudge rim around her mouth.

"Tyber!"

"Just testing out Mark's instant camera." A whirring sounded and her picture popped out of the Polaroid.

"Ha! Your eyes are closed, Zanita!" Mark grinned. "Looks like you're in brownie ecstasy."

Zanita giggled. "I am."

Chuckling, Tyber tossed the picture onto a side table next to the couch.

"I wonder why ghosts always choose the 'dead' of night to make appearances." Zanita yawned. "Pun intended."

Calendula laughed as she checked one of the instruments for calibration. "Actually, they don't.

There have been numerous sightings during daylight hours. However, the majority do seem to occur during the wee hours of night."

"Any theories as to why that is?" Zanita took out her notebook and began jotting down notes for her story.

"Yes, actually, I do. I think that is the time when they can communicate best with us. Our conscious barriers often are lowered at those hours."

"Have you been able to pick up anything psychically on the ghost, Calendula?" Mark called from the corner.

She frowned. "Nothing clear. It's as if I'm being blocked by interference of some kind. We may have more than one spirit at work here, Mark."

"More than one ghost?" Zanita swallowed and cleared her throat. Somehow the idea of *many* ghosts was . . . well, spooky.

"Perhaps. I'm not sure. I've been picking up several different energies. It may just be confliction, though."

"Confliction?"

"A term I use to describe obstructed energy patterns."

"Sort of like bad reception on a TV set?"

"Exactly. Zanita, why don't you monitor this camera? It will give you a feel for what we look for."

"Okay. What do I do?"

"Just keep an eye on the motion sensor. If the camera starts to move and focus, we may have a presence. Staying calm is the first rule. Just let us know if you see anything."

"Oh, I'll let you know all right. How do you decide where to set up the cameras?"

The grandfather clock chimed half past midnight. "I mapped out the ley lines earlier this evening."

"Ley lines? What are those?"

"Nonsense is what they are," Hubble harumphed.

Calendula exhaled wearily. Hubble was starting to seriously irritate even this complacent woman. "Ley lines are ancient lines of energy that crisscross the earth in a gridlike pattern. The Chinese in their feng shui refer to them as dragon lines and actually believe that the dragon which represents the chi resides in the earth itself."

"What physical proof do you have of these ley lines?" Hubble sat himself down beside a dessert cart that Todd had thoughtfully filled with drinks and an assortment of homemade cakes and cookies. The psi-cog wasted no time in plopping one of the frosted goodies into his mouth.

"The lines themselves cannot be measured magnetically or electronically, if that is what you are implying; but they can be felt psychically and have been known to a affect the movements of pendulums and dowsing rods."

"Of course they do! These pendulums and dowsing rods are held by people who *expect* them to be affected. It's all power of suggestion!"

Calendula's nostrils flared. "That does not explain why so many paranormal events throughout history seem to occur directly on these ley lines."

That caught Tyber's attention. "More than what would be statistically expected?"

"Yes. What's more, it is believed that psychic occurrences such as ghost sightings may be triggered by psi-sensitive humans who actually activate phenomena along the grid points."

"That's interesting." Tyber thought about the supposition, taking it one step further. "It might explain why those who have demonstrated high 'psi-q's' are inconsistent in their abilities; sometimes scoring high, sometimes low. If their alignment to the grid was important—"

"Excellent point, Doctor. We mainly utilize the ley lines as an aid to predicting possible paranormal activity for our research. I'll have to mention your suggestion to the board. It merits further investigation. If it proves to be correct, you will, of course, be credited with the finding."

Zanita beamed at him.

Tyber wasn't at all sure he wanted to gain a

credential from the Society for Fantastical Research. He had simply been playing "what if" and had taken it from there. Hubble, however, looked at him as if he had just turned traitor to the cause. Too bad the man was such an insufferable prig. It made it extremely hard for Tyber to go along with him, even though he basically agreed with his scientific approach. Blame it on his pirate nature, but he detested pretentious authority.

"We think that in some cases these psychic energies may give the imagination actual physical substance." Mark walked over to the cart and scooped out a glass of punch from the bowl.

"Whoa." Tyber put his hands up. "Now you've gone too—"

Zanita interrupted him. Her "husband" had a way of starting spirited debates without even trying. She didn't want to lose the focus of the conversation. "How did the study of ley lines come about?"

Tyber narrowed his eyes; he knew exactly what she had done. Damned if she didn't know him too well! He rubbed his jaw. That could prove to be . . . interesting.

Calendula elaborated. "A man by the name of Alfred Watkins described the alignments of ancient stone circles such as Stonehenge in a published work called *The Old Straight Track*. Of course, it has long been wondered if these primeval sites are aligned to certain astronomical events."

"This is so fascinating!" Zanita turned to Tyber. "Do you remember what I told you about Joe Sprit's hogs?"

Tyber blinked once. *Completely nonlinear.* "How could I ever forget it?" he drawled as he crossed his arms over his chest, waiting patiently for the other shoe to drop.

Zanita turned back to the group. "My grandfather's neighbor Joe has these defiant hogs. Every now and then, for no reason anyone can figure, they bust loose and make a foray through the countryside, causing all kinds of trouble. Snorts and mayhem! It's been going on for years." She circled her hand in the air to indicate the endless procession of pig feet throughout time.

Tyber rubbed the bridge of his nose. "She said snorts and mayhem," he mouthed to himself incredulously.

"Well," Zanita continued blithely on, "last month, Joe brought in a feng shui specialist and—"

Tyber stared at her. "Joe brought in a feng shui master for the Hogs?"

"Ahuh. It seems their pen was set up all wrong and the energy was bouncing all over the place, making the Hogs edgy. That's why they kept busting out. So Joe realigned the pen and they haven't caused any trouble since. He's swearing by it."

"He realigned the pigpen so the energy would be right for the Hogs," Tyber deadpanned.

"Yes. And all this time we thought they took some kind of demented glee in cutting loose."

"Ooo-kay." Tyber stood up and got a glass of punch, wishing Todd had spiked it. At least then there would be a reason for what he was hearing.

"And he painted the wood slats red because—"

The lights in the room began blinking.

Everyone stilled as the lights continued to flash in rapid succession.

Then they just stopped.

"Any readings, Mark?" Calendula asked in a quiet voice.

"There was a slight fluctuation when it started, but that was it. Not enough to call one way or the other."

"But what else could have caused it?" Zanita wondered out loud, looking into her own monitor.

"Todd, do you have any electrical problems?" Tyber calmly asked. "I imagine being out on this end of the island . . ."

"Occasionally, but when I do, it's not in the form of rhythmic blinking lights. I have noticed that when these odd light pulses occur, they often precede a manifestation of some kind. We'll just have to wait and see."

They waited. An hour went by with absolutely nothing happening. Zanita, sitting on the couch next to Tyber, started to nod off in typical Zanita fashion. Tyber leaned over as if he intended to whisper quietly in her ear.

In actuality, he ran the flat of his tongue along the sensitive skin of her neck. Right under her ear.

"EEEE!" Zanita's eyes popped open. "I hate when you do that!"

"Like I always tell you, baby—no sleeping on the job.'

"I wasn't sleeping; I was thinking!"

"Mmmm-hmmm." Tyber stretched out, placing his hands behind his head. "Next time you think, try not to snore so loud."

"I don't snore!"

"If you say so, baby." This was an ongoing thing with them. Tyber constantly teased her that she snored when she knew positively that she did not.

"You always mistake a slight snuffle for a snore."

He raised an eyebrow. "Slight snuffle? Sweetheart, it registered on their monitors like the San Andreas rupturing."

"It did not," she hissed back. "You're only making that up to get to me."

"Why do you think I had to wake you up? That's very sensitive equipment."

"Oh, hush." Zanita peered around the room just to be sure. Everyone was busy with some task or other. Mark and Calendula were checking the cables to the equipment, Todd was making notes on the next day's menu, and Hubble was reading a paperback book. She threw Tyber an "I should have known better" look.

His lips twitched.

Zanita's chin notched up. "I did not believe it for a minute."

He closed his eyes and grinned. "Did too."

"Did not." She turned way from The Wedded Annoyance in a huff, feeling his low laughter ripple up her spine.

Suddenly Mark's motion detector sounded an alarm. They all raced across the room to huddle around the scopes.

"There's something really large moving around in the kitchen." Mark spoke sotto voce.

Tyber glanced down at the top of the paranormal researcher's head in disbelief. Apparently, Mark must have discovered that ghosts could be "spooked" by loud voices. Tyber rolled his eyes.

Mark was getting excited; he turned a dial to sharpen the focus. "It's really big!"

In sync, Tyber and Zanita shifted focus to the corner, automatically checking to see that Hippolito was still lying prone on the floor. He had fallen there in a dead stupor (with all four feet pointing straight up) over an hour ago and hadn't stirred a muscle since. The little pink tongue still poked out of his mouth, silent proof that the act of grooming after dining had proven a bit too much for him.

This was a cat who took his digestion very seriously. Not even a whisker was allowed to twitch as the all-important activity went on.

Tyber and Zanita's eyes met. Both pair were flashing with humor. *Cats*.

"It's moving to the refrigerator now . . . look!" Mark pointed to the screen. "There's a smaller anomaly next to the larger one. I've seen this once before, in England. It was a double-linked spirit. They are always joined in some common pursuit or purpose. This is very rare." His voice rose in pitch with the uncommonness of the sighting.

Tyber bent over his shoulder and viewed the screen. His well-shaped lips lifted in a secret smile. "I believe I've seen this particular 'anomaly' many times, Mark. And you're right—they do have a common purpose." With that, he got up and strode determinedly toward the kitchen.

"Stop!" Mark warned, trying not to speak too loudly. "You'll ruin the experiment. If you go in there, you'll chase the spirit off."

"I don't think so," Tyber called out over his shoulder as he skirted the circular staircase. Striding through the dining room, he pushed open the swinging door to the kitchen. What he saw did not surprise him in the least.

Blooey and Hambone both looked up in shock. *Caught in the act.* The refrigerator light perfectly illuminated their nefarious deed, removing any doubt as to what they were doing. Of course, the raspberry tartlet crumbs lining the two guilty mouths put the period to the statement.

"Captain!"

Tyber crossed his arms over his chest and leaned against the door frame. "Blooey . . . and his accomplice in skulduggery, Hambone." He clicked his tongue. "Tsk-tsk. What have you two come to?"

Man and cat swallowed with guilt.

Blooey reached up to the nightcap he always wore to bed and fidgeted with the material. "It was all Hambone's doin', sir! I was sleeping like a babe when the scurvy swabee whapped a paw across me mouth! Sat on me chest and stared me straight in the eyes, he did. Swear he hypnotized me! Next thing I knew, we was coming down here and ravaging the rations."

Tyber raised his brow and stared down at Hambone.

The pirate cat had the nerve to grin up at him. The fact that the cat was missing several teeth added to the charming picture.

135

"Blooey, I know Hambone and you do this every night."

"You do, Captain?"

"Aye, I do."

Blooey scratched his chin. "Takes some of the fun out of it, doesn't it, Hambone?"

The cat didn't answer. He was busily wiping the crumbs off of his face and licking clean the evidence. Like most cats, he was going to try to disavow any knowledge of the deed once all trace of it was gone. Strange how cats thought they could do this even when they were caught red . . . pawed.

Stranger still was the fact that it usually worked.

It was difficult to refute a kitty who looked smugly up at you as if to say, "Prove it." Tyber always marveled at the feline sense of selective relativity. For a cat, the past was just so much fantasy—especially if it involved some wrong doing.

Mark's head poked around Tyber. "A snacker!" There was a wealth of disgust in the observation.

"Sorry, pal." Tyber nodded at him over his shoulder. "The double reading combined with the refrigerator was a dead giveaway—you'll forgive me the pun. Better luck next time."

"Geesh." Mark stormed back into the library.

Zanita shook her finger at the two culprits, but her eyes were dancing with mirth.

When they got back to the library, Hubble did not even glance up from his book. "False alarm, by chance?"

"Blooey and Hambone out for a midnight snack."

"Hmf." Hubble went on with his reading, a treatise on the life cycle of the gnat.

Zanita thought it was particularly appropriate reading material for this man.

"He's not even polite enough to pretend he's interested in what we're doing," she sputtered to Tyber in an aside.

Tyber glanced over at the psi-cog. "Mmmm."

"It's as if a little cloud hangs over his head, waiting to rain on everyone he comes in contact with. What is it with him, anyway?"

"I don't know, baby. Maybe he's just one of those straight-by-the-book academic types." He shuddered theatrically.

"Really, Tyber. You're much too serious, you know that?" His only response was a sexy wink.

An entire shelf of cooking videos crashed to the floor.

Zanita jumped. "My god, what caused that?"

Tyber began walking over to the fallen videos to investigate, but Calendula yelled out a warning. "Watch out, Tyber! Behind you!" Tyber turned and veered just in time to see a kitchen spatula whiz by his head.

"Poltergeist activity! Mark, are you recording?"

"Yes! The readings are off the scale!"

"I don't believe this!" Zanita watched dumbfounded as several objects hurtled through the air. Tyber yanked her out of the path of a flying nutmeg grater.

"Did you notice—it's all kitchen equipment?" As if to verify her words, a whisk whipped by her nose.

"Yes, I did notice that." Tyber put his hand on top of her head, protectively holding it down as a shelf of books crashed to the floor. "Maybe this ghost of yours is a disgruntled chef who was unjustly stripped of his Michelin stars."

"That's not funny."

"My cookbooks!" Todd moaned.

He started to pick them up but thought better of it when Mark yelled out, "Forget it, Todd! Wait until it stops—you might get hurt!"

Through it all, Hubble sat in the corner cool as a cucumber, reading his paperback.

Zanita raised her head. "Why is he just sitting there?"

Tyber murmured, "Better question might be: why aren't any of the flying gadgets going near him?" He ducked on top of her to avoid a lemon zester.

"Because he doesn't believe in it?" Zanita mumbled facetiously against Tyber's shoulder. "I don't believe in spooks! I don't! I don't!"

Tyber grinned against her curls. "Okay,

inverted cowardly lion; you're safe." He kissed the top of her head. "You know, baby, it's occurring to me that all of these gadgets have exactly the same trajectory."

"Tyber, how can you think of physics now? We are experiencing a genuine paranormal event!"

"Well, I suppose I could think of sex."

"Tyber!"

"Haven't you seen the statistics on men's thought patterns? Every three minutes we think of physics or—What is that scent?"

"Um, avatar of roses."

"No, that *other* scent. It smells like burnt eggs."

Sure enough, the sulfurous stench of burning eggs filled the library.

"Argh!" Zanita buried her nose in Tyber's chest, trying to inhale his delicious, clean scent instead of the noxious fumes.

"This happens sometimes on cases I've been on, Zanita." Calendula actually seemed joyous amid the otherworldly odor. "It's a type of haunting which stimulates the olfactory senses. Sometimes it's a perfume that the deceased wore; a spirit will use that to let the target know it is present. It's called a sign. I've also experienced the scent of pipe tobacco at hauntings." She took a big whiff of the malodorous aroma. "This is the first time I've encountered a negative scent." She paused. "I'm afraid we have an angry spirit here, Todd."

"What makes her think that?" Tyber groused as a cherry pitter bounced off his shoulder.

As suddenly as it started, it stopped.

Slowly, everyone stood up, warily looking around for stray basters zinging through the air. Hippolito, of course, remained in the same position: slack-jawed, on his back with all four paws in the air. Not even poltergeist activity was going to get this dude to move.

"Wow!" was all Todd said. Tyber wasn't sure if he was referring to the sacked-out cat or the ghost.

"Have you experienced anything like that before, Todd?" Zanita brushed off her dress.

"No. Nothing like that." He thought a minute. "Maybe the presence of the equipment has angered it?"

"Possibly." Calendula bent over the instruments, examining the results.

Zanita walked over to Hubble. "Why weren't you affected, Hubble? Do the psi-cogs have some immunity we are not aware of?"

Hubble put down his book. "Yes, Mrs. Evans, as a matter of fact, we do. You see, we don't believe in such nonsense and therefore we do not allow ourselves to be affected by it."

"That is ridiculous. You had to see what was happening. How can you dismiss this?"

"Oh, I don't dismiss it. On the contrary. I just

don't believe that the cause of it was 'other-worldly.' "

Mark snorted. "Yeah. Right."

Tyber cleared his throat. "Hubble may be right."

Everyone stared at him doubtfully.

"I noticed that the trajectories of the objects were all identical."

"Was does that mean in plain English, Doc?" Todd asked.

"It means that they all came from the same source."

Hubble stood. Walking around his chair, he exclaimed merrily, "Now we are getting some-where!"

"Do these poltergeist activities usually involve a single end source?" Tyber inquired.

"Not usually," Calendula responded. "Usually the activity seems to initiate from several differ-ent places at once. But that's not a hard and fast rule."

"Where do you think the objects launched from?" Zanita asked. Something wasn't right here. She could *feel* it.

Tyber's beautiful blue eyes gazed upward, fol-lowing the path of the circular staircase.

"What's up there?" she asked Todd.

"Just a narrow platform and the upper level of the bookshelf."

"And an octagonal window . . ." Tyber began climbing the staircase, taking two steps at once.

"Be careful!" Zanita watched him anxiously. Spiral stairs always made her dizzy.

Tyber reached the landing and carefully examined the small alcove. There was nothing out of the ordinary that initially met the eye.

First, he went to the window and looked outside. It was too dark to see much of anything, but he did note that there was a foot-wide ledge possibly within jumping distance of the window—if one could squeeze through the narrow opening. Right above the ledge was another, wider window. "Where does that window over the ledge lead to?" he called down to Todd.

The chef had to think a minute. "That's a closed wing of the house. I doubt anyone could make such a jump safely. The ledge isn't stable."

Tyber wasn't so sure about that but shrewdly responded, "You're probably right."

"I was planning on making repairs to that section next spring. That is, if my business increased." Todd sighed. "I guess I won't have to worry about that if these weird things keep happening. Who in their right mind would want to stay here with all this going on? I can't even serve a decent squash casserole."

Upstairs, Tyber shuddered. *Squash casserole!* He hoped Blooey wasn't within hearing distance. His cook had an unnatural affinity for butternut squash that threatened his sanity.

"Don't worry, Todd, we'll get to the bottom of it," Mark consoled his friend.

Inside the small alcove, Tyber knelt down in front of the bookshelves and ran his hand along the entire back edge. He had noticed that the wood wainscoting was slightly uneven where the platform bisected the bookcase.

There it is. A hidden catch to a secret cubby or passage. The entire top of the bookcase must swing forward!

He could hear the guests talking below. At least one of them was in on this, he was positive. He opened the hatch slightly and peered inside. It was dark, but he could definitely see a passageway.

He decided to wait to investigate during the day when the library was empty. Carefully he latched the door, making sure no one saw him.

Zanita looked up at him as he made his way down. "Find anything?"

Everyone waited for his answer with fervent anticipation.

He shrugged. "Nothing. I must have been wrong."

Zanita looked at him knowingly. For one thing, the Doc would never admit so easily to being wrong.

For another, he was *never* wrong.

It was one of those genius drawback things that she had to live with. Her rogue of a husband had found something. "We'll talk later," she whispered to him so no one else could hear.

"Damn," he murmured softly. Zanita raised her eyebrow.

Tyber's forehead furrowed. The woman was really on to him! *This is not good.* He was going to have to come up with a much better plan of attack if he hoped to win their challenge. And win it he would.

His eyes narrowed, and the slightest of smiles graced his outlaw lips.

It was time to weigh anchor.

Chapter Six

An arm came around her waist and pulled her under the bed.

Zanita started to scream, let out one abortive bleat, then hesitated. Was she dreaming? She blinked. No, this wasn't a dream.

Her hand balled into a fist and punched the wall of muscle leaning over her. A slight "oomph' was the only response from her sneaky husband.

"I-am-going-to-kill-you." She uttered her words with all the vehemence she could muster.

"Did I surprise you?" he whispered in her ear, letting his lips graze the sensitive folds.

As soon as they had returned to their room, she had pulled all the shades down, blocking out the dawn light. Then she had swept off her clothes and flopped onto the mattress. She had been lying in the high tester bed, drifting off to sleep, while Tyber washed up in the bathroom.

"You scared the bejesus out of me! What is the matter with you? I can't believe you did this!" She pushed ineffectually at the solid naked chest. It was too dark under the bed to see anything but his outline.

"Good." His butter-soft lips skimmed over her in a raider's kiss.

She gasped as his intent became clear. "You—you can't be serious, Tyber!"

A playful tongue caressed the corners of her mouth. "Mmm-hmm."

"Under a bed?" She sucked in her breath as she felt the palm of his hand slide over her breast. The peak hardened instantly. And so did her captain.

"Yes, under a bed . . ." He kissed her deeply, letting his tongue insinuate itself between her shocked, parted lips. Zanita made one of those little sounds of pleasure, the kind that always drove him wild.

"Why?" she asked raggedly while his mouth coasted in a lively pattern down her exposed throat. He blew softly on the moistened skin, making her shiver.

"For one thing, it allows me to explain the Heisenberg Uncertainty Principle to you." His voice had a low, sensual rumble to it. She recognized that growl. Tyber didn't just have bedroom eyes. He had bedroom voice.

He also had a "thing" about teaching her physics by using very unorthodox methods. "*Oh noooo.*"

"Oh yessss." He caught her lower lip between his teeth and sharply tugged on it.

Zanita smiled to herself. How did the man manage to irk, entice, and entertain all at the same time? She was positively convinced that in a past life the Doc roved the bounding main. What was she saying, *in the past*? All the man needed at this very moment was a cutlass to make the picture complete!

She moved against him. "Tyber, I don't know how you can draw parallels between—"

"That's it, baby, just like that . . ."

"—making love and . . . oh, god, *what* are you doing?"

"Demonstrating. Heisenberg said that it's impossible to know *both* the position and momentum of—"

"*Oh, my.* He was right." Zanita stretched up, circling her arms around his neck.

He smiled against her forehead. "Yes, he was. In order to have a sense of the event, one can either take the perspective of one or the other; like this. . . ." He did something utterly sinful with his lips.

"Oh!"

"Of course, he was talking about subatomic particles . . ."

"Who cares? The man was obviously a genius, too." She moaned as Tyber changed one variable but not the other.

"What do you mean, too?" He nipped her shoulder.

She giggled. Then sighed as he changed the other variable while maintaining a constant. "Dr. Evans, how did you get to be so bad?"

"I told you, I ate my vegetables when I was a little boy."

"And I told you, you were *never* a little boy. Speaking of vegetables, I saw you shudder when Todd mentioned squash casserole. Maybe he'll make some for us?"

Tyber shuddered again.

But not for the same reason.

He was breathless when he said in her ear, "Don't ever mention squash again at a time like this."

The perfect opportunity to get even for the trick he'd played on her by tugging her under the bed fell right into her lap. So to speak.

"Squash! Squash! Squash!" she mercilessly repeated.

Tyber groaned. "Arghhhh!"

Zanita recognized when she had the victim at her mercy. "Squash! Squash! Squash!"

He stilled.

Zanita laughed. The man actually could not move. Immobilized by a gourd!

"You think that's funny, huh?"

"Yes, actually, I do." She grinned up at him.

Even in the low light, she could see his nostrils flare. Now, this was an interesting turnabout! Thank goodness he couldn't discern the smug look on her face.

"You don't have to look so smug about it."

Her jaw dropped. "How did you know?"

"I didn't. Now I do."

Geniuses. "Tyber, I hate when you do that!"

He chuckled. "What?"

"Trick me into telling you stuff."

"Oh. I didn't know I could do that. Now I do."

"Very funny. And stop looking so smug."

"I'm not."

"Oh."

He roared with laughter.

She bucked her hips against him.

He arched his brow.

"Do you know what Heisenburg really meant by the Uncertainty Principle?"

"I have no idea." Her voice was clipped and terse.

"He was referring to the nature of the universe in terms of probability." His mouth came over hers in a tender kiss. "For instance, there was a very high probability that once I met you, I would want you forever."

That melted her. "Tyber, what a sweet thing to say." She placed her hands on his cheeks and planted butterfly kisses all over his handsome face.

"Baby, I love you."

"*Tyber.*"

His mouth teased at her lips, tempting her to deepen his touch. He kept giving her hints of himself, delicious sweeps of tongue, fascinating glimpses of passion, tantalizing impressions of sensuality.

Yet she was never able to guess where he would go next. What he would do. How he would feast upon her. He lingered over every inch of her skin. In loving tribute, he laved each tiny erogenous spot until she was crying out, begging him both for more *and* less. Bless the Heisenberg Principle!

"You see," he drawled, "you're married to a physicist who holds these principles in high regard. So what's it to be, Curls, more or less . . . ?"

White teeth scraped along the sensitive line of her groin. His hot of tongue flicked back and forth over the susceptible area.

Zanita shivered.

"Hmmm?"

"Ohhh . . . I think more."

His white teeth captured a tiny dark curl and pulled on it. The sensation was exquisite.

"Definitely more!"

"Mmm . . . I like that choice better." His fingers threaded through the thick patch of soft hair covering her mound, tangling in the silken strands. He tugged sharply twice, just enough to cause heightened feeling not discomfort. The action intensified her response to him even more.

While he did this, his middle finger strummed along the folds of her feminine lips in contrasting, gentle sweeps. Soon her natural dew covered his hand. That was when he slid his finger into her, sinking *deep*.

Zanita writhed closer to him, "You feel so good . . ."

"I want to say that to you." His voice was a bare breath, raw and sexy. "But you feel better than good; you feel right."

She moaned again, his words exciting her as much as his actions. His lips skimmed her nether curls; a faint touching. Followed by the stirring sweep of a hot tongue.

At his first press, tremors raced through every part of her. Unconsciously, Zanita sifted her fingers through the strands of his long hair, marveling as she always did at the silky texture of the gold-kissed chestnut mane.

Even in this, Tyber remained unorthodox, choosing not to wear his hair in the fashionably short, buzz-cut style favored among men today. Such styles were not for pirate captains.

Zanita sighed. It was impossible not to love a man who so valued individuality.

And who was such an extraordinary lover.

A maverick lover. Tyber's nature was wild and unpredictable. At the same time, he was always a considerate and passionate lover. The combination was an irresistible handful. Not many women would be able to take this man on, Zanita knew. Still, she had always felt that her friend Mills was right when she'd told her that she had had one hell of a horoscope the day she met Tyberius Augustus Evans.

His tongue flicked precisely on her, pressing in on that small hidden nub. It pulsed like an instrument being played to his rhythmic ministrations. At the same time, his tapered finger explored lazily inside her, palpating a certain mysterious spot that made her go completely out of control.

"Oh! What are you . . ." She couldn't finish her question. Her body wouldn't let her. Tensing and curving into him, Zanita felt a powerful release building within her. Trying to hold it at bay, she desperately panted, "Less! Less!"

Tyber was so surprised that he stopped and blinked. Zanita felt his long lashes sweep against her inner thigh.

"Wh-what?" she gasped.

"Baby, you understood the Uncertainty Principle." He grinned against her skin, planting a smacking kiss at her juncture. Knowing Zanita's predilection to run screaming from all forms of science, he almost crowed. "Damn, I'm good."

"Yes, you are." Her hand fisted into his hair and brought his face firmly back down to where she wanted it. "Now let's see if we can ace the exam, Doc."

He chuckled against her.

And aced it.

They both drifted off to sleep under the bed.

Though it was slightly stuffy, neither one of them had the energy to move. Before she nodded off, Zanita had made one joke about their lying in state like a couple of Hammer Film vampires caught without their coffins at sunup.

That was the last thing either of them remembered until a persistent pounding sounded at their door. This was followed by a loud bang as the door was energetically flung open to crash against the wall.

Tyber automatically reached for Zanita in a protective move. "What in the hell was—"

"I know the two of you are in here, so there's no sense in your pretending you're not!"

Zanita gasped. "That sounds like Auntie!"

"*Auntie?*" Tyber was horrified. Not that woman who ordered everyone about in an affected

Boston accent spoken through locked jaws! *Not her. Please don't let it be her.* "Are you sure?" he whispered frantically.

"Yes, it's her."

Tyber slapped his forehead with the heel of his hand and made the sound of a tortured prisoner. "What is she doing here?"

"I don't know! We'd better—"

The sharp point of a Ralph Lauren umbrella dived under the bed, poking Tyber square on his left cheek. And it wasn't the cheek on his face. "*Ow!*"

"What are you doing under there? Come out at once! I need to speak to you, Zanita."

Zanita started to slide out when Tyber stopped her by grabbing her by the thigh. "You aren't dressed, remember?"

"Oh. You're right. You'd better go."

He gave her a look. "Earth to Zanita. Wake up, sweetheart. There's a barracuda up there waiting to devour us, and we are both naked."

"Hush, she'll hear you! It will hurt her feelings; you know how she adores you," she whispered back, then spoke in a louder voice to the woman standing expectantly over the bed. "We ... um ... we kind of aren't wearing any clothes, Auntie."

"You mean Tyber is *nude*? At this hour?" Auntie sounded as if her sensibilities had been bruised beyond repair. No man should ever have the audacity to be naked in his own bedroom after luncheon!

Tyber knew an opportunity when he heard one. "Yes, I am," he called out. It was worth a shot to see if it would scare the barracuda away so they could come out and reconnoiter.

No such luck.

Barracudas chewed up and spit out such flimsy excuses. *She* shocked *them*. "You needn't be ashamed with those buns, my marvelous man. Get out here and stop dawdling!"

Tyber coughed. "I don't believe that woman is related to you," he gritted out.

"Of course she is! She's just upset about something."

"Auntie, dear, may we have a few moments to—"

"No. Grab one of those dangling sheets that are hanging down over the bed and stop being such babies. Come out of there!"

They did.

In very short time they were both standing in front of the woman who always wore three hats as her trademark. Tyber wrapped the sheet closer around his waist and glared at her.

"What's going on, Auntie?" Zanita smoothed the sheet over her hips.

"How could you get married without inviting me—your only aunt!—to the wedding!"

Zanita bit her lip. "How did you—"

"Blooey told me the other night when I called." She threw her arms up in the air. "Horrors! What a thing to hear while you're unpacking a parcel from Neiman's!"

Tyber made a mental note right then and there to murder Blooey. Slowly. Without mercy.

"It's not what you think, Auntie."

"Thank gaaaaaawd!" She threw herself into the nearest chair. Making herself right at home. Tyber progressed from gritting to gnashing his teeth.

"I need a bourbon," the Aunt from Planet Attitude proclaimed. She looked expectantly at Tyber.

Muttering under his breath, Tyber grabbed his jeans from the closet and dragged them on. As he was padding barefoot to the door, she called out, "Straight up."

He nodded curtly.

Auntie raised an eyebrow. "Marvelous buns! I just adore that boy."

Tyber cringed and sharply closed the door behind him.

Zanita grinned. "He loves you too, Auntie." Afraid a bolt of lightning was going to strike her, she added, "In his own way."

"Of course he does, the darling thing." She squinted her eyes. "I do hope you were smart enough to snag him, Zanita. One needs to remember that *Cosmo* survey."

"Auntie! I hate that attitude! Men are not to be 'snagged' like wild boars!"

"Well, some of them are wild bores. And let's face it, dah-h-rling, you are a bit ditsy."

Zanita's lower lip stuck out.

"Come on, admit it. Everyone in the Masterson clan has a touch of it. Something in the blood, no doubt. We put the dys in dysfunctional. Did you know a couple of our forefathers bayed at the moon? In any case, it's nothing to be ashamed of as long as you fess up to it. Doesn't seem to have anything to do with intelligence, which we are all graced with in abundance. Have you seen the new Dolce and Gabbana collection? What were they thinking?"

Zanita sank into a chair opposite her aunt and let out a long breath. "Tyber says I'm nonlinear. I think he likes it. The marriage is temporary."

"Those fluffy streams of chiffon have to go— what did you say?" If it caused Auntie to stop her review of the latest in haute couture, it was going to be trouble.

"Tyber and I have this challenge going. He's trying to convince me that nothing will change between us if we stay married."

Auntie's mouth dropped. She stuck her feet out and leaned her head back in the chair. "Yes, it's the Masterson curse, that's what it is." She bent forward and patted Zanita's arm. "You can't help it, you poor thing."

"What are you talking about? I think it makes perfect sense."

"Yes, well, to you it would, darling."

"In any case, Tyber in turn agreed to help me investigate this ghost tale. You know how resistant he is to these kinds of forays."

"Ghosts?"

"Yes. The inn is haunted." She scratched her head. "But that's not important right now."

"What do you mean it's not important? Are you saying I find myself in the middle of a haunted inn?"

"Hmm? Yes, I think so, Auntie."

"How wonderful!" She clapped her hands together.

"He's so good at this. I don't know why he always pretends to be doing something else when I ask him if he wants to investigate something of a paranormal nature . . ."

"I will help, of course. I'm mar-r-r-velous at these undercover things."

"I think he really likes it but won't admit it—stubborn pirate that he is."

"What do we do first?" Auntie's eyes flashed behind her "fashion-plated" chrome and rhinestone glasses.

"We?" Zanita snapped to attention, peering at the woman sitting opposite her. "And when did you start wearing glasses?"

"Oh, these are the latest thing. Sort of an Elton-Marilyn look."

"You can't help us, Auntie! This is very complicated."

"Nonsense. I helped you with that eel LaLeche, didn't I? Reeled the piranha in like so much fish!"

Zanita bit her lip. Tyber was not going to be happy about this.

Auntie stood up just as Tyber was coming through the door with her drink. She grabbed the glass of bourbon as she passed him on her way out, saying, "Ghost-busting! How mar-r-r-velous! Had no idea that lovely boy Todd was haunted! This is going to be so much fun. See you at dinner, children. Ta-ta!"

Tyber's mouth opened as the big kahuna Auntie wave gathered momentum and rolled to shore.

Then his head snapped back to his wife. "What did she mean—see you at dinner? She's not . . ." A horrified expression crossed his face. "Tell me she's not."

"Now, Doc, she was very good with LaLeche."

"That's because he could not be classified as human." He paused, thinking over his own insightful words. "I suppose if anyone can lure a denizen of the dark out of hiding, it's her."

"Tyber! Stop that. You know you love Auntie."

"Mmmm-hmm. The same as I love squash."

It was time to throw her genius off by diverting him. "By the way, what was that second reason?"

The ice-blue eyes clouded over and he rubbed his ear. A sure sign he was hiding something. "What second reason?"

"You know, when I asked you why we were making love under the bed, you said, 'for one thing.' So what was the other reason?"

"Ah . . ." He shook the kinks out of his shoulders. "Can't seem to remember," he said in an undertone.

She folded her arms over her chest. "Really."

"I, ah, need to check out something . . . I'll be back in a little while—"

"Oh, no, you don't! Stop right there. What *did* you find last night?"

Tyber pivoted about on his heel. Damn. When did it become hunting season on physicists? he wondered.

Hell, this was his battle. In true pirate manner, he matched her by crossing his arms over his chest. "You didn't answer my question about your aunt."

The Captain's lady held her ground. "You didn't answer mine."

"You're trying to distract me, and its not going to work, baby."

"Fine, then we'll forget it."

He arched one eyebrow, looking very much the rogue.

"So what did you find?"

He shook his head. When a woman had inquisition on her mind, it was as if a man were entering the fray with no weapons. He did best to cut his losses right from the start to avoid further bloodshed.

"There's a secret panel behind the bookcase on the landing."

Her face lit up with excitement. "Really? Wow! Let's go investigate!"

"*I* am going to check it out. We don't know what's behind that door and—" A pillow bounced off his head. He blinked. "Did you just throw a pillow at my head?"

"Um, noooo. It must be the ghost."

"Zanita, we don't know who is in on this, and it's too dangerous to—"

"*We* don't have to worry. Auntie's here now. She'd never let anything happen to us." She grinned at him.

He paused. "You might be right. Who, living or dead, would dare mess with her? A woman who *murders* Harley Davidsons." His eyes narrowed.

Tyber still hadn't gotten over the death of his beloved motorcycle under Auntie's wheels. The first time he had met her, the woman had run over his bike with her ancient Mercedes.

Remorselessly, she had left it there, belly-up in his driveway, for dead. It was not the best of introductions.

Furthermore, it had taken him and Gregor two months just to assemble the new parts for it, let alone to begin the task of seeing if they could revive it. He was of the opinion that it was all over but for the wake. Gregor was more optimistic.

Tyber sat on the edge of the bed, slipping on his argyle socks and boots. "We'll check the veranda when we come back."

She handed him his shirt.

He took it from her, not letting go of her hand. "I want you to be careful, baby." The blue eyes held a wealth of sincerity and concern.

"Of course I will," she responded.

So he kissed the inside of her palm, letting his tongue tickle the center. "Let's go." He grabbed a flashlight from his suitcase on the way out.

They were both thankful that the library was vacant.

It was around two in the afternoon; the other guests were undoubtedly still sleeping off the night watch. Ghost-busting could play havoc with your internal clock, Zanita acknowledged. Pretty soon your days would be completely turned around.

Not that that was a bad thing. She had always

been something of a night bird, and the idea appealed to her.

They were amazed to see Hippolito in the same position in the same spot under the side table. "He couldn't still be there!" Zanita peered at the lackadaisical feline to see if it was still breathing. "He must have gotten up at some point . . . ?"

Tyber squinted at him. "Yep. He did."

"How can you tell?"

"He has a bit of egg clinging to his whisker. Must be from breakfast."

"Gawd." Zanita was tempted to lean down and tickle the little pink tongue sticking out. Hambone did her one better.

Hearing familiar voices in the library, Tyber's cat had come in to investigate. No slouch himself in the food department, the pirate cat scanned the perimeter, his one-eyed gaze going mischievously to the supine cat.

He padded over, using what he must have thought was incredible kitty stealth. In actuality, the rag-tag cat hadn't been light of foot in some time.

But Hambone didn't acknowledge the effects of aging and a pugnacious life; in his convoluted cat mind, he was a feather falling on fresh snow.

Fortunately for him, in the realm of cats, Hippolito was not exactly a rocket scientist. Hambone stood over Hippolito, staring down at the tubby cat with a mixture of naughty glee and disgust.

Then—without warning—WHAP! Right across the kisser.

"Oh, oh." Tyber turned to Zanita. "He gave him the Slap of Obeisance. We're in trouble now. Hambone will expect full worship status as befitting a cat who dares execute a command cuff on a slumbering puddy-tat."

Zanita goggled at him. "*Where* do you get this stuff?"

He pointed to the scene before them. They watched to see what would happen.

Hippolito blinked.

His whiskers twitched.

His round eyes widened.

As an afterthought, his chubby back legs wiggled in the air. The pink tongue remained exactly where it was, peeking out of his mouth.

Zanita and Tyber watched incredulously as the round eyes slowly drifted shut again. All was as it had been before.

"Shane does not return," Tyber murmured conclusively, apparently solving a longtime conundrum.

Zanita clunked her head against his shoulder.

Hambone, observing all of this with equal interest, seemed to frown. He hesitated as if thinking it over, then swished his tail in self-proclaimed victory (although what the victory was in tabby terms was anyone's guess). Head held high, he strutted out of the room with a "who's-the-cat" swagger.

"That feline of yours is just too weird, Tyber."

He grinned at her, displaying two deep dimples. "Gotta love him."

"Uh-huh."

He snorted and started up the circular staircase. "Right this way—fun, excitement, secret doors, and ghosts."

Zanita put one foot on the bottom step and glanced up. Which was a mistake.

A wave of dizziness assailed her.

Then she thought of Tyber checking out that exciting discovery on his own and took a deep breath to still the reeling. No way was he going to have all the fun! Grabbing on to the railing for dear life, she slowly made her way up, almost closing her eyes as she reached the top.

Tyber pulled her onto the platform.

"Why didn't you tell me you were afraid of heights?"

"I'm not. I just don't like circular stairs. They give me vertigo."

"Vertigo? You could've fallen. Why didn't you let me . . ." He hesitated when he saw her mulish expression. "Okay, but I'll help you on the way down by going first." He knelt in front of the bookcase, springing the hidden latch. "Here we go."

"How did you ever find this?"

"I noticed that the wainscoting on the book-case and the stairwell were not properly lined up. See?" He pointed to a very minuscule discrepancy that most people would have overlooked. Most people, however, were not Tyberius Augustus Evans.

"Amazing, Doc. What about this window? That ledge . . . ?"

"It's possible, but my money is on this passageway."

"Just because it's here doesn't meant it's the source of last night's phenomenon."

"Perhaps not," he conceded. "But in my book, it's too convenient. When something is that convenient, look to it first for the solution."

"Is that the famous Evans Convenience Principle?" she teased.

His lips curved. "Yes. I'll demonstrate it to you later." He began to crawl into the passageway, saying over his shoulder, "I would have said 'after you,' but in this case, I am going to be the gentleman by going first."

Zanita knew he would never willingly let her take any kind of risk.

Initially, the passage was low and narrow, but it soon widened out considerably. After a few yards, they were able to stand as they walked along. Tyber's flashlight? bounced off the walls as he used it to break up several webs.

If the house isn't haunted, it should at least get an award for interior creepiness, Zanita thought. She brushed several large spider webs away from her. Good thing Tyber went first. The last thing she wanted was a sticky web in the face. Especially if it came equipped with *arachnid horriblus.*

"Hold up! The floor drops off here." He pointed the light beam down. "I hate to tell you this, Curls, but it's another circular stairway. Only this one looks a hell of a lot more rickety and nowhere near as stable. There's a lot of rust on it. I don't want you to get on it. Stay here while I—"

"Are you insane? Stay here while all the *things* that made these webs are somewhere nearby? No, thank you. I'm going with you."

His nostrils flared as he exhaled noisily. "I really don't think that staircase is going to hold both of us. It might not even hold one of us."

She held her chin up. "Then I should go first."

"I admire your bravery, but forget it."

"I'm the lighter one. It makes sense."

"No. Besides, there's only one flashlight. If the staircase moves, you will need two hands to hang on. We can't take the chance of the light dropping and shattering."

He was not going to talk her out of this. Zanita got a sneaky idea. "All right, I'll hold the light on you while you go down."

Tyber nodded and started to hand her the light.

"Then I'll toss you the light, so you can hold it for me."

His lips thinned. "What if I miss?"

"You? No way."

"I don't like it, baby." But he handed her the light and faced the stairwell.

It was dark.

It was probably very dangerous.

It looked like the perfect vacation spot for Nosferatu.

Chapter Seven

"Be careful, Tyber," Zanita whispered as he stepped onto the rusty platform.

He stepped lightly onto the first step. The ancient stairs creaked ominously. Several streams of rust sifted down to whatever was below. Altogether this area was more than creepsville; it gave her the heebie-jeebies big time.

"Tyber, maybe we ought to reconsider this. I don't want you getting hurt."

Tyber used one foot to bounce up and down on the staircase, testing its steadiness. "I think it will hold, baby, but we have to be very careful here. I don't know how secure the moorings will be as the weight point shifts with the path of the circular stairs, and the only way to find that out is to start down the staircase. If it starts to dance, I can leap over the railing."

"How far is it to the bottom?" She shone the flashlight down so he could see.

"Doesn't look too bad," he answered vaguely.

Zanita wasn't sure she believed that. "I don't—"

"Here goes."

Lightly he put his full weight onto the first step. There was a slight protest, but the structure held. He began the downward spiral. When he got about a third of the way down, the moorings protested by shifting suddenly with a loud, creaking groan. The entire staircase swung around about twenty degrees, but the base stayed in its socket.

Expecting to hear a crash any minute, Zanita called worriedly into the darkness.

"I'm okay. It just shifted. It's holding."

The rest of the trip down was accomplished very slowly. When Tyber reached the bottom, Zanita heard his boots clang off the stone floor and sighed a breath of relief.

"How far down is that, anyway? It sounds like you're in a dungeon."

Tyber glanced around him in the dim light. He was surrounded by damp stone walls and musty air. Dungeonlike enough for him. "Close to it."

"I'm coming down now—are you ready to catch the light?"

"Just a second." He positioned himself to one side of the staircase. "Okay, just lean over the side and drop it straight down."

She did.

He caught it securely. *Knew he would*. Zanita smiled to herself. Tyber was just that kind of guy.

He steadily trained the beam on her while she carefully made her way down the looping stairs. In a way she was glad that it was mostly dark; she couldn't see all the sharp spiral turns. All she could view was the narrow patch of stars that Tyber illuminated for her as she stepped down.

It took a few moments for her to realize that he had twisted the head of the flashlight, adjusting the beam to a sharp, narrow focus for just that reason. He was helping her get down those stairs.

As she'd said before, it was hard not to love someone who was so smart.

At one point the stairs shook slightly, but all in all she had no problem. At the bottom, Tyber winked at her and trained the now widened beam on the stone walls and down the corridor.

"Where do you think we are?" She spoke barely above a whisper. Just in case someone or some *thing* was listening. There was no telling how many critters with beady eyes might be down here, and she didn't want to disturb them unnecessarily.

"I think we're under that other wing we saw

from the window," he said in a normal tone. "Todd had said that the window ledge led to a closed-up section of the house. This must be part of it."

Zanita peered around cautiously, walking on tiptoe.

He chuckled. "If you're worried about rats, forget it. You saw how meticulously Todd keeps the house and ... you know, that *is* odd. If he keeps the house so clean, why close off the other wing and not clean it? It's bound to cause trouble with infestation; especially in the winter months."

"You just said there are no rats down here!"

"Well, I wouldn't think so. I was talking more about the webs."

"Yes, that is strange. I don't see any down here, do you? And another thing: He certainly seems to do all right with the inn, or at least he did before the hauntings started."

Tyber frowned at her word choice.

"Well, that's what it is until you prove otherwise, Doc. So *why* did he close off the other wing in the first place?"

Tyber flashed the beam toward the end of the path. "We have to turn right here. He did say he was planning on renovating soon. So that might explain it."

"I don't know ... it doesn't ring true. You would think he would want to have it open to fill with guests as soon as possible. Money doesn't seem to be a factor for him. Why not do it all at once?"

An ear-piercing shriek shattered the quiet around them.

Zanita almost jumped on top of Tyber. "My god!"

It sounded again from behind them. A hideous, wailing cry. "What kind of unearthly creature could make a sound like that?"

"Hambone."

"Hambone?"

Tyber exhaled in resigned patience. "He must have slipped in beside you before I closed the door. The rogue."

"Hambone can make that kind of split-your-eardrums-crackle-your-bones sound?"

"Yes, if the circumstances warrant it. Wait here; I'll go get him. It will just take a minute."

"Oh, no, you don't! I'm not going to be that stupid. I'm going right with you."

"Why? I'll just be gone a sec—"

"Don't you ever pay attention to all those horror movies we watch? This is exactly how the first victim always gets it. The person is left alone for a 'moment' while someone else goes and gets something, and *whammo*! Victim Pâté. And it's usually a woman, too. For the scream effect."

He was trying very hard not to laugh. "I think

173

you've been watching too many of those *Gonna Git You* movies, baby. C'mon."

"Well, you have to admit the first one was good. After that they kind of lost it with the sequels: *Gonna Git You in the Food Court* and *Gonna Git You in the Home Depot*. They weren't as—"

"Uh-huh." He placed his hand on the back of her neck and steered her back down the hall.

Sure enough, there was their scruffy orange tabby sitting halfway down the stairs, tail swishing as he waited patiently for rescue.

"Must've gotten halfway down and realized he didn't like it very much." Tyber went up to get him after giving Zanita the flashlight. "Come on, you scalawag."

Hambone hissed-purred as Tyber hoisted him up, but all in all looked pretty happy that his human had come back for him.

As they reached the bottom, Zanita swung the light around and jumped. She almost dropped the light. Written on the stone wall—in what looked like dripping blood—was the word *Nan*. It hadn't been there a few minutes ago when they first came through.

"What is it?" Zanita showed him by illuminating the stone.

"Nan? Is that someone's name? Short for Nancy?"

"How did it get here?" she whispered. "It wasn't here before when we came through."

"It was here and we just didn't see it."

She threw him a "try another one" look. "There is no way we would have missed that! It's a word printed in dripping red whatever!"

Tyber set the cat down and firmly took the light from her. "Get behind me, Curls. Right now," he said in a low, commanding tone.

She did as he bade, nervously peeking over his shoulder. "What is it? Do you see an apparition?"

Tyber's arm encircled her, and he slowly turned them both in a wide circle, training the light into every dark corner.

"No. Hambone didn't come in with us. Someone else let him in, which means . . ."

"We're not alone down here."

Tyber kept searching the dark nooks under the stairwell, keeping himself constantly in front of her. There was another partially hidden smaller passageway under the stairs to the left, but it appeared undisturbed. He exhaled. "I don't see anything, and the passage is too narrow for anyone to have gotten by us. Whoever it is must have written that on the wall and left, not realizing that Hambone had snuck in underfoot."

"Or the ghost opened the passage to purposely let the cat in after it wrote this message, knowing that the cat would cry out for help and we would see it."

Tyber choked. "Would you listen to yourself?"

"What?"

He arched that eyebrow.

"It's as plausible an explanation as yours, given our circumstances."

"I'm not even going to respond to that."

He began walking the pathway again, but stopped momentarily to examine the dripping letters.

"Is it blood?" She gagged.

"I don't know. It might be. Don't touch it."

Zanita and Hambone followed slightly behind. Both of them kept looking behind their shoulders every few seconds. It appeared that Hambone didn't like spooks either. Despite what Tyber thought, that yell from the cat was pure fright. She had once read that cats have a special sense of the paranormal, and many believe that they can see things that humans can't.

Besides, Hambone was a pretty fearless cat. His chewed-off ear was testimony to that. Whatever he had seen had scared him!

"I believe you, Hambone," she muttered to the pirate tabby.

Hambone acknowledged her with a meow-purr.

After turning right, the passageway went on for quite a while under the main part of the house.

They heard rapping noises from the walls as the passage continued along. "Where is it coming from, do you think?"

"My guess is that there are heating ducts on the other side of this wall. The ghostly raps are probably nothing more than expanding and contracting pipes."

Zanita bit her lip. "I don't know, Tyber. They don't sound exactly the same as the ones we heard last night."

"Well, they wouldn't on this side of a stone wall."

She had her doubts.

The passage suddenly veered to the left. They all followed along. Actually, Hambone was starting to trot, happy to be in on an adventure with them. Strange how cats could always tell that. They must have adventure-o-meters built in, Zanita marveled, snickering to herself.

The floor started to slope and they began walking up an incline. Suddenly the passage simply ended. A heavy wooden trapdoor was directly above them. Tyber opened it and hoisted himself through.

"Well. Well. Well."

"What is it?"

"Hang on to Hambone with one hand and I'll pull you up."

Zanita was a little apprehensive about lifting the irascible cat, but he seemed to understand and let her. Tyber pulled them up.

Muted light trickled down on them through wooden slats. Above them was another trapdoor.

"Where are we?" she wondered.

"We are right beneath our veranda, baby. Unfortunately, I can't lift that door because I dragged the hammock back over it last night; remember?"

She bit her lip. "Try it anyway."

He stared at her. "Okay."

He did, and much to his surprise, the door swung open.

"How did you know?"

She shrugged her shoulders. "I had a hunch that whatever it was that led us back through the passageway wanted us to see those letters. Maybe someone else didn't."

"What do you mean?" He helped her out onto the veranda. She blinked in the bright sunshine then shivered. It was winter and they did not have any jackets on.

"We would have gone straight through—if not for Hambone. Maybe Calendula's right; there are two ghosts here. One that wanted to give us either a creepy warning or clue, another that wanted to help us get through or prevent us from seeing those letters."

"Some of that may be right in regards to motive, but I think our source or sources are living, breathing entities, and I think they are working together."

"We'll see." She let the cat down. "At least *I'll* keep an open mind." She walked off the veranda and began to trudge around the side of the house. Their room was locked from the inside, and they would have no entrance this way.

"What do you mean?" Tyber came up quickly behind her. "Are you implying that I am not open-minded?"

"Yes. No. I don't know."

"Huh?"

"It's just that you have these nice little explanations for everything, and I'm not sure they fit all the time."

"Don't you think it's better to accept a logical explanation when there is one to offer?"

"Not necessarily."

"Why not?"

"Because it *may* not be the right explanation. And being a reporter, I want the truth. Whether it fits into your scientific paradigm or not."

He put his hands up in defense. "Whoa. I want the truth, too. But if there's a logical explanation for the things that have been happening here, I'm not going to embrace a half-baked theory instead."

"Don't get pissy with me."

"*What*? I'm not getting pissy! I'm simply trying to get you to understand that . . ."

"What?" She stopped and stared at him with her enormous violet eyes.

"That while some things are unexplainable, it doesn't mean that they are paranormal."

"Excuse me, but I thought that was a definition you just gave."

She was good, he thought. He laughed. "Perhaps. We'll see. I promised you to keep an open mind and I will."

"I love you." She smiled up at him, taking his breath away.

Hell, for this woman he'd debate with Ghoul, that happy-go-mad TV horror host.

He just hoped he wouldn't have to.

"Oooo. You look cold." Todd greeted them at the front door. "What were you two doing outside without your coats?" Before they could answer, he put up his hands.

"Stop. Don't want to hear any more. I know you're newlyweds . . ."

"Todd!" Zanita feigned embarrassment, for which Tyber gave her high marks. "Actually, we were investigating that secret passageway. You know, the one that leads from under our veranda to the landing on the top of the spiral staircase in the library."

Todd's brow furrowed.

"You didn't know about the secret passageway?" Tyber was skeptical.

"Not that one. There are several of them in the house, though most of them are under the closed wing. I've had plenty of nightmares about guests discovering a secret panel and getting lost or hurt inside for days before being discovered. Thank goodness that wing is completely sealed up on that side of the house. When I have time, I'm going to map out and mark off the dangerous areas. That's one reason why we haven't renovated over there yet."

That answered several of their questions. Todd would be concerned for his guests' safety. But Tyber wondered what the other reasons were.

"Who's we?" Tyber shrewdly asked.

"What?"

"You said, 'we haven't.'"

"Oh, that would be Sasenfras."

"*Who?*" Tyber and Zanita asked at once.

"Sasenfras. He's my caretaker. You haven't met him yet, have you? Dotty old coot, but pretty dependable. Been with my family forever. He came with the house."

"You mean as in 'including all furnishings and Sasenfras'?"

Todd smiled. "Something like that. Do you think the hidden passage had anything to do with the poltergeist activity last night?"

"It might. We'd like to talk to this Sasenfras, if we could."

"Sure; but he's mostly around here during the day. He doesn't like being here at night because of the ghost. Sasenfras is very superstitious, I'm afraid. He's probably already left for the evening."

"Where does he live?"

"He's got a small cottage near the bluffs. I can give you directions later, if you want to go see him after dinner. It's a nice walk."

"That'll be great."

"I'm impressed you found that passageway, Tyber. Clever of you to keep silent about it. You two are good! Now, just find the ghost and get rid of him for me and I'll cook you the best squash lobster bisque you ever had. Blooey told me how much you love squash, Tyber."

Zanita grinned broadly. "Deal!"

Tyber was much more subdued.

"You missed cocktails, but we were just going in to dinner. It's chicken l'orange tonight."

Zanita licked her lips. "That's my favorite!"

"I know; Blooey told me." He smiled back at her.

As they followed him toward the dining room, Tyber casually asked him, "Do you know anyone by the name of Nan or Nancy? Past or present."

"No. Can't say that I do. Why do you ask?" Todd glanced over his shoulder at Tyber as he led them through the parlor.

"No particular reason." Tyber gave Zanita a "let's keep that one to ourselves for now" look.

"By the way, Zanita, who is that outrageous woman with the three hats?"

"Umm, that's my aunt, Todd."

"Ah! I met her at lunch. She was sitting in the dining room, waiting to be served like the Queen of Prussia, actually."

Zanita swallowed. That was Auntie. The world was her oyster. "Was she very, um . . . demanding?"

"Oh, hell, yes." Todd waved it away. "But I adored the diva anyway. She's mar–r–r–r–velous!"

Zanita laughed.

Everyone was just sitting down at the table when they entered the dining room.

"Hey, you missed the hors d'oeuvres, you two." Mark winked suggestively at them.

Zanita blushed again.

"Horrors! Look at your clothes!" Auntie gave them both a disapproving sniff.

"We were out doing some of our own investigating this afternoon." Tyber handed Mark the bowl of mashed potatoes.

"Find anything interesting?" Hubble served himself a large helping of chicken l'orange.

"Not really," Tyber hedged. His eyes met Todd's across the table, signaling him that it might be best to keep the knowledge of the passageways hidden for the time being. The chef nodded slightly. He was still a suspect in Tyber's book; Tyber just hoped Todd wasn't involved. The guy was too damn likable and he cooked a mean chicken l'orange. *Chicken.*

"Great dish, Todd. Are these birds free-range?"

"Yes, as a matter of fact, Tyber, they are. One of my neighbors here on the island raises chickens. We often swap. Some of the herbs and vegetables from my garden for his birds. Works out very well."

"I've mentioned something similar to Blooey; thought he'd like to do a swap with a local farmer near us."

Blooey stared at Tyber agog. "Captain, you never—*oomph!*" Tyber kicked him under the table. "That is, you never know until you try it."

Todd refilled the plate of steamed beans on the table and took his seat.

"I recommend it very highly, Blooey. Just know who you're dealing with and it works beautifully. Almost like a cooperative."

Tyber took a bite of his meat. "Does your neighbor dress them for you?"

"God, no. I have to do that myself. But I prefer to sacrifice convenience for quality and freshness."

"Gads, let's not talk any more about dressing and undressing fowl! I don't mind eating the beady-eyed, filthy things on occasion, but surely there is better table talk."

Tyber threw Auntie a murderous look from beneath veiled lashes. He'd been trying to lead Todd down a specific path of questioning, and the Barracuda had just put an end to it. Aunts!

Zanita watched her husband curiously, wondering what all the chicken talk was about. Whatever it was, he was steaming. She decided to take some of the heat off Auntie by asking Calendula, "So what's on the agenda for tonight?"

The parapsychologist looked very tired, and Zanita wondered if the woman had slept at all. Calendula carefully patted her lips before replying, "The same as last night. Since the equipment is already set up and calibrated, it'll be a little smoother for us."

"Did you get any abnormal readings today?"

"No, nothing; but I wasn't expecting any. Todd said that nothing occurred today to upset his dinner preparations, and I'm not surprised after all that activity last night. We often see periods of quiet after heavy activity."

"I can't wait to experience this!" Auntie clapped her hands together. "Why, when Zanita told me . . . what's that, dear?" She looked down at Hambone, who miraculously gave her the sweetest of cat looks. She gave him a tiny piece of chicken. "Here you go, darling. Now where was I? Oh, yes, the ghost! This is sooo mar–r–r–velous! You know, Todd, I am going to tell all my friends about this wonderful place! Not only is the food fabu–u–u–lous and the accommodations superb, but a ghost!"

"Now, Auntie, I don't think Todd wants that to become common knowledge. He's trying to get rid of the ghost, remember?"

Auntie dismissed the notion. "Of course he's trying to get rid of it. That won't matter. Just the idea that there *was* a ghost here will bring them in droves. Do you mind, dear boy?"

"Well . . . I suppose not," Todd mumbled.

Auntie gave Zanita a pointed look, which was meant to convey a secret message. The old dear was trying to help them by ferreting out a motive, and she was right. If word did get out, Todd would be mobbed by curiosity seekers. Which placed him high up on the suspect list again.

She glanced at Tyber to signal him, but the Doc was watching Hambone as he pranced with his prize piece of chicken to the corner of the room to dine alone with the purloined goods.

What good was all this dinner-table signaling if you couldn't get the person's attention? Zanita groused to herself.

"So far, I have not seen one thing that comes close to convincing me that anything paranormal is going on here." Hubble had the annoying habit of speaking with his mouth full.

"What about all the activity last night? Don't tell me you can dismiss that, Hubble." Mark bristled.

"On the contrary. I simply don't believe that its origins were supernatural. Take those noises that you insisted were ghostly raps. I did some investigating myself and discovered them to be nothing more than some cellar pipes expanding and contracting with the heat."

Tyber caught Zanita's attention and nodded slightly. He had pointed that out to her earlier.

"You see, my dear"—Hubble gestured expansively, speaking directly to Auntie—"there is always a logical explanation to be found."

Zanita looked back and forth between the two of them. It seemed her aunt had made a conquest during cocktails. Zanita wasn't surprised. Auntie always attracted the scientist types.

Across the table, Tyber shook his head and rolled his eyes.

Well, *some* scientist types.

As Zanita watched, a framed photo of Todd standing in front of a famous culinary school slid across the top of the sideboard, crashing to the floor. Her mouth dropped open.

The others jumped at the sound. "Whatever was that?" Auntie turned around, looking everywhere for the culprit.

"A picture just slid across the sideboard," Zanita croaked, still shocked at what she had witnessed.

They all gazed down at the smashed picture.

"Must have been a plane overhead or a truck going by on the main road which caused a heavy vibration," Hubble surmised.

There was the infamous truck theory! "I don't think so." Zanita met her husband's eyes.

"Why not, baby?"

"Because I watched it scoot all the way across the top of the sideboard as if it were being pushed along by an unseen hand before it toppled over."

"Call to arms! Call to arms! There's a bloomin' phantom on board!" Blooey crossed his eyes and fainted dead away.

As he watched the spectacle of his rotund cook falling off his chair to the carpeted floor, Tyber deadpanned, "Oh, the humanity."

Zanita and Tyber hiked through the mixed oak and cedar woods under the moonlight, following a well-laid path through the Menemsha Hills. Tyber had brought his flashlight but didn't need it. The moonlight was lighting their way perfectly.

They both thought it was a lovely walk. Through a break in the trees, Tyber pointed out some white-tailed deer taking their evening feed.

"No, there are no poisonous snakes on this island."

"That's good to know." Zanita grinned at him

because he had anticipated her question. They were so in tune sometimes, it was eerie.

The corners of his lips curled. "There are, however, lot of ticks." He gestured to the deer. "And deer ticks, at that. Fortunately, it's cold enough not to have to worry about Lyme disease."

They rounded a bend; below them was a gorgeous lake. Zanita's nemeseis, the Canada geese, were honking their collective heads off. A few black-crowned night herons were still about.

"This is turning into a real adventure, Doc. Isn't this island fabulous? It's so beautiful here!"

"Yes, it is. Maybe we should buy a winter home here?"

"A winter home? Don't you mean a summer home?"

"Why be like everybody else?" He grinned at her. "I like the solitude out here right now. With you."

"True." She snorted. "Not that I could afford even an outhouse on this island."

Tyber stopped. "Baby, *we* can afford it. We're married, remember?"

"For the time being."

He took her in his arms and kissed her deeply. "For all time."

"We'll see."

He frowned at her.

189

She put her palm on his wide chest. "I admit that so far you are doing a very good job of presenting the unexpected. But the weekend isn't over yet. Sooner or later we'll turn into the epitome of the Mundanes, a married couple trudging wearily through life doing the same thing over and over again because its *expected*, not unlike those poor, doomed creatures in Dante's Inferno."

"You are twisted."

"I know."

"I love it." He grinned.

"I know."

"Now, what would your aunt say if you announced we suddenly aren't married anymore?" he drawled.

"Oh, she fully expects it. I told her all about our challenge."

"*You what?*" Tyber groaned. "I wish you hadn't done that."

"Why not?"

"It's, ah, embarrassing." That was not all it was. It was Trouble with a capital T. Especially since there were some things a barracuda aunt should not guess before the wife does.

"Phooey. She completely understands. After all, she is a Masterson."

"No doubt there," Tyber grumbled.

"You might think twice about shackling yourself to us. We have a genetic disorder of some kind that makes us all, ah, nonlinear—only in different ways."

"I'll take my chances with the dreaded blight." He glanced at her derriere playfully. "Especially when it's such a cute little awesome pest . . . i . . . lence."

Zanita wagged her finger in his face, but she was smiling slightly. "Your call. Don't say you weren't warned."

"Okay."

They walked along for a bit, enjoying the soft crunch of the snow underfoot. Puffs of air left trails of steam breath as they took in the winter night by the sea on the Vineyard.

Finally Zanita spoke.

"So how do you explain the cobwebs?"

Tyber's light blue eyes flashed with appreciation. "I was wondering when you were going to bring that up."

"Yes, I bet you were. There was no way someone could have come through that secret passageway to rain kitchen gadgets down on us without disturbing those webs. Yet we had to break through them when we went by."

A dimple appeared in his cheek. "Scary, isn't it?"

"Tyber!" She stopped and poked his chest. "You don't have an explanation, do you?"

He rubbed his ear. "Actually, I do, but you're not going to like it."

She placed her hands on her hips. "Go ahead."

"There are only two rational solutions. The first is that whoever was up there *never* went through the passageway in the first place, but entered the door from the platform in the library earlier and waited for us to appear. When we did, the culprit opened the door a crack, which would not be seen by us below, and showered us with the Julia Child rainstorm. Which is damn odd, now that I hear myself say it."

"The theory?"

"No. The gadget deluge."

"Oh."

"The theory is fine."

"Nope. Not going to wash. Where did this culprit go when you found the doorway? By your theory, he would still have been there. Otherwise, he would have had to disturb some of those webs. They were unbelievably thick."

"Which brings me to my second theory. I don't recall seeing those webs last night when I first discovered the passage. They might have been there; I didn't examine the passageway too closely. But my guess is that they weren't."

"What are you saying, that somehow the webs appeared overnight? That's impossible! Not that thick screen."

"That's exactly what I'm saying. They did appear overnight. All it takes is a can of web spray."

"Web spray?" Zanita laughed. "Sounds like something Paul Mitchell would devise for *avant* ducks. What is it?"

"Just what it sounds like. Kids use it all the time at Halloween. It doesn't look exactly like a web, but it's close. At the time, we took it for granted that the webs were real. We weren't even paying attention to them except to get them out of our way. The darkness aided the deception, too."

Zanita scoffed. "You're reaching."

He shook his head. "I don't think so."

"There's one way to prove it."

"Yes. We go back in the morning when everyone's asleep, take a sample back to our room and check it out."

"You're going to lose this one, Doc. Those were real webs. Women know these things, trust me."

"A kiss says I'm right."

She hesitated. "One of those curl-your-toes-and-leave-no-one-standing kisses?"

He smiled smugly. "Of course. Why else would I bet?"

"You're on." She put out her hand, and Tyber shook it to seal the wager.

"Deal."

Ahead of them, on the bluffs, was a small wooden shingled cottage backed by scudding clouds and the roar of ocean tides. As they stood there viewing the place, a dog bayed at the moon right on cue.

"Castle Sasenfras, I presume."

Zanita chuckled. "No telling how tangled the tale will get now, Doc."

She had no idea how portentous those words were.

Chapter Eight

"Sent ya hey-ah, did he?"

Sasenfras scratched his grizzled jaw. Just as Todd had said, he was a rheumy old coot. In fact, he looked remarkably like the Gloucester fisherman on the frozen-fish boxes ... or perhaps like Igor. Igor, the Transylvanian fisherman—that was a whole new concept. Zanita shook her head.

The man spoke with the thickest down-home Yankee accent she had ever heard.

"Yes, Mr. ... Sasenfras. He said you might be able to answer some questions for us about—"

"Well, then, might as well come on in." He opened the door to a small yet vivid living room which screamed psychedelic sixties. Both Tyber and Zanita stared uncertainly at the spectacle. The garishly bright furnishings seemed completely at odds with this snaggletooth of a man, who would be more at home in a medieval dungeon.

"Sit down there." He pointed to a splashy flower-patterned couch that looked as if it had been imported directly from sixties' Haight-Ashbury. Glass-beaded curtains separated the living room from the kitchen and there was an abundance of those modish orange and blue tones that always made Zanita want to gag. Next to the coffee table was an old lava light that was still chugging away; blobs of red floated sickeningly in pink water.

This erstwhile Transylvanian fisherman was not a hip, kitsch decorator. The stuff was all original. Zanita felt as if she had slipped into a time warp. The astounding part of it was that in no way did Sasenfras seem like the aging ex-hippie type. He seemed more like the old European servant to Dr. Frankenstein type.

Zanita would bet that these furnishings had been placed here by someone else. As they sat down, she noticed an old, faded poster in the corner which advised the viewer to "Turn On! Tune In! Drop Out!"

She whispered in Tyber's ear, "Oh, wow, man. This is so-o-o far out!"

Tyber tried not to laugh. This had to be one of the strangest things they had yet encountered—and the list was long.

Sasenfras's penetrating gloomy stare pinned them to their seats, taking away all notions of humor. "I know about it. I hate the way it is, but that's the way it is. So that's it."

Tyber and Zanita blinked. Was he speaking about the furniture or something else? And why was it that the words "caretaker" and "bizarre" always seemed to go hand in hand?

"Why'd you come up here?" he barked at them suddenly, then answered his own question before they had a chance. "As if I don't know."

Zanita and Tyber looked at each other. Obviously, they had come into the middle of a conversation that Sasenfras was having with himself.

Tyber cleared his throat. Being a scientist, he supposed it was up to him to try to put the bell on Igor's neck. "We were wondering if you knew—"

"Of course I know! What do you think, I'm, an idiot?"

Tyber wasn't sure. He rubbed his ear, pausing. He would try again. "Do you think that—"

"The answer is no."

"But I'm not—"

"Sure you are! I've told him time and again. So you can just forget it. Came down hey-ah for nothing, is what you did."

Tyber turned to Zanita and lifted his palms up as if to say, why don't you try? Zanita smiled prettily at Sasenfras. "Mr . . . um, Sasenfras . . ."

"Just Sasenfras. No airs for me. Wouldn't need them, would I?"

How was she to answer that? "Um, no, I suppose not. We would simply like to ask you if you—"

"Sorry, won't work. You're a pretty little thing, but the answer's the same. Won't sell, and there's the end to it."

"Sell?" Tyber got in the single word/question before they could be interrupted again.

"That's right. Know he wants it, but he ain't getting it! Was left to me, and that's that."

Zanita leaned forward to ask what he was talking about, but Tyber put a restraining hand on her arm. He had just figured out how to communicate with the caretaker. Simple. No more than three words at a time, directed at specific points. This man had elevated the knack of obscure, dipped Yankee conversation to a fine art.

"Wants what?" Tyber slashed back.

"The portion of the house old Sparkling gave me. The original wing."

Zanita's eyes widened. "You *own* part of the Florencia Inn? How did you—"

Tyber cut her off before Sasenfras could. This was a race to the punctuation mark. He didn't want to send the guy off again. "Todd's father?"

"Grandfather. Didn't think he'd really do it, but he did."

Zanita looked back and forth between the

two of them, amazed that they were actually communicating.

"Nice of him," Tyber probed.

"*Nice of him*? Twisted bastard! Liked to steal what wasn't his. Like all them Sparklings!"

That took them both by surprise. Especially Zanita, who was not at all sure she was following this exchange. Sasenfras did not appear to be the beloved family retainer, after all.

"Didn't want it?" Tyber watched him carefully.

"Does a man want his leg shackled to the grave?" Sasenfras was getting extremely passionate about the subject. Whatever it was.

"Hmmm." Tyber responded noncommittally, impressing Zanita by not taking a stand in a conversation that as far as she could tell had no focus.

"And all the goings-on there. Played me false, she did. Won't let him touch it!"

"I understand." Tyber nodded sagely. Zanita watched him open-mouthed. *He did?*

"They say there's strange things happening. Don't doubt it . . . but it chills a man's bones all the same. Won't go in there again . . . It'd be just like her . . . Promised me she'd take it one day. No doubt she will . . . she will . . ."

Zanita nodded stupidly. What was he babbling about?

"Got it first?" Tyber spoke softly.

Sasenfras's expression narrowed and sharpened suddenly. "Never said that. Was an accident." He seemed to be mulling something over, then mysteriously added, "Todd's not like the rest, but he won't get it just the same. It's mine!"

"Something's there?"

Sasenfras's eyes widened in fright. Apparently, he took Tyber's question as a statement. "I know." His hand shook. "I've seen it. Won't go in there again, I tell you."

"Scared you some?"

"Yes." He wiped his brow uneasily. "Hideous thing. Never forget it. I can still hear that scream . . ."

Trembling, Sasenfras reached over to the electric blue coffee table and grabbed a bottle of pills. He slid one shakily under his tongue.

"Bad ticker?" Tyber watched him alertly.

"That's a fact."

"We'll leave now."

Sasenfras thought a minute. "You can come again, if you have a need to."

Which seemed a strange invitation.

Tyber nodded and stood, bringing Zanita up with him. "Thanks. Appreciate it." He took a bewildered Zanita's hand and led her to the door.

As they opened it, they heard Sasenfras chuckling softly behind them. "Nice view from that bedroom window at night," he said insinuatingly. "Never quite seen that before. You're something else, boy."

Zanita gasped.

Tyber's shoulders hunched slightly and he stared off to the right, his cheekbones turning a dull bronze. "Um, yeah. Thanks."

He quickly pulled Zanita outside.

"He saw us!" she gasped again.

Tyber dragged her rapidly along the path. "Ah . . ."

Zanita dug her heels in and glared at him.

Tyber decided the only chance he had was to quickly change the direction of the conversation. Damn, but he'd thought the view was obstructed that night. "Do you think he did it?" he asked, trying to throw her off the topic.

"Did what?" She put her hands on her hips, still fuming. "I didn't understand one word of that conversation, if you could call it that."

"It appears Sasenfras was left part of the house by Todd's grandfather."

"That was the only thing I did get. It's that closed-off wing, isn't it?"

"Ahuh. And that is why Todd hasn't refurbished it yet. He can't. It doesn't belong to him."

"I wonder why he didn't tell us that."

"I don't know. The whole thing is peculiar and getting more so by the minute. He had to know that Sasenfras would tell us; so why send us here, then not mention the bit about the will?"

Zanita thought about it. "Maybe Todd and Sasenfras interpreted the will differently?"

Tyber raised his eyebrows. "Not likely. One

thing we do know is that Todd wants that wing. He'd be crazy not to; it's part of his heritage, and I imagine he wants to expand."

"What was that about some woman talking it one day? I was completely lost there."

"It seems ol' Sasenfras's wife and Todd's grandfather had a thing going on, and my guess is that it was going on a *lot* in that old wing of the house. In fact, I'd bet that was where the grandfather had his private quarters."

"But why would he leave it to Sasenfras? Doesn't sound like your typical benevolent bequest, and the grandfather didn't sound like the type who would feel guilty for cuckolding his servant."

"Sasenfras hinted that his wife may have come to a nasty end. It might be worth it for us to see if we can get into the wing and have a look around."

"How would we do that? It's sealed off."

Tyber grinned wickedly at her. "Not from the ledge, it isn't."

Zanita's mouth opened, then closed, then opened again as she thought about it. "No, no. It's much too dangerous. You heard Todd say the ledge might not be sound."

"Aren't you forgetting something?"

"What's that?" she asked puzzled.

"I'm a physicist. We live for this. I'll work out the logistics."

"What logistics? A rope around your waist, tied to the railing of the circular stairs?"

"Hmmm. That *would* work. Thanks, baby." He smiled brightly at her.

Zanita exhaled sharply. She was not going to let the rogue do it! It was too dangerous. Besides, it bore too much of a resemblance to a pirate throwing a grappling hook and . . . on second thought, he *was* the right man for the job. "We'll talk about it later."

"Yes, ma'am," he drawled out the words. "I love when you decide to get on top . . . of a discussion."

She ignored *that*. "By the way, didn't Sasenfras say something about *not* going in there again because he had seen something horrible, et cetera, et cetera?"

Tyber rubbed his jaw. "Yeah, he did say that." He grinned wickedly. "But I take that as an invitation. What about you?"

Her chin went up. "I'm going in. Although I'm not sure I'll love it. Something about a scream he'll never forget rings in my head. Was that supposed to be back then or now?"

"Ah, both, I think. It's safe to say that Sasenfras is a true believer."

"So the ghost is his wife?"

Tyber shrugged. "Let's not forget that there's a motive here for provoking Sasenfras to see a ghost. For one, he'd be more apt to unload his percentage if he was scared enough. And *something* scared him. Whether it was human or otherworldly, I'll leave it up to you to decide in the end."

She did a double take. "What end?"

"This end." He pinched her behind.

"Tyber!" She jumped and slapped his hand away. He chuckled low. Zanita was a teaseable woman, and he adored taking advantage of every opportunity.

"Sasenfras seemed pretty stubborn about not wanting to sell." Zanita stopped short as something occurred to her. "You know, he never actually said that it was Todd who wanted to buy him out."

Tyber's blue eyes flashed in appreciation. "You're right. I hadn't thought of that. Maybe Todd isn't the only one trying to buy him out. Good work, Curls."

"One thing's for certain, Todd's grandfather doesn't seem like a very nice guy. I wonder if I can get some information on him in the library—"

Tyber stopped her short. "There is something we've both overlooked here."

"What's that?"

"*Kitchen gadgets*. In some way, cooking implements are tied into all this." He whacked the side of his head with the heel of his hand. "I can't believe I actually had to say that. Can we go back home now?"

Zanita ignored the request. This was a perfectly good case, in her opinion. "Maybe whoever wants Sasenfras out also wants Todd out. What better way to get to a chef than with his own arsenal?"

Tyber gazed across the field as they emerged from the forest path, trying not to think too deeply about her last comment. It suddenly occurred to him to wonder *what* he was doing here. He should be working on a Unified Field Theory. Compared to chef's being under attack from denizens of the underworld traipsing around an inn, it should be a breeze.

He pinched the bridge of his nose. He never should have turned down that chair at the Institute for Advanced Studies. Somehow, *this* was his cosmic payback. He just knew it.

The house was bathed in moonlight. A ground fog swirled around the foundation. Several windows had lights shining in them, but the overall effect was gothic. And from this angle, eerie.

"Instead of the Florencia Inn, Todd should have renamed it Collinwood II," he remarked dryly.

"Very funny."

"Maybe Barnabus has a coffin hidden in that wing over there." He pointed to the west wing. The sealed wing.

Zanita grinned. "Nahhh, the closed wing is always a sure sign of another dimension coexisting and overlapping with this one."

Tyber chuckled. "And will certainly produce a story that trails off to yet another story." They both watched the *Dark Shadows* reruns late at night, curled up in bed. In the supposedly scariest parts, the acting and effects were so bad that they laughed their heads off.

"By the way, Tyber, what was all that to-do at dinner about the free-range chickens?"

He viewed her through half-lowered lids. "You know, you look damn sexy under this moonshine."

"Of course I do. Don't change the subject, Doc. Talk."

He sighed. "It had to do with that blood on the wall."

"So it was blood?" She shivered.

"Yes."

"Yech!"

"Chicken blood, to be exact. And again, all chicken feet are pointing to Todd. He had access to the fowl while he was preparing them."

Zanita shook her head. "I don't think it's Todd, Tyber. It's too easy. Someone wants us to believe it's him."

"Maybe. At least now we know what Hambone was doing in the passage. He followed the raw chicken, like any good cat."

Zanita chewed her lip. "You know, several voodoo ceremonies use chicken blood—"

"Don't even start with that. I'm having a hard enough time with the ghost and the gadgets."

Zanita watched a shooting star streak across the sky. "There is a true mystery going on here, Tyber. Don't be surprised if it turns out to be supernaturally based. There are several things you haven't been able to explain."

"Yet."

She looked at him out of the corner of her eye. "Perhaps."

He bent down and brushed her lips with his. "We'll see, Mrs. Evans," he whispered enticingly.

"Mmmm. Yes, we will, Doc."

"I think I'll take a shower and change these dusty clothes before we go downstairs for the night vigil. Do you mind, Tyber?"

"Of course not."

They had just entered their room after watching a brief meteor shower. Tyber had joked that the meteors were a material symbol that physics would blaze the trail to solving what was happening at the Florencia Inn.

Zanita had laughed and snapped back, "Or the meteor shower is a metaphysical sign that we are about to uncover a wondrous paranormal discovery that will streak across the planet!"

"Ah, that would be an article straight to *The*

Patriot Sun?" he teased her. *The Patriot Sun* was the small-town newspaper she worked for.

Zanita grinned. "You got it."

She went to the closet and grabbed one of the terry robes that the inn provided for guests. One thing she had to say for Todd, he was an excellent innkeeper. During their absence he had even lit a fire in the stone hearth. She started to unbutton her shirt.

"Do you want to clean up, too?" She viewed him from under her dark lashes, violet eyes sparking with suggestion. "We haven't tried out that whirlpool tub yet, have we?"

Tyber strolled up behind her, placing his hand over hers. "No, we haven't." He took over the task of unbuttoning her shirt. Only when he did it, the job took on a whole new dimension. His warm, capable hands ministered to her with tender care.

And intent purpose.

"Aren't you concerned this will give me a slight advantage in our challenge?" He stroked the backs of his fingers along the sensitive area he exposed, massaging her in a line from her chest to her stomach in the lightest of caresses. The soft skin quivered delicately under his expert touch.

Zanita gave him a look of pure feminine desire.

Tyber's eyes dilated with hunger as he watched her silently.

"No," she purred.

His slow, sensuous motions heated the surface of her skin. Every spot he touched radiated with his body warmth—a blazing heat that he had always been able to transfer to her instantly.

"Why not?" His voice was hoarse.

Zanita closed her eyes and stretched slightly into him. "Because I *surprised* you."

His gaze fastened on her full lower lip, and she knew he was remembering the feel of that lip on certain parts of his anatomy. The icy blue eyes hazed and flamed. "Yes, you did."

Masculine fingers lazily worked their way up to her exposed collarbone, sliding back and forth. Light and torturous prickles followed his path as he occasionally scraped the edges of his nails on her. The tips of his fingers feathered along her neck, sending tingles all the way down her spine. He was inciting her with these simple touches alone. She wanted to moan aloud.

She did.

He observed her, knowing exactly what he was doing to her.

"Be careful," he warned her with a sensual growl in his voice. "You might get more than you think." He continued to indolently play at the back of her neck, letting his fingers tangle loosely in her hair.

Imitating what he had done to her the last time, he gently tugged at the curly strands. A breath of excitement passed her lips as his determined action evoked that incredible memory. "That's not fair," she whispered indignantly.

"Where did you ever get the idea I play fair?" he drawled back. He blew on her neck—a hot, sustained stream of moist air that sizzled her senses.

No, he didn't play fair.

He was a renegade.

A marauder who seized and then had the audacity to *tease*. As far as Zanita was concerned, the compelling combination was the most dangerous one to be found in a male.

Impossible to resist.

And lethally sexy, to boot.

But how could one be "married" to a modern-day buccaneer? Like everything else concerning Tyber, the problem was empirical.

His palm cradled the back of her head and he dragged her back at an angle. The perfect angle. Slanting over her, his lips swept across her mouth in a raw, damp laving. Rich yet erotically subtle.

"That feels so good." Zanita closed her eyes so she could concentrate fully on the sensation, the inspiring textures of this incredible man.

"It's going to be better than good," he promised her, his smooth, low voice husky now.

She shivered at his words.

His other hand came around her waist to settle low in the curve of her back, his splayed fingers cupping her derriere. He pressed her to him, arching her again at the *precise* angle. Precision, that was Tyber. She could feel him, strong, hard, throbbing.

He watched her from under veiled lids. Eyes bright like burning crystal. Those eyes always captivated her. The way they changed . . . His keen intelligence was ever present in them, but when his passion rose high, they blazed. It always made her think that somewhere inside him there was a special internal energy reactor, and it was exclusive to Tyberius Augustus Evans. Such incredible eyes, with their spiky, thick lashes, were the window for her to see but a small portion of the fire and intensity that was within him.

Every time they made love, she watched those eyes flame out of control.

When he ignited, he took her with him on the wildest of journeys. And yet, he always maintained his command. A true mentor, his teaching skills were not relegated to the classroom.

Already she knew quite a bit of physics.

Unfortunately, she could only relate her knowledge to certain very private activities. She smiled to herself. *I hope I am never called upon to explain Newton's Laws.* She would die of embarrassment.

Doc Evans's passion always ran high. For learning. For life. For love.

His fingers undid the top button on her jeans. The rasp of the zipper followed. "Take them off." His smooth, low voice was raw with desire.

Never taking her gaze off his, she lowered her jeans to the floor and stepped out of them. He studied her actions, marine eyes sparking with combustible intensity. "Now . . . the . . . panties." The tone was three-quarters order, one-quarter request.

Giving him a secret smile, she slid the new pink lace panties down her silken legs and brazenly kicked them aside. Her buccaneer groaned deep in his throat. The depth of sultry sound was in direct proportion to the slide of the silky undergarment.

Zanita briefly wondered if there was a hidden mathematical "principle" involved with the motion of lace panties. She quickly squelched the idea, lest Tyber somehow intuit it and explain the physics of it to her.

He watched her through half-veiled eyes, his long lashes almost concealing their bold gleam. "Actually, baby, there's a physics term that—"

Her bare foot stepped on his.

He cocked an eyebrow. "Not now?" he drawled.

"Not now," she agreed.

His sensual lips curved ever so slightly. It was one of those enigmatic Tyber smiles that always made her tingle right to her toes.

He caught her gaze with his and slowly lowered his own zipper.

Inch by inch.

When Auntie had barged in on them and he had dragged his jeans on earlier, he had not bothered with briefs. At the sight of the crisp, golden-chestnut curls and velvety-hard skin, Zanita parted her lips with a trembly sigh. Seeing him this way always excited her.

And the rogue knew it.

Lowering his eyes, he unbuttoned the top button at his waistband and purposely left the jeans to gap open so as to partially conceal him from view. Then he gradually lifted his eyes, giving her a smoky, "hot syrup" look.

In fact, his maple syrup look.

Once experienced at the Marble Manor Inn, the maple syrup look was never to be forgotten. Her hand fluttered to her throat. There was sheer power in *that* look.

Without preamble, he slid to his knees in front of her. Strong hands clasped her thighs to bring her to him. Molten lips immediately trailed down her naked legs in a passionate love-sweep. Teasing. Playing. Tasting.

Possessing.

Zanita's breathing sped up considerably at the sultry touches that somehow were hot-dry and damp-wet at the same time. "Tyber." Her voice came out as a thready whisper of sound.

"Mmm?" He rubbed his face against her lower belly, the roughness of his beard-shadow a luscious abrading.

A small moan came from her lips.

"Unbutton my shirt." He inhaled her scent deeply, then placed his lips on her navel. There he flicked the depression with his tongue.

Zanita reached down and undid his buttons, opening his shirt. But when she tried to remove it, he stopped her. "Uh-uh. I want to feel you just like this . . ." He slid his chest back and forth, brushing against her nether curls and lower belly. Sensitizing her everywhere he grazed.

Zanita felt every muscle under his golden skin bunch and ripple.

"You're driving me wild, baby." He stared up at her; his pupils were hazy, dilated. Zanita answered silently, her violet eyes also clouded with wanting. Wanting him.

Only him.

Tyber had had that effect on her since the first time she had seen him, and she suspected he always would. He had often joked that they had the perfect "spin" together, and she knew he was equating them in his way to some weird subatomic particle thing; but she preferred to think of it as good old-fashioned chemistry.

They *cooked* on every level.

Right now, they were smoking.

Tyber's short fingernails languidly scraped

down the back of her thighs. His white teeth grazed the tender underside of her belly. He placed a damp kiss just above her hairline, near the pubic bone. Zanita's sob of sheer, too-sweet pleasure rent the air.

He gazed up at her, giving her such a look of utter love that Zanita felt tears rush to her eyes. The expression was so pure and so intense that it scared her with its sheer beauty.

"Don't, Tyber," she pleaded, softly running her hand over the back of his head, over the heavy fall of chestnut hair.

"Why?" he whispered softly. He slid his finger back and forth over her nether lips. In an instant he was dew-covered and slick.

Still, he watched her.

"Why?" he repeated as he brought his finger to his lips and suckled hungrily on the wet tip. "I could live on the taste of you."

Zanita's face flamed.

"Did I shock you?" Low and deep in his throat, a rough sound of satisfaction rolled.

She knew then what the rogue was implying. Their challenge. Tyber was the cleverest of opponents. But she could be just as clever in this regard.

The hand at the back of his head tugged his hair back so that his face tilted up to hers. She had hoisted her own Jolly Roger.

And would give no quarter.

215

"You meant to." Zanita bent over him and moved her mouth delicately over his in the barest of killer kisses. Cannon kisses. Short fuse—big impact.

Tyber moaned helplessly into her mouth—a prisoner of love.

Then he seized her face and commandingly brought her to him. Tight.

She smiled against such a fierce plunder. A prisoner of love, yes.

But always a pirate of passion.

Spent, Zanita fell asleep in his arms. They had both been rather energetic.

Tyber picked her up and gently placed her on the turned-down bed. Before he covered her, he lightly kissed her forehead so as not to awaken her. Getting dressed as quietly as he could, he slipped on his socks, grabbed his boots, and softly closed the door behind him. She needed some sleep.

Something brushed against her face.

Zanita wiggled her nose.

Again.

Her hand slapped the air in front of her. She was too tired to open her eyes. And she was going to kill him. Where did that man get his energy?

"Tyber, if you even think of dragging me under

216

this bed again, I swear I will murder you," she mumbled sleepily.

The annoyance was persistent.

"That does it!" She opened her eyes, ready to do battle. A hazy light morphed in front of her.

"What . . . ?" It wafted in the darkened room, which was lit only by the waning flames in the fireplace. She sat up.

"Oh my god . . . Tyber," she whispered fervently. "Tyber, wake up! It's the ghost!"

When there was no response, her hand slid out to her side and felt around the covers. Empty.

Terrific.

The one time her husband had decided to leave and the ghost made an appearance! She swallowed, amazed at what she was seeing. It was as if there were two Zanitas. The sane, rational Zanita who was wondering how she was going to convince her scientist lover that this had really happened, and the other, less rational Zanita who wasn't sure if she should be screaming or not.

The hazy light wafted along the carpet and traveled up the bookcase-lined wall. A strong scent of herbs filled the room. It was a pleasant scent; not like that other one they had smelled in the library. Was this a different spirit? Whatever Tyber was intent on investigating, she was certain this would add a new twist to it.

As she watched, spellbound, the light hovered

over a section of the bookcase. Suddenly the light went out and a heavy book flew out of the case to crash on the hard wood floor. It landed spine side up, its sides tented out slightly, supporting the weight.

Everything was silent as the dust motes settled. Zanita blinked. All was stationary.

Whatever had been in this room with her was now gone. She switched on a bedside light. Gingerly she pushed the covers off and padded carefully across the floor to the edge of the hand-hooked rug, glancing behind her frequently.

Kneeling down, she examined the title of the book. *Prominent Homes of Nantucket (1930–1965).*

Zanita's brow furrowed. What significance did this have? Somehow, she didn't think this book was a random toss on the ghost's part. She believed the entire scene had been enacted to get her attention, the focal point being this tome on the floor.

Still kneeling, she glanced up at the wide bookcase above her, briefly noting the empty slot in the otherwise full case. Then she picked up the heavy leather-bound book.

Sitting in the large chair by the fireplace, she opened the book and began flipping through the pages, looking for some connection to everything going in this house.

She couldn't find it. At first. There was no mention of the Sparklings or the Florencia Inn. No relatives, no second Nantucket home, nothing. Then she realized something.

"*Nan . . . tucket!*" *That was the message written in blood in the passageway!* Whoever (or whatever) was leaving the messages, was trying to lead them to Nantucket Island. But why?

"What is so special about this book?" she muttered to herself. "I've gone through it twice and there is no connection to anything. If you hear me, spirit, please help me here!"

She had begun flipping through the pages again when the photos in the center of the book caught her eye. She hadn't studied them very carefully, except to glance at the names. Now she looked at them more closely.

The typical island estates were pictured, as well as some fishing boats with images of the catch of the day surrounded by proud fishermen. One picture on the pier showed a great white shark mugging it up in a very dead way for the camera—along with the guy who'd caught him. Some blueblood who was convinced his manhood was attached to that trophy of a catch.

There was a small quote from him under the picture which said that even the best fisherman on the island would have a hard time topping this one. "Not even Sasenfras could catch this big boy. We had a bet going and I won. He cooks dinner tonight!" the young man quipped.

Zanita inhaled a rush of air. *Sasenfras*. But it couldn't have been Todd's Sasenfras. Could it?

Had this other Sasenfras also worked for Todd's family? Maybe this fisherman was the ghost? But why was he haunting this inn? What did Todd's grandfather have to do with it? And what had so terrified the present Sasenfras when he had gone into that wing?

It was time to find the Doc. He might not buy the ghost thing, but he'd figure it out.

Physicists couldn't help themselves when it came to that.

"I just don't figure it that way."

Tyber closed his eyes and rested his head against the couch back. It was all he could do not to groan. The Barracuda was grilling him.

So far the Attitude Queen was not accepting his reasoning. He sighed. *In-laws*. They came with a marriage like some symbiotic life form you wanted to get rid of but knew you couldn't, not if the organism was to survive!

He didn't think Zanita would forgive him if he offed her aunt. It would make for an uncomfortable atmosphere at the breakfast table. Especially during the holidays. He exhaled heavily.

"I simply don't understand how you can possibly think she would not have a clue as to what you think she would think to do!" Auntie said.

Tyber opened one eye and squinted at her. Yep. Definitely runs in the family.

"I never said that." Having long ago lost the thread of the conversation he deemed that to be an answer that would keep her going for a while.

"Tyber, really." The lock-jawed voice dragged out the words as if they had a hundred syllables. "This one's going to come back and bite you on those mar-r-rvelous buns of yours."

He frowned down at her. "No, it will not."

Auntie's eyes twinkled behind her rhinestone wing-shaped glasses. "What shall we bet?"

Tyber arched his eyebrow. "Hmmm." He folded his hands behind his head and stretched his long legs out. "A case of Wild Turkey if I lose."

"Done. And"—she gave him a sly look—"that special Harley Davidson oil gauge you've been trying to locate but can't."

He sat up. "How'd you know about that?"

"I am a wonder in three hats. Do we have a deal, my dear?"

He rubbed his jaw. "You'll never be able to produce that part. Gregor and I have tried every place we can think of—"

Auntie snorted. "That explains it, then."

Tyber's eyes flamed fire.

Auntie brushed the impending system crash

221

away. "Of course, if you're so concerned about losing that you can't take a simple bet . . ."

His lips firmed. "Done. And don't say you weren't warned. I'll expect that part within thirty days."

Auntie snorted.

Tyber just smiled.

"She'll be on to you, you'll see. She's more analytical than you think—"

"*Tyber, I've seen the ghost!*" Zanita came rushing into the library, eyes alight with wonder. She was haphazardly dressed in jeans and a misbuttoned shirt, and her feet were still bare. Clutched tightly to her chest was an old leather-bound book.

This had all the earmarks of the popcorn brain incident.

Tyber nonchalantly turned to Auntie. "Who were you calling analytical?"

Chapter Nine

Auntie viewed her niece askance and sighed deeply.

Auntie's Elton-Marilyn glasses slid halfway down her nose. Then, like a true Masterson, she rallied behind the Bohemian Code of Battle. "I will remind you of the road less taken." She pushed the words through narrow lips like slivers of shaved ice.

"Ah, yes, I know." Tyber's face revealed his fondness for the "obscure road" as he watched his wife come to a screeching halt in front of him. "It does make all the difference."

"The ghost gave me this book!" Zanita beamed at him. "Isn't that incredible!" Her pretty face glowed with excitement.

Tyber glanced down at the title, his long, dark lashes obscuring his reaction. Slowly his gaze rose to hers. "Tell me all about it, baby," he intoned softly while patting his thigh for her to come sit on his lap.

"We don't have time for that now!" At her comment, several of the guests in the library tittered. Realizing what she had just blurted out, Zanita blushed slightly.

Tyber's lips lifted in amusement. Zanita was and always would be his primary enjoyment in life. Not a day went by that he was not thankful she had taken up the cause of entropy and blundered into his classroom.

"What happened, Zanita? Tell us!" Mark came forward, almost leaping to her side in his enthusiasm.

"Well, I was taking a nap in bed after we . . ." She paused, her gaze meeting Tyber's.

The Doc gave her a lazy wink.

She cleared her throat.

"Um, after . . . bathing. The next thing I knew, it felt as if someone was brushing something across my face!" Excitement overtook her again. She bounced forward on the pads of her bare feet. "Naturally, I thought it was Tyber trying to drag me under the bed again—"

Tyber coughed, alerting her.

Zanita came to, glanced around her at the sea of stunned yet pruriently interested faces, and cleared her throat again.

A Special Offer For Leisure Historical Romance Readers Only!

Get Four FREE* Romance Novels

A $21.96 Value!

Thrill to the most sensual, adventure-filled Historical Romances on the market today…
FROM  LEISURE BOOKS

As a home subscriber to the Leisure Historical Romance Book Club, you'll enjoy the best in today's BRAND-NEW Historical Romance fiction. For over twenty-five years, Leisure Books has brought you the award-winning, high-quality authors you know and love to read. Each Leisure Historical Romance will sweep you away to a world of high adventure…and intimate romance. Discover for yourself all the passion and excitement millions of readers thrill to each and every month.

SAVE AT LEAST *$5.00* EACH TIME YOU BUY

Each month, the Leisure Historic Romance Book Club brings you four bran new titles from Leisure Books, America foremost publisher of Historical Romance EACH PACKAGE WILL SAVE YOU AT LEAS $5.00 FROM THE BOOKSTORE PRICE! Ar you'll never miss a new title with our conv nient home delivery service.

Here's how we do it. Each package w carry a 10-DAY EXAMINATION privilege. the end of that time, if you decide to kee your books, simply pay the low invoice pri of $16.96 ($17.75 US in Canada), no shi ping or handling charges added*. HOM DELIVERY IS ALWAYS FREE*. With today top Historical Romance novels selling f $5.99 and higher, our price SAVES YOU LEAST $5.00 with each shipment.

AND YOUR FIRST FOUR-BOOK SHIPMENT IS TOTALLY FRE

IT'S A BARGAIN YOU CAN'T BEAT! A Super $21.96 Value!

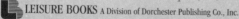 LEISURE BOOKS A Division of Dorchester Publishing Co., Inc.

GET YOUR 4 FREE* BOOKS NOW—
A $21.96 VALUE!

Mail the Free* Book
Certificate
Today!

4 FREE* BOOKS 🌹 A $21.96 VALUE

Free Books Certificate

YES! I want to subscribe to the Leisure Historical Romance
Book Club. Please send me my 4 FREE* BOOKS. Then each month
I'll receive the four newest Leisure Historical Romance selections
to Preview for 10 days. If I decide to keep them, I will pay the
Special Member's Only discounted price of just $4.24 each, a total
of $16.96 ($17.75 US in Canada). This is a SAVINGS OF AT LEAST
$5.00 off the bookstore price. There are no shipping, handling, or
other charges*. There is no minimum number of books I must buy
and I may cancel the program at any time. In any case, the 4 FREE*
BOOKS are mine to keep—A BIG $21.96 Value!

*In Canada, add $5.00 shipping and handling per order for first ship-
ment. For all subsequent shipments to Canada, the cost of membership
is $17.75 US, which includes $7.75 shipping and handling per
month.[All payments must be made in US dollars]

Name _____

Address _____

City _____

State _____ *Country* _____ *Zip* _____

Telephone _____

Signature _____

If under 18, Parent or Guardian must sign. Terms, prices and conditions subject to change.
Subscription subject to acceptance. Leisure Books reserves the right to reject any order or
cancel any subscription.

(Tear Here and Mail Your FREE* Book Card Today!)

Get Four Books Totally
F R E E* —
A $21.96 Value!

(Tear Here and Mail Your FREE* Book Card Today!)

PLEASE RUSH
MY FOUR FREE*
BOOKS TO ME
RIGHT AWAY!

Leisure Historical Romance Book Club
P.O. Box 6613
Edison, NJ 08818-6613

AFFIX
STAMP
HERE

A dimple appeared in Tyber's left cheek as he silently dared her to continue relating the event without getting herself in trouble. He reclined into the couch with an air of unsuppressed enjoyment of the outlandish scene that was unfolding.

"Anyway," she continued more slowly, obviously monitoring her words carefully, "The next thing I knew, there was this light in front of my face—"

Tyber sat forward, instantly alert. "What did the light look like?"

"Well, at first it was sharp, very defined. Then it seemed to soften and spread as it moved over to the bookcases along the wall by the desk."

"Was it directly in front of you?"

"Not exactly, it—"

"Did it have any scent?" Mark interrupted in ghost-hunter euphoria.

Zanita scrunched up her nose as if she were trying to recall the scent and the only way to do it involved "proboscis tae bo." Tyber thought it was extremely cute. Not that he would ever tell her.

"There was an herbal scent, Mark, as well as the smoky smell of the logs burning in the fireplace."

"Weren't you frightened, Mrs. Captain?" Blooey was bug-eyed with morbid fascination. Even Hambone seemed to lean in toward her so as to not miss any scrap of this deliciously grim tale. Pirates always love a good yarn, especially if it involves something spine-tingling.

"It's strange, Blooey, I thought I would be terrified being alone and confronting this supernatural phenomenon, but I wasn't. Oh, I admit, at first I was kind of in shock and my heart was beating a tattoo, but I never felt in any kind of danger."

"And you weren't." Calendula put her hand on her shoulder. "As I said, there has never been a recorded incident in which a spirit has ever truly harmed anyone." She chuckled as she added, "Although many people have harmed themselves by being panic-stricken. All kinds of silly accidents have occurred, but you really can't blame a ghost for that."

Hubble rolled his eyes. "No, you can't." This conversation was too much for him. The others crowded him out and ignored him, interested to hear the rest of the juicy tale.

"The ghost sort of hovered for a few instants, then drifted over to the bookcases slowly. I realize now, it was trying to tell me something."

"Your shirt's misbuttoned," Tyber drawled.

"No, not that." Zanita bit her lip. "I was naked at the time, so—"

Hubble coughed this time.

Zanita's cheeks flushed.

Tyber chuckled, a deep, low, sensual sound

that caused Calendula and Auntie *and* Todd to actually suck in their collective breaths. Not many were immune to physicists, it seemed.

"I mean your shirt's misbuttoned right now, baby."

"Oh." She narrowed her eyes at him. This was not the first time they had been on an investigation and her shirt had ended up misbuttoned! And both of those occurrences had evolved around Tyber and a bathtub.

Each time, the rascal had the nerve to bring it to everyone's attention! By the satisfied expression on that oh-so-arresting face, there was no doubt that he knew what she was remembering. Marble floors and steam heat.

The man had a penchant for causing trouble.

"So then what happened, Zanita?" Mark could not wait another second to hear the rest of the story.

"Well, the hazy blob seemed to get brighter for a second. Then, just like that"—she snapped her fingers—"it went, disappeared completely! That was when this book crashed to the floor as if an unseen hand had pulled it off the shelf."

They all gasped. Except for Hubble, who snorted, and Tyber, who appeared pensive. Hippolito remained, as ever, unconscious on the floor.

"The book—what is it, darling?" An exhilarated

Auntie tried to read the title upside down. Unfortunately, it was now covered by Zanita's palm.

Everyone waited with bated breath.

Would the book be something arcane and slightly annoying like *Faust*? Or would it be foreboding with a nightmarish aftertaste like Poe? Maybe it would be witty and silly like Coward! What had the ghost chosen?

"*Prominent Homes of Nantucket*," Zanita merrily informed them.

A dead silence filled the room not unlike that which occurs when the plug is pulled out of a life support system.

Finally, Todd spoke. "I, ah, don't recall that book in our collection."

"Why would you?" Hubble scoffed.

Todd scratched his ear, completely at a loss. "What is it about? Is it a novel? Have you had a chance to look at it yet?"

"Yes, as a matter of fact, I have. It's exactly what it seems, I'm afraid. A collection of boring stats and vignettes on the property of prominent families that lived on Nantucket between nineteen thirty and nineteen sixty-five. It doesn't have much to recommend it."

"Geesh." Mark seemed deflated. "I was hoping there would be a reason why he picked that particular volume."

"We don't know that 'it' is a he," Calendula

added. "Are you sure there is nothing of interest in there?"

"Absolutely nothing. I went over it three times with a journalist's eye for ferreting out details. Believe me, it's a dud." Zanita hesitated. "But still, it's all very exciting. Maybe the ghost is farsighted and picked the wrong book?" She shrugged.

Tyber watched her but said nothing.

"I think we should go to your room and see if there are any residual readings." Calendula turned to Tyber. "Do you mind?"

"Be my guest."

"Mark, let's take the Geiger counter. I think that's our best bet, since the event is past. By the way, Zanita, did you feel any change in temperature in the room?"

"What do you mean?"

"Did it get colder suddenly?"

Zanita's brow furrowed. "No. No, it didn't."

"Okay. Just thought to ask. Let's go." They all marched out of the library to go to the room.

Hippolito remained behind to keep close tabs on the library carpet.

He began as he ended.

With a snore.

"So what was in the book?"

Tyber caught up with her in the hallway, pulling her behind as the others went ahead.

229

"How do you know something was in the book?" She brushed some curls out of her eyes as she gazed up at him.

"The same way you knew there was something at the top of that circular staircase."

She batted her lashes at him.

"C'mon, baby." He snaked his arm around her waist. "Give," he mouthed at her.

"All right." She stood on tiptoe and brushed her lips against his ear. "There's a connection to our lovely and radiant entry from the State of Massachusetts, namely Sasenfras."

"Sasenfras, hmm?"

"Yes. It seems our dour, more-than-strange caretaker originally hailed from Nantucket. Or his family did."

"And . . . ?"

Zanita rocked back on her heels to stare him in the face. "And what?"

"What is the relevance of that?"

"I have no idea, but I am sure there is some."

The right side of his mouth tipped up in a half grin. Yep. Enjoyment. "You think, huh?"

"Mmmm-hmmm."

"I see."

"And you're going to figure it out."

"Really." He rubbed her nose with his own in a very teasing way.

She caught the tip of his nose in a quick nibble-kiss. "Yessss!"

230

"You're just smug because you think you've seen a ghost." He sipped at her bottom lip.

"*Think?*" She paused and frowned up at him. "I did see a ghost, Tyber."

"Show me," he breathed against her lips. Zanita was not at all sure he was talking about the haunt.

"Okay." She slipped out of his arms and, taking his hand, led him down the hall to their room.

"Tell me how the book fell, Curls."

"Well, I was still in bed across the room when it happened, but as I said, the light seemed to diffuse right over that spot." She pointed to the empty slot in the bookcase. "That was when the book came shooting out and fell to the floor."

"Hmm." Tyber walked up to the built-in bookcase and stared pensively at the wall. He ran his finger lightly over the wall behind the empty space and checked the books on each side of it.

"I didn't see anything unusual. Do you?" Zanita came up to stand beside him. The others were all with Mark, checking the Geiger counter.

"No. Looks okay." He rubbed his jaw. "So you went to get the book when the coast was clear—which reminds me, I'm not leaving you alone in here again."

Zanita smiled softly. "I was never in any danger, Doc. You heard Calendula."

"Yeah, I heard her. And I'm not leaving you

alone. And be sure to tell your aunt to lock her door at night."

Zanita beamed. "Tyber! You're worried about Auntie!"

A dull flush washed over his face. He chose not to respond to *that*. "So you went and picked up the book. Was it lying on the carpet or the floor?"

Zanita put her hands on her hips. "Really, Tyber, I don't see what—"

"Humor me, I'm a physicist." *Hmm, great bumper-sticker.* He decided then and there to make one up for all the guys at the local.

"It was on the floor."

"Are you sure?"

"Yes. It fell straight down like a leaded . . . book."

"You took me literally, didn't you?"

"What?"

"Never mind. Let's reenact this. You bend down, pick up the book—"

"No, first I glanced up at the empty slot above my head."

"Good. And?"

"Then I picked it up."

"Okay."

Zanita rolled her eyes. "Sometimes I think you just bait me."

"Why would you think that, baby?" He knelt

down and carefully examined the floor, running his fingertips over the wood.

"Did you find anything?" she asked.

"Nope. Didn't expect to."

"Why are you doing it, then?"

"So you'd ask me if I found anything." He grinned at her, revealing perfect white teeth.

Zanita exhaled heavily in mock annoyance.

"By the way, was the front cover facing you or away from you when it fell?"

"Neither."

His focus remained on the floor. "To the left, right, what?"

"Actually it was up."

"*Up?*"

"Ahuh. It fell open like a tent."

"It fell spine up?" He seemed surprised.

"Yes."

Still kneeling on the floor, Tyber looked up at the slot just as she had done. Whereupon he grinned from ear to ear. "Thanks." He handed the book back to her.

"What? What does it mean?" Zanita hopped next to him as they left the room.

Tyber bent down and placed a kiss on her forehead. "Uh-uh. Not until I piece it all together."

"But you have a segment?" She worried her lip.

"Yep." He walked a few steps forward, stopped, and turned back. Over his shoulder, he gave her the most sensual, male, "I got that one and I'm not gonna tell you, don't you love me?" look.

"Hmf." Zanita swished by him, book clutched tightly to her chest.

His provocative laughter followed her down the hall.

If there was anything more irritating than a sexy physicist-pirate (who is was also a genius), Zanita had yet to meet it.

"Did you find anything, Mark?" Zanita tossed the book onto an end table in the library.

Mark tramped back into the room. "No. No readings on the Geiger at all. I was hoping we could still pick up something even though the event had passed."

"Does that happen at times?"

"Yes. When Calendula and I were in England this past spring, we had a case where we were able to catalog several reverberations many minutes after the sighting actually occurred."

"How long have you been working with Calendula, Mark?" Tyber sank into a nearby Morris chair.

"For about five years now."

"How did you two hook up?"

Mark crossed the room and sat in the chair opposite Tyber. "It was one of those remarkable career stories that you always pray will happen to you. Calendula had been an astrologist for several years before she realized she had medi-umship abilities. One thing led to another, and it wasn't long before she was sought out by the Society. She began doing investigations just as I was graduating from tech school. Of course, she was already well known by then. You can imag-ine my surprise when she wrote to me, asking me if I'd like to join her team as a technical investigator."

"She asked you?" Tyber flicked on the light that rested on the table between them.

"Yes. She had heard about me from a mutual friend and knew my knowledge of electronic equipment would be invaluable to her research. I was always interested in the supernatural, so I jumped at the chance to work with her. So it was because of her that I got into this field in the first place."

Tyber viewed him thoughtfully. "And you brought her into this case."

"Yes. When Todd told me what was happening here, I naturally asked her if she would help him. She was hesitant at first, but then agreed to take the case on."

"Interesting." Tyber steepled his fingers under his chin.

Zanita's eyebrow rose. It didn't seem that interesting to her. Just what was the Doc up to?

"Yeah, she's one of the best—both profession-ally and as a friend."

"She is very nice," Tyber agreed, prompting the conversation along.

"Yes, she's helped me through some tough relationship times. She's a brick."

"Are you talking about me over there?" Calendula smiled from the doorway.

"Yep, but nothing bad." Mark grinned at her.

Hubble and Auntie came in, briskly approaching the group. Zanita gave her aunt a questioning look, but Auntie ignored it. Obviously, the woman thought she was doing her own snooping.

Mark glanced down at the end table and a line of puzzlement appeared on his brow. "That's odd," he commented.

"What, Mark?" Calendula asked.

"I could have sworn that in this Polaroid picture Tyber took of Zanita last night, her eyes were shut."

"They were." Zanita walked over and glanced at the shot lying on the table exactly where Tyber had left it last night. "Oh my god, my eyes are open in the picture! Look at that!"

Tyber picked up the photo. Sure enough, Zanita's eyes were wide open. And it was the same shot, right down to the fudge-brownie nut crumbs on her luscious mouth.

"Is it the same picture, Tyber?"

"Appears to be."

"How could a Polaroid instant picture change?

This is too weird." Zanita glanced at it again and gave a little shiver. Her own violet eyes gazed straight back at her.

"Perhaps there was more than one shot taken?" Todd asked hopefully.

"No." Mark shook his head. "Just this one." He bent down and began untangling the equipment cords along the wall.

"A hidden camera could have taken it," Hubble articulated, trying to impress Auntie.

"Could have, but didn't," Tyber announced. "That's the same angle and same shot. I took it rather close. No hidden camera."

"Horrors! Isn't this bizarre?" Auntie announced to the room, succinctly summarizing what most everyone was thinking.

"There have been instances where physical phenomena such as this have been reported," Calendula said. "I've never seen one quite like this, but I have seen many photos that, when developed, have shown images that weren't initially physically present to the eye."

"Most of them are faked!" Hubble barked. "Or there is a very logical explanation for the anomaly in the picture."

"We disagree on that, Hubble." Calendula lifted her chin. "I know you think all of these occurrences are nothing more than so much fantasy, but I have personally witnessed genuine instances of the paranormal."

Hubble harumphed.

At that point, Zanita happened to glance at the inlaid wood console cabinet that she had left the book on, only to discover that it was gone! "The book's missing!" she yelled, causing everybody to freeze.

"What do you mean, it's missing, baby?" Tyber stood up immediately and came to her side.

"Look." She pointed to the empty surface. "I left the book there a few minutes ago, and now it's gone."

"Gone?" Mark straightened at the news.

"That's downright creepy." Todd paled. "What could have happened to it? We were all on this side of the room. Since we came back in here, no one was even near that table."

Zanita nodded in agreement. "He's right, Doc."

Tyber walked over to the table, checking on the floor to see if the book had somehow fallen off. It was nowhere to be seen.

To be seen . . .

He opened the two cabinet doors, and there, lying on the top shelf, was the book. "I'll be damned," he said in a quiet voice.

Zanita peered over his shoulder cautiously. "But how could it get there? No one was over here, and there was no way someone could open these wooden doors and put the book inside without one of us noticing."

"Yes, Dr. Evans, can you explain that one?" Mark goaded him good-naturedly.

"I suppose you are all ready to call it supernatural!" Hubble scoffed.

"Well, duh," Mark shot back.

Auntie took a healthy swallow of her bourbon. "It does seem like the only one who could have possibly done it was—"

"Maxwell's demon," Tyber finished for her.

"Who?" everyone said at once.

"The ghost's name is Maxwell?" Zanita scrunched her nose. "How do you know that?"

Blooey, who had just walked into the room, surprised everyone by rushing over to view the scene of the shifting book. "Maxwell's demon, eh, Captain? Ha, but wouldn't it be just like me to miss that once-in-a-zillennium event! Went to let this grifter out." He gave the cat a disgusted look.

Hambone nonchalantly licked his paw.

"Will someone please tell me who Maxwell is and why he is haunting my inn?" Todd beseeched anyone who would listen.

Zanita spoke at the same time, saying to Tyber, "I can't believe that you are finally going to have to admit that we just have witnessed a genuine . . . Wait a minute! Isn't Maxwell one of those physics dudes?"

Tyber's eyes flashed. "I see those *lessons* are

239

finally sinking in." He winked lazily at her, causing her to blush.

"Gads, what does this have to do with that *bor-r-r-ring* subject?" Auntie held out her empty glass for Hubble to refill.

Tyber gave her an indignant look, then went on to explain. "Clerk Maxwell is the father of the theory of thermodynamics. Along with Faraday, he introduced the concept of fields. He also introduced the concept of a statistical demon. The demon is not a real demon, but a figure of speech. He was referring to the possibility of heat being made to flow against temperature, thereby invalidating the second law of thermodynamics—you remember that one, baby—the principle of increasing entropy."

Zanita remembered *that* one very well. She examined her toe.

"I was using the term to refer to zero-point motion."

"Zero-point motion; sounds like an ice-skater's jump to me," Todd quipped.

Blooey closed one eye and stared at Todd with the other. All that was missing was a knife between his teeth. For a man who believed himself aboard a pirate ship, Blooey took his science way too seriously. "Why don't ye explain the situation to this landlubber, Captain."

"A body in an enclosed space has a certain motion associated with it—"

"Don't go there," Zanita warned under her breath.

Tyber glanced at her out of the corner of his eye. "No?" he whispered seductively.

She shook her head.

A naughty dimple grooved his cheek. "One of the most intriguing aspects of quantum theory is that it is impossible to contain anything within an enclosure *if* there is enough motion/energy available after it might have crossed the barrier."

"What does that mean in English, Doc?"

"It means it's theoretically possible for anything to 'leak through' a barrier. What we have here is a statistically astonishing event. The book leaked through the wood to the shelf below. We should all be amazed that we were able to witness such an event. The odds of it happening are—"

"You'd go to any lengths not to accept this as paranormal, wouldn't you?" Zanita shook her head back and forth in disgust.

Hubble had the opposite reaction. "Bravo, Doctor!"

Calendula just raised her eyebrows and went over to the sideboard to pour herself a drink of water.

Everyone quickly dispersed after that eggheaded proclamation.

"I can't believe you came up with that one!"

Zanita shoved the flat of her hand against his forehead. Physicist attitude adjustment.

Tyber seem perplexed. "What?"

"That was so ridiculous!"

Tyber shrugged. "It's physics."

Zanita stuck out her tongue at him.

He hummed a low tune under his breath. It sounded suspiciously like "Jeopardy." "I never said how long that event would take to happen, did I?"

Her head snapped up. "What do you mean?"

"Try about a zillion years. That's about how long it would have taken that book to leak through that table top."

"Oh." She viewed him speculatively. "Then you don't believe it, either?"

"Not likely."

"You were observing something at the time?"

"Mmm-hmm."

"Gonna tell me?"

"Not yet."

She was beginning to hate that answer. "Well, how did the book move?"

"Guess that will remain a mystery for now."

Zanita sighed. "I really think there is a ghost here, Tyber. I don't think you're going to explain this one."

"We'll see."

"What about the photo? You know my eyes

were closed. How do you explain that one? Supposedly Polaroids can't be altered because there is no negative *to* alter."

He smiled slowly, looking remarkably like Hambone when he was about to pirate-pounce.

"You're not going to tell me that either, are you?"

"Nope. Not yet."

She tapped her foot. "When?"

He folded his arms over his chest. "You know, you sound just like a"—he shuddered theatrically—"*wife.*"

Zanita's features narrowed. She had accused him of sounding like a boyfriend in the past in much the same manner. He was baiting her again. Sexy, irritating thing. "You're not throwing me off by annoying me. When?"

"Later, in our room," he whispered. "Where I can really *annoy* you." He blew her a kiss.

"Hmf!" She turned away. The rogue took advantage of the opportunity to trail his palm over her backside. And give it a little slap.

In full view of the rest of the room.

Zanita's mouth opened in shock; she stared at him over her shoulder.

"Sorry, baby. My hand just leaked through this space here." He swept the air between them to illustrate. "Must be the li'l Maxwell's demon in me."

The brigand audacity to grin.

* * *

"Want me to demonstrate zero-point motion?"

"No."

Tyber chuckled and caught her pouting lower lip between his teeth. They were lying in bed. The rest of the night had been relatively quiet after the discovery of the picture and the book. Even Calendula thought it best not to provoke the spirit further by having a channeling session, since whoever it was seemed content to leave clues at its own pace.

"Now, why are you sulking, baby, hmmm?" He played with her lip a bit before releasing it.

"Because you are being your usual impossible self, Mr. Evans."

"How is that, Mrs. Evans?" His nose nuzzled her neck.

"And don't try to use the 'nuzzling nose of forgiveness' on me—it won't work!" She sighed blissfully and stretched her toes out against his calf.

"Oh. I see."

"I've been waiting ever since we came back to the room and I haven't heard one peep out of you yet."

"Peep."

Zanita tried to wiggle out of his arms but he held her fast, laughing. "Tyber! You know what I mean. Tell me about the photo!"

"Tell me about this cute little beauty mark." He poked the small dot on her chest lightly with his index finger.

"Argh!"

His handsome face reflected his amusement. It was hard to stay mad at a man who seemed to enjoy you so much. However, there was one way to catch the Captain at his own game. She caught *his* lower lip in her mouth and suckled sweetly on it.

Tyber sucked in his breath. "Mmmm."

"Ahuh." The tip of her tongue slipped between his lips and licked inside.

"Mmmm . . . ?"

"That's right."

Tyber paused, breaking away from her mouth. "Am I to assume that you are going to try to coerce the information out of me by teasing me into compliance?"

"There's no trying about it." She gave him a knowing grin. "You're done for, Doc."

"We'll see about that. I'm made of pretty stern stuff. Go ahead and do your worst . . . or best, baby," he whispered as he feathered his lips over hers.

Zanita delicately licked the small indentation next to his mouth. Tyber narrowed his eyes a bit. Ever alert.

Next, with the lightest of touches, she

strummed the backs of her fingers up and down his broad back, letting her fingers dip into the lower curve of his spine.

"Mmmm, nice." He attempted to capture her mouth with his velvet lips, but Zanita turned her head simply to deprive him of the gratification. She knew her pirate; it would soon drive him crazy.

Sure enough, a frustrated gust of air was exhaled through his flared nostrils.

"Ready to give in?"

"Not even close."

Sliding her palms down, she cupped his naked, firm buttocks, pressing her fingertips deep into the muscular globes. Whereupon she ran her index finger lightly over the center line of his cheeks.

Tyber's breath hitched erratically.

"Ahuh?" she asked too sweetly.

"Uh-uh." He rubbed his nose up and down the edge of her throat to try to distract her. Zanita was not about to be distracted. She wanted that information!

Her tongue traced a teasing path over his sensitive earlobe, flicking around the folds. That always drove him wild. He tried to hide the shiver that raced through him. Then the tip of her tongue poked slightly at the canal. A small groan was ripped from him.

"It's working."

"No, it isn't," he panted unsteadily.

Zanita moved one of her hands around to the front of him and slid it between them.

Pausing, she looked up at him before taking this next step. She was opening up her heavy artillery and thought it only fair to warn him. Especially since he was her husband. "Last chance, Doc—spill what you've got or else."

Tyber's mouth dropped. "Excuse me?"

Zanita realized what she had actually said and turned beet red. Leave it to him to befuddle her! He knew exactly what she had meant. "I mean it, Tyber, this is your last chance!"

"I'm shivering in my boots," he rasped hoarsely.

That did it! The battle lines had been drawn.

Zanita scraped the fingernails of one hand down his hard buttock, while at the same time she scraped the nails of her other hand up his inner thigh. *All the way up.*

Tyber's light blue eyes darkened, and for a second it almost seemed as if he had difficulty breathing. A sound suspiciously like a stifled cough came from his throat. He wheeze-snuffled, trying to recover from the exquisite, almost painful sensations. Lips firm, he fought to inhale.

"All right, pal, sing like a canary."

"Those weren't your eyes, dammit!"

Chapter Ten

"They weren't my eyes? *Ewwwwww!*"

That was too creepy even for a haunted inn. She pushed Tyber off of her and sat up in bed. "Whose eyes were they?"

"Well, no one's, technically."

"Yech!" Zanita's tongue fell out in a display of revulsion.

Tyber rolled over onto his back and folded his arms behind his head. By the stunned look on his gorgeous face, he was trying to figure out how he had lost that last bout. He should chalk it up to W.I.F.E. Women Initiating Force Equations.

An extremely powerful field that was never to be underestimated.

"How could my eyes be replaced?" She shuddered. "It sounds like something from Franken-stein's lab: 'It sees! It sees!' Bwaaaaa."

Tyber viewed her carefully from under lowered lids. "You okay, Curls?"

A pillow bounced off his head.

"Now, you yourself said it was the same picture. How are those not my eyes?"

"I said it *appeared* to be the same picture. Those are not your eyes because someone opened them."

"I beg your pardon? How could someone open them?"

"Whoever it was is very skilled. The finish is amazingly smooth."

"Wait a minute. Are you telling me someone altered that photo? But how? I've heard of photos being enhanced, of course—that's why photos, for the most part, aren't allowed as evidence in the courtroom anymore. We had already discussed that. But this was the original Polaroid picture, wasn't it?"

"Yes. I believe the alteration was done right on the picture. Tricky but not impossible. And whoever did it was so good that not many would have been able to figure out how it was done."

"So how is it that you know?"

He shrugged his shoulders nonchalantly. "Learned here and there," was all he would reveal.

Zanita's eyes narrowed. "Does it have anything to do with Sean, that FBI guy you know?"

Tyber started to brush a feather, which had

escaped from the pillow, off his chest—then hesitated. He picked it up and began to tickle her arm with it instead. No sense letting an opportunity to irritate pass by. He grinned sexily. "Don't you want to know how he did it?"

Zanita tried unsuccessfully to wiggle away from the irksome, *interesting* stimulation. The fact that he had evaded her question about Sean did not get by her. *Nice evasion, Doc.* "Of course I do! How?"

"With oil-based pencils, gloss spray, and a very clever little trick. Normally, the shape of the eye and the pupil can be read by examining the closed lid." He swept the tiny feather over her brow bone.

"How so?" She crossed her legs and hugged her pillow to her.

"When the eyelid is closed, the curve and shape of the eye are visible through it. The shaded line above the closed eye is identical in shape to the edge of the opened eyelid. If the eye is opened, this line becomes the eye fold. If you can locate the prominent bulge in the lid, you can easily map out the iris's dimensions as well as the pupil and its highlight. Here, see?"

Putting the feather carefully down on the bedside night table for later use, he got up off the bed and padded over to the desk. Taking out a pad and pencil, he roughly sketched a closed eye, drawing a large circle over the area of the eyeball.

"Okay, I can see how you can approximate the size and shape, but how did they get my exact eye color?" she asked, joining him.

"They didn't have to. Photos rarely capture exact eye color. Especially Polaroids; although Mark is using a Pro 100, which tends to have fairly correct color. However, all that was needed was the color tone, which anyone looking at you can see is a lovely shade of violet. What was left out was that special sparkle. That's how I knew it wasn't really your eyes."

"My special sparkle?" She liked that.

"Yep. The retoucher got the highlights all wrong, and more important, he left out a very important step in the process."

"What was that?"

"He forgot to shadow in the upper iris. It gave you a rather dazed look." He paused. "Well, more of a dazed look than you usually get from chocolate."

Zanita stuck her tongue out at him. He grinned. "But how did he actually change the photo itself, Tyber?"

"It's a complicated process. First you have to sketch what you think the natural shape of the eye is, using neutral spotting dye. On a lacquered print, it must be sprayed with a solution to make it porous for the dyes. The line above the eye fold now becomes the edge of the opened eyelid. Then you sketch in the iris over what was the closed lid, putting in the pupil and highlight by finding the catchlight—usually at eleven o'clock or one o'clock depending on where the light is coming from. Using a very fine brush, you add lashes and darken the pupil. After spraying with retouch lacquer, you can deepen or lighten the different areas using an oil-based color pencil."

He demonstrated on his sketch pad.

"Wow. This is very clever."

"Yes, it is an interesting technique. And very well done. However, this would be easily spotted if we weren't examining the image by eye. Whoever did this knew we don't have that kind of photo detection equipment with us . . ." He hesitated as something occurred to him. "That may have been the reason why our room was searched."

"Sounds plausible." She chewed on her lower lip as she thought it out. "But we would have discovered the alteration eventually."

"Not if the picture disappears. In fact, I'll bet you that when we go back downstairs the picture will be missing."

"We'll see. I still don't see how it looked so real."

"When you add further steps, using white oil

paint, q-tips, oil, pencils and pastel, and then a final coat of smooth lacquer spray to even out the finish, what you have is—"

"A Zanita with her eyes wide open?"

"Exactly."

"The picture was left there yesterday morning when we went up to sleep so whoever did it had—"

"The whole day to work on it before putting it back where it was sure to be spotted by somebody."

"Unbelievable."

"They might, in fact, have taken an exact picture of the altered picture." He shrugged. "I'm not an expert in these things."

Zanita snorted. Who else but Tyber *would* figure out this stuff? The scope of his knowledge always amazed her. "Like someone else would know all this?"

He ducked his head sheepishly. "I don't know. There's a lot you can do with the right equipment."

"Tell me about it," she murmured, scanning his naked length.

He almost blushed. "Be good."

"I am." She batted her lashes at him.

He threw her a sultry look before rubbing his jaw. "I wonder who did it?"

"You don't know? I thought you had that already figured out," she teased.

"No, not yet," he responded seriously.

She hid her grin behind her hand.

"Well, it was Mark who pointed the picture out to us, to get our attention focused on it. And it's also Mark who has photography and computer imaging expertise. It has to be him."

"It's too pat. Besides, why would a man who was smart enough to figure out that alteration, be dumb enough to draw our attention to it?"

"True. Okay, let's say it wasn't Mark for the time being. In fact, let's not focus on who did it right now, but *why* someone did it."

"That's easy." He wrapped his arm around her neck and pulled her to him.

"So we would think the ghost did it?"

"Mmmm-hmmm." He kissed her forehead.

"So all we have to do is figure out who that person is." She stretched up and pecked his chin.

"Giving up on your ghost theory, baby?" He pecked her back.

"No. Not entirely. There's something weird here, I feel it. In fact, there might be something even more weird than a ghost . . ."

"What's that?" He brushed her hairline with his lips.

"Someone with a motive who wants to make this haunted inn appear more haunted."

Tyber stopped and blinked.

A slow smile etched a cross his face. "Good work, baby!"

"I said something?"

"Um-hmmmmm."

"What? What did I say? I gave you a clue, didn't I? I knew I—"

His lips fastened on hers in a hot taking. "Now it's my turn." With that pronouncement, he lifted her in his arms and carried her back to bed.

And even though he tortured her with his sweet lips and silken tongue, Zanita was not in the least inclined to surrender without a proper love-battle. Tyber was ecstatic.

Engaging the opposition always makes a pirate captain's day.

She had never seen anyone use a tiny feather like that!

The man ought to come with a smoke alarm attached to him, Zanita groused and mumbled to herself as they went down to the library.

"C'mon. Tell the truth. You loved it." His mouth swept her ear in a zippy little pass.

"I have nothing to say." Her lip jutted out mutinously.

"Really?" His eyebrow arched. "You had a lot to say just a little while ago."

"That does not qualify as speaking." She pierced him with her glare. "As such."

A dimple slowly grooved his cheek. "You're just ticked because I had the feather and you didn't . . . *Mrs. Evans.*"

"Stop calling me Mrs. Evans; it sounds like a Bette Davis role in which she plays the *other* woman."

"What other woman?" he asked tongue in cheek.

"The one who . . ." She stopped when she realized he was baiting her.

"The one who gets teased with feathers?" he suggested huskily. "Tsk-tsk. Where was the Hayes office during all this?"

"I am not going to respond to that."

Zanita walked into the library, a mischievous Tyber trailing after her. "I bet good ol' Bette never had the 'feather flapjack.'" he drawled in her ear.

She stopped and gaped at him over her shoulder, horrified. "Shush! Someone will hear you." Her face pinkened at *that* memory. She was quite sure he had made up the "feather flapjack" although he wouldn't admit to it. "There is no such thing as a 'feather flapjack'!"

His eyes twinkled. "Seemed pretty real to me. Especially the way you screamed when I—"

Her shoe came down on his instep. "Shush!"

He chuckled. "It's okay, baby. I know the after-effects linger for a while."

For a while? Her whole body was still shaking from what he had done to her with that damn little feather. "The next time I throw a pillow at you, I'll make sure it's polyester fill."

He blinked slowly as if *ideas* were coming to him. "Polyester fill? Hmmmm . . ."

"You're impossible!" She stormed over to the side table to get a glass of iced tea. His masculine laughter followed her the whole way. Todd approached, carrying a tray of cookies, which he placed on the table. This man was born to be an innkeeper.

Tyber sauntered over and took one, crunching on it. "You know, Todd, this morning I checked out that passageway at the top of the circular stairs."

Zanita stared at him, surprised. When had he had time to do that?

"I didn't see any spiderwebs there," he went on. He had wanted to examine them, although he'd pretty much guessed what he would find. Nothing.

Todd hesitated as he arranged a bowl of floating flowers. "What? Oh, when I saw how mussed up you and Zanita were yesterday, I sent Sasenfras up there to clean. I can't stand the thought of any part of the house being so dirty." He shuddered with distaste. "Who knows what condition that closed wing is in?"

"Speaking of which, why didn't you tell us that Sasenfras owned that wing?"

"Hmm?" Todd snipped the head of a white flower off the stem and floated it in the bowl. "Well, he owns it, yes; but we're trying to work something out. He's been surprisingly stubborn about the whole thing. Out of concern for the property value of the whole inn, I even offered to renovate it while he retained ownership. He refused, though." He rubbed his chin. "I never understood why Grandfather willed it to him. It's an odd bequest. He won't even go near the place. Unless he sells it, what good is it to him?"

"Perhaps there are painful memories there for him," Zanita suggested.

Todd appeared slightly embarrassed. "From the family rumors I've heard, that's probably true. But it's all the more reason for him to sell it to me."

A god-awful groan of near death erupted from the kitchen.

"Oops! It's Hippolito's lunch time. I'll talk to you later." Todd scurried back to his kitchen.

"Well, that was odd."

"Hippolito's wrenching plea for sustenance?" Tyber gazed out the window, his mind working.

"No, nummy! Todd must be the one Sasenfras spoke of—the one who wanted to buy the wing."

"Not necessarily. There may be more than one person after that wing. The question is *why*. Todd was right, though, about one thing."

"What?"

"It is strange that Sasenfras won't sell. He appears to loathe the place."

"And be terrified of it."

They stared at each. They both spoke at once.

"There must be something in that wing, Tyber!"

"We need to get in that wing, baby!"

They left the library and hurried to the far side of the house. As they rushed along, Tyber murmured, *"Nummy?* What do you mean, nummy?" He mussed up her hair with his palm.

There was a solid wall where a door to the upstairs wing should have been.

Tyber checked it carefully, running his fingertips along the edges, searching for any panels that might open. There were none.

Zanita was slightly disappointed. How were they going to gain entrance to the wing? Chopping through the wall would be illegal, as far as Sasenfras was concerned. They both doubted he would ever give his permission for that.

"They really did seal this off tight, didn't they?" she said, sulking.

"Yes. I don't think we're going to gain entrance through any acceptable channels."

She grinned up at him. "Can we find some unacceptable channels?"

He rubbed his jaw. "Well, there is that ledge outside the window at the top of the library stairs."

"That seems very risky. The ledge might be icy, Tyber."

"Yeah. Maybe as a last resort. I wonder where that left fork in the secret tunnel went to? We never did follow that pathway when we were down there."

"There was a passage to the left? I never saw that."

"It was behind and under the stairs to the left. I noticed it when I went back for Hambone, but it must go in the direction of the . . . kitchens. The kitchens! Store that one for later, baby—this is coming together."

"It is?" She furrowed her brow.

"Yes. If that passage does lead by the kitchens, it could explain a lot of the culinary poltergeist activity. Someone would have easy access to the food and its preparation. Let's check it out. It may even lead us to another passage and to that wing."

Zanita was not overly thrilled about going into that dark, dank passage again. It was creepy down there. She sighed. What journalists do for their work! "All right, let's go."

They retraced their steps back to the library and mounted the steps to the top. Tyber unlatched the secret hook, and the small door squeaked open.

It was too inviting by half.

"You go first," she offered magnanimously.

Tyber cocked his brow.

"I'm the writer." As if that were an explanation.

"Oh, yes. That's right." Tyber's lips twitched as he ducked into the passage. "The writer must be preserved at all costs! I remember reading that throughout history, whenever there was danger, a shield of human protection went instantly around the writer. Even before the supplies."

Zanita slapped his shoulder as she followed him in. "You wretch."

He laughed. "It's true! Scribes were always protected so that they could bring the tale back. I know I want to bring your tail back."

"Tyber! Get serious!"

His hand covered his heart. "You wound me."

"You'll survive. Hey, you were right . . . all the webs have been cleaned out. It's right purty down here if you ignore the dark dankness and musty odor."

Tyber sniffed. "There's a slight tinge of Formula 409, overlaid with a strong bouquet of Spic and Span."

She snickered. "When did you find the time to check this out this morning? I don't recall your leaving the room; on the contrary, you seemed determined to stay." She gave him a pointed look.

The rogue didn't even try to deny it. He had been very happily and very actively engaged with her. Featherwise. "I didn't."

"Then how did you know the webs were gone?"

"I had a good suspicion that whoever put

them there would have them removed. Just like that picture. Don't know if you noticed, but it was already gone."

She hadn't. "So Todd is still a prime suspect? He admitted to having this tunnel swept out."

Tyber narrowed his eyes. "He's still a prime suspect."

"But what's his motive?"

"That we need to find out by getting into that wing." Zanita sighed. "What's the matter, baby?"

"I just wish it weren't Todd. I like him so much."

"I know; me too. But we can't let our feelings interfere with this. We need to be objective while we collect our facts. Isn't that what you wanted?"

"Yes. I just didn't know that it would hurt a bit."

"Welcome to the world of investigative work. When you dig to find answers, they are not all going to be pretty or otherworldly, Curls."

"I know." She stiffened her shoulders. "Let's go."

Tyber smiled appreciatively at her attitude as she took the lead down the corridor.

They traversed the circular hidden stairs much as they had the first time, with Tyber going first and Zanita carefully following.

When they both reached the bottom, Tyber trained the light behind the stairwell. There off to the left was another passage. It was partially hidden by the stairwell, and if Tyber had not been searching for Hambone's nemesis, he probably would have missed it.

"Wow. Spooky. Do you think the whole house is riddled with these passages?"

"A good portion of it, although they are very well hidden. Todd will have a time with his complete renovations. There's no telling where these will all lead to or what the support structure is." He started down the left fork. This time he had brought a compass and shone the flashlight on it every now and then to check their direction.

"I think we're coming up close to the kitchens."

"Tyber, why do you suppose the webs were placed there in the first place?"

"I wondered about that for a while. Then I realized that there *must* be another passage down here that leads to places someone didn't want us to discover. I think they hoped to scare us off."

"Hey, it worked for me. I don't like being down here."

He put his arm around her shoulder. "Neither do I."

"Oh, yeah? Then why are your eyes sparkling and why is your step so lively? You're not kidding me, Doc; you love this. The adventure, the danger, the puzzle. It's right up your analytically paved alley."

He spread his arms wide. "What? I said nothing."

She scoffed.

They came upon a low trapdoor in the side of the wall, which stood all of three feet high. Tyber bent down and clicked the latch. The place beyond was dark and narrow. "Stay here," he called behind him as he scooted into the space.

"We already had that discussion." Zanita was close behind him. She felt as if they were two rats scurrying along a maze. *Rats*. Gulp. She hoped not.

"Where do you think we are?" she whispered.

"Right-about-here." He slowly moved forward and looked up. They were in the bottom of an ancient dumbwaiter.

"I hope no one wants lunch."

"Why?"

He pointed to the top of the shaft, where a small wooden platform hung. It was operated by pulleys. "I don't feel like getting beaned on the head by that."

"Is this a way into the kitchen?"

"You got it."

"Hmmm. So what do we do now? Do we back up and pick up the main tunnel we just left?"

Tyber glanced at his compass and then gazed speculatively upward. "Nope." He backed out of the shaft into the narrow passage. "Can you scoot up here next to me? It's a tight fit, but we've been tighter." His white teeth flashed in the dark. The pirate.

"Yes. I'm sure I can." She squiggled back alongside him. It was a very snug fit.

"Mmmm. Maybe we should take a break." His breath licked at the curls along her hairline.

"No. No. And no. There may be rats in here and all kinds of oookie stuff."

"Oookie stuff?" He grinned, showing that dimple. "I thought you loved oookie stuff." He tickled her midriff.

She slapped his hand away. "Not this kind of oookdom. So what do you have in mind?"

He looked altogether wicked in the dim light.

"I meant, why did you ask me to squeeze into this small space with you?"

"I'm going to pull that dumbwaiter down. This rope looks pretty thick; it may be able to handle our combined weight if we squeeze onto it together."

"May be able to? That sounds warm and fuzzy."

"I'll get on first, then pull you onto my lap. No surprise *feelies* while I'm pulling the cord, sweetheart, or we'll both plummet to serious injury."

"How are you going to lift us both up in that thing?"

He flexed his arm muscles. "I can do it. Just try to stay still."

He pulled the dumbwaiter down and slid onto

the small, level platform. Zanita scooted over to the edge, and he pulled her up and over onto his lap. They were like two sardines in a can.

Tyber grabbed the pulley ropes and began yanking them up.

"Where do you think this dumbwaiter leads to? One of the rooms in the closed wing?"

"I'm counting on it," he puffed as he pulled them up. It was harder than he had thought; the wheels were rusty, and the task required extra strength.

Zanita watched her husband's muscles bulge with the effort. Even though he was probably killing himself, she thought most women liked seeing their men engage in such displays of strength. There was something about bulging male arm muscles dotted with a sheen of sweat that felt like a ride on Space Mountain. Totally unexplainable but true.

"What are you smiling about? I'm killing myself here." Tyber glanced down at her.

"I know. I was just thinking about Space Mountain."

Tyber gave her the famous Mysterious Face of Mars look.

Men never had a clue.

When he reached the top, he wrapped the rope tightly around a wall bracket designed for that purpose. A small sliding slatwood window faced them. Tyber leaned over to pry it open, causing their platform to sway.

Zanita almost lost her balance and slid off him. "Hold on to me, baby, and don't let go!"

Tyber expected the window to be stuck from age. He expected that he would have to use a lot of elbow grease to get it open. So he was surprised when it slid up easily on its runners.

He twisted around with Zanita still on his lap, letting his legs fall out the other side.

Training his flashlight around the room, he instructed her it was safe to jump off.

Zanita landed feet first in a boarded-up bedroom. Small beams of sunlight streaked through several holes in the wood slats covering the windows. Not enough light to completely see by, but enough to illuminate some areas of the room. She walked around a dusty old bed and peeped through one of the window holes.

"Look, here. We're in the room directly across the ledge from the library stairs platform."

"Yeah, I kinda thought we would be."

Zanita shook her head at his directional perception. After that maze they had just navigated, she had no sense of direction whatsoever.

The massive bed facing them was covered in dust and spiderwebs. So were the period furniture pieces. By the well-worn opulence, Zanita guessed that this was part of the owner's suite.

The room had a musty air from being sealed up so long—underlaid with another odor she couldn't put a name to. An almost sweet, sickening smell.

The room looked like a chamber in a haunted house.

It was cold, very cold.

Chills ran up and down her arms, but she was not sure if the chills were caused by the low temperature alone.

"Not exactly a homey place, is it?' Tyber came up to her, encircling her in his warm arms.

"These must have been Todd's grandfather's rooms." She walked over to an inlaid side table. Through the seventeen dust layers, she could still tell that it had once been a very fine imported Moroccan piece. "Some of this stuff is valuable. I wonder why Sasenfras wouldn't want to come in and get it. He could get some money for this stuff."

"At the very least, he could redecorate."

They both gave each other a look. That sixties furniture that he had in the shanty was horrible.

"Well, there's no accounting for taste."

"True." He grinned, his eyes trailing a path down the bright purple shirt and turquoise pants she had decided to wear.

"Not one word."

He put his hands up. "I didn't say a thing, baby."

Her lower lip pouted out. "No, but your look had a chapter's worth."

"Aw, baby, I love your clothes." He encircled her in a bear hug. "They're you."

What was that supposed to mean? "Hmf." But she enjoyed the caress just the same.

"I wonder how much action that bed has seen."

"Tyber!" Zanita pushed away from him.

He realized how she had interpreted his comment. He chuckled. "No, no. It was just that, by all accounts, Todd's grandfather was quite a . . . swinger . . . in his day. I don't think Sasenfras's wife was the first dalliance."

"But she seems to be have been his last."

"How do you know that, Curls?" Tyber walked over to the bedside table and examined the dusty contents on the top. They were an eclectic mix of oddities. The Karma Sutra, some sex devices that even Tyber had a hard time figuring out, an old prescription bottle in the name of grandfather Sparkling and . . .

He grinned. A large peacock feather.

"Hey, baby, check this out." He held up the moth-eaten feather and waggled his eyebrows.

Zanita's mouth formed an O of amused surprise. As he was standing there holding up the feather, several of the filaments drifted to the floor one by one, then the rest suddenly all dropped off at once. Tyber was left holding nothing but a long quill.

Zanita burst out laughing. "Can't cause much trouble with that, now can you?"

He gave her the Evans "wanna bet?" look—a curved dimple and flashing eye.

"Better be careful." She wagged her finger at him. "If you knew what happened to Todd's grandfather after he played with that thing, you wouldn't be so smug."

"What did happen to the old reprobate?"

Zanita walked over to the closet and opened the door. A shower of dust and a scurrying sound resulted. She brushed her hand back and forth in front of her face to dispel the worst of the dirt. "Well, Todd said that according to family lore, his grandfather went out at night in his boat, not long after the dalliance with Sasenfras's wife, Winifred, began."

"Winnie Sasenfras?" Tyber shook his head. "Now, that sounds like a vixen to curl your toes."

"Hush. They say she had a certain *je ne sais quoi*. Anyway, apparently a gale sprang up and his boat sank." She peered further into the closet.

"Don't go rummaging through there," Tyber cautioned.

"Why not?"

"Because I just saw two pairs of beady yellow eyes sticking out from the tangle of cloth at the bottom."

270

"*Eeee.*" Zanita jumped back two steps and slammed the door shut.

Tyber walked over to a connecting door and opened it to the next room in the suite.

Zanita glanced at the bed hangings, shocked to see lewd pictures under the canopy. "Todd told me they had a burial at sea, although he was only a few years old at the time and has no real memory of it. His grandfather's body was never found."

"I—wouldn't—say—that."

Zanita turned around swiftly. Tyber was poised in the doorway to the next room, frozen in place.

She ran up to him. "What is it?"

His chin gestured in the direction of a round burled walnut table in the center of a sitting room where he had trained the flashlight.

There, sitting at the table in a silk smoking jacket, was Todd's grandfather.

Chapter Eleven

Unfortunately, he was a skeleton.

Tyber bounced the light off the faded brocade smoking jacket. On the table nearby was an elongated cigarette holder, the kind that was popular in the fifties and early sixties. Its cigarette had long since turned to a pile of powdery tobacco. He was facing the door to the sitting room.

"Dapper bag of bones, isn't he?"

"My god, Tyber, do you know what this means?"

"I have a good idea." Without touching the remains, he carefully examined the skeleton. After he was done, he glanced over at the table top, noting an empty teacup. Next to the teacup was a teapot. The contents had evaporated ages ago.

Tyber lifted the lid and sniffed. A faint scent assailed his nostrils. *Almonds*.

"Self-inflicted or murder?" Zanita asked.

"It *looks* like a natural death or suicide, but it's definitely murder."

"How can you tell?"

"My gut feeling and the way he's sitting in that chair. There are scuff marks on the floor beneath his slippers, like he was wrestling with someone or had been surprised by something. He was writhing and clawing at his robe, too; see how the ascot is skewed? If it was suicide, he wouldn't have been so actively fighting it. Of course, a heart attack would produce that reaction as well. But-I-don't-think-so."

She nodded. "How was he done in?"

"There is still the faintest trace of an almond scent in that teapot."

"Arsenic?"

"Probably."

"Poor Merville."

"*Merville?*"

"Mmmm. That was his name. Todd told me."

"Merville, you suave skirt-chaser, you." Tyber bowed to the skeleton.

A vase crashed to the floor.

They both jumped. Almost out of their skins.

"Apologize at once, Tyber! You've offended our spirit!"

Tyber gave her a patient look. "Baby, just because this man was murdered doesn't automatically mean he's a card-carrying member of the haunting set."

A picture fell off the wall, slamming onto a sideboard. It knocked off several knickknacks while raising a cloud of dust.

"Just do it!" Zanita hissed.

"Fine. But I still think it was caused by the sudden vibrations of our footsteps, as well as our intrusion in a rat-infested area that has been undisturbed for a long, long time."

She crossed her arms over her chest and tapped her foot.

He faced the skeleton and swept him another bow. "Merville, I apologize." As he straightened up, his flashlight swept the right edge of the table top. *Something was there.* Tyber walked over to get a better look.

"Be careful," Zanita cautioned in a little voice. Skeletons in smoking jackets did not inspire a warm fuzzy feeling as far as she was concerned.

"I will, baby." Tyber thought the warning was rather sweet.

He trained the light over the spot. The dying man had tried to write a word in the once polished surface of the desk. Undisturbed all these years, it was still perfectly legible. As he was dying, Merville had penned the word *Dam.*

Tyber thought it was an apt evaluation of the man's situation. He pointed it out to Zanita.

"Do you think he was cursing his murderer with his last breath?" she asked.

"Looks that way."

"He left the 'n' off."

"I don't think he was worried about spelling at the time, sweetheart."

She shivered. "If he was cursing someone with his last breath, no wonder he haunts the place."

"Too bad he never got to tell us his murderer's name. Would have made this a whole lot easier."

"Hey, what's this here?" Zanita gingerly peered over the skeleton's shoulder. There was a faded piece of paper on the table in front of him. Next to it was a small lock box. Merville must have taken the paper out of the box and laid it on the table to look at it. "I wonder if he took the paper out before or after the poison hit him."

"I don't know, but the answer to that will be crucial. Whatever is on that paper was important enough to him that he kept it under lock and key." He pointed to the key next to the open box.

Zanita examined the yellowed piece of paper. A series of numbers were scrawled across the top. "52329625 223105 2225 52351910186235," she read out loud. More numbers followed in a scroll pattern down the page.

Tyber looked over her shoulder. "Well, what do you know?"

"Is it the combination to some kind of safe, do you think?"

"Nope. It's a code."

"A code? Of what?"

"That is what I am going to find out." He very carefully lifted the ragged sheet of paper, hoping it wouldn't fall apart. It held together.

"This should give us some answers, I think."

Zanita nodded. "Poor Todd. What do we tell him?"

"Nothing for now."

"*What?*" She turned and gazed up at him. "We have to let him know about his grandfather. And we should call in the police; there was a murder here. There's no statute of limitations on murder."

"Baby, we need to keep this to ourselves until we figure out what happened here. Once everyone knows about the murder, our advantage will be lost. Merville's waited this long for justice; he can wait a little while longer."

She nodded, seeing the logic in that. "Does that mean we have to leave by dumbwaiter as well?"

He winced, rolling his sore shoulder muscles. "I'm afraid so."

They walked back into the bedroom, both glad to be out of eyeshot of that macabre skeleton. It reminded Zanita of that spooky Disney ride through the haunted house where all the ghosts were seen stationary in one place, then suddenly began to cavort about. Only Disney was fantasy and this was real. She shivered.

Tyber's hand rested on her shoulder. "He can't hurt you, baby. I'd never allow it."

Zanita smiled up at him, patting his hand on her shoulder.

As they made their way to the dumbwaiter, Tyber noticed a painting on the sitting-room floor, its front facing the wall. It was obvious by the faded wallpaper above it that someone had taken the picture down and turned it away from sight.

Which meant that it was a clue.

He knelt down in front of the canvas backing. "Wonder who or what it is?"

"In this house it could be anything." She hugged herself, warding off a sudden chill.

"Wanna take bets it's the femme fatale Winnie?" He winked at her.

Somehow the name "Winnie" and "femme fatale" seemed a contradiction in terms. Zanita giggled. "I say it's *himself*."

"Then why turn it around to face the wall? Bad hair day?"

"Uh-uh. Whoever did him in didn't want the portrait watching as the dark deed was done."

Tyber rubbed his jaw. "Bet?"

"Okay." Zanita toed the old carpet. "If I win, you willingly go on the next investigation with me."

He winced. "Ouch. That's steep."

She almost pushed him over with her foot but he grabbed it in time.

"All right," he conceded. "But if I'm right, you take belly dancing lessons."

Zanita blinked. *"Belly dancing lessons?"* Where had that come from?

A truly wicked smile inched across his sensual face. "Ahuh."

She raised an eyebrow. "I see Merville is not the only one with secret fantasies."

He blew her a kiss.

"Okay, you're on, but no feathers."

He laughed out loud. A rich sound of enjoyment. "Agreed; no feathers." He gave her a calculating glance out of the corner of his eye. "That'll be the next bet," he murmured to himself.

"What did you say?"

"I said, 'it's a good bet.'"

She didn't believe that for a minute. Not from this pirate.

They both were horrified when Tyber turned the picture around.

And not because one of them had won the bet.

There, painted in deep, lustrous color, was an enormously fat black cat. A pink tongue lolled from its mouth. It was the exact image of Hippolito.

Zanita gasped. "It couldn't be."

Tyber's brow furrowed. "How many cats could look like that?"

She glanced at the bottom right corner of the work. The painting was titled, signed, and dated by the artist: *Merville's Folly, Winifred, 1964.* "So Winnie painted this. I wonder why it was taken down from the wall and turned over."

Tyber shrugged. "Just more to add to the mystery, baby. And how can Hippolito's portrait be dated 1964? This is getting more and more tangled."

Zanita poked him in the side with her elbow. "C'mon, admit it. You love it!"

"Well . . ."

"Ha!"

Tyber frowned at her back as she pranced toward the dumbwaiter. To his mind, her saucy step had way too much know-it-all bounce.

The edges of his mouth lifted as a thought occurred to him. The proof was right in her attitude. Somehow, in her eyes, he had become a partner. *A husband.*

He was going to take great pleasure in making her realize it.

"Oomph!"

"Dammit!"

The dumbwaiter came to a halt at the bottom

of the shaft near the kitchen with a *whump-bang!* Since Zanita was perched prettily on his lap while he sweated and strained in an effort to bring them down safely with the pulleys, he had the delightful experience of absorbing the full brunt of the jolt when the board hit rock bottom.

Since he was on the bottom, his *bottom* took the initial wallop. This was followed by the rebound, which caused Zanita to plop down onto his lap in a really uncomfortable way.

You might say poor Tyber took it two ways to the middle.

He tried not to be too vocal about it—there was no telling who was beyond the small lift door in the kitchen. He rested his damp forehead against Zanita's and counted to ten.

"Bad landing, huh?"

He nodded his head silently.

"Poor thing." She patted his back over his shoulder. Then she tried to scramble from his lap.

Tyber clenched his teeth. "Wait—a—second."

"Okay." She wiggled her rump, getting cozy once more.

"You'll pay for this," he croaked.

She grinned. "Stop being such a baby. I didn't land that hard."

"It was the angle . . . but never mind that."

"Oh?" Her face took on a puzzled look—until she realized where the flashlight was. "Oh my! Are you okay?"

"I will be . . . in about five days," he groaned.

"What made you put the flashlight *there*?"

His blue eyes narrowed. "I didn't. You did."

"Oh," she said in a small voice.

Tyber took a few deep breaths and carefully lifted the hatch just enough to see if anyone was in the kitchen.

"Thank God it's empty. Now we don't have to go all the way around. Quick—jump into the kitchen." He lifted the hatch the rest of the way for her and she sprang out. A small groan followed her from the direction of the shaft.

Tyber followed, although not as quickly.

His freedom of motion had been severely restricted. He had just lowered the hatch when Todd came strolling into the kitchen.

"Hey, you two, looking for an afternoon snack?"

"Ah, sure, Todd," Zanita said. "We thought we'd take a pot of tea and those finger sandwiches back to the room with us."

Tyber limped slightly over to Zanita, his complexion a bit paler than usual. "Yeah, we thought we'd relax until dinner, maybe soak in the tub awhile, take a nap."

"Tyber's sore from his workout this morning." Zanita kept her voice perfectly bland.

Dara Joy

Tyber pinched her bottom discreetly.

"Sure thing!" Todd set out a tray and retrieved the sandwiches from the fridge with enviable flaire.

Hippolito, who was lying feet up in the sun by the window, opened one eye and twitched his nose. Todd tossed him a scrap of turkey. The cat caught it like a performing whale at Sea World, upside down, mouth opening and closing in a snap. Snack accomplished, he drifted back to sleep.

Tyber and Zanita watched the cat speculatively.

"Todd . . . how long have you had Hippolito?"

"Oh, forever!" Todd put a kettle on for their tea. "You might say he came with the house."

Zanita and Tyber eyeballed each other. "But how long has he been in the family?" Tyber probed.

"Gee, the Litos have been with my family for ages."

"The Litos?" they both said at once.

"Yes. There was Grandelito, Collosolito, and then before him, Megalito . . . that was grandfather's cat." Todd smiled slightly. "Grandfather was fond of cats, from what I've heard."

"You mean the Litos actually are able to get up and procreate?" Tyber looked at the sprawled feline doubtfully.

Todd chuckled as he removed the kettle from the stove and poured boiling water into a strawberry-patterned teapot. "Yeah, I guess, but only once a generation, it seems. After that, I guess they figure it isn't worth the effort."

"Not worth the effort? What's wrong with those Litos? Twice is always the charm. They obviously didn't have the right love partner," Tyber declared with mock seriousness. Zanita wagged her finger at him.

Todd laughed. "Guess not. The Litos seem to have only one offspring in the litter, and it always comes out looking exactly like pappy. Somehow, junior always shows up at our door. Guess the Litos are part of the Florencia Inn." He handed Tyber the laden tray.

"It would seem so."

"Thanks, Todd!" Zanita gave him a thank-you wave of her fingers as they left the room.

"What did you find so funny about the once-is-enough tale?" Tyber asked her, grinning.

"Oh, just that Hippolito needs some new techniques to pique his interest."

"Uh-huh. And what techniques would those be?" He limped along.

She giggled.

"Whaaaat?"

"I just realized you got the shaft in the shaft."

"I'm not laughing, baby."

* * *

Is Hippolito spelled with one p or two? Zanita
made a note on her laptop to ask Todd.

Tyber sighed and snuggled deeper into her
side, his head half on her lap. She was sitting up
in bed taking notes on the story, which would
later turn into an article and possibly part of a
book. After taking a nice long bath in the
whirlpool—which he constantly tried to cajole
her into—Tyber had crawled naked under the
sheets next to her and promptly fell asleep.

Not even the rapid tapping of the keys was
having any effect on him.

They really hadn't had much sleep these past
two days, not to mention that their schedule had
been changed around from day to night.

Zanita sighed as his muscular forearm cradled
her waist, over the loose T-shirt she was wearing. He murmured something unintelligible just
before the gentle puffs of air started again, indicating he was once more in La-la Land.

She gazed down at him. He was a physically
stunning man awake, but he was an even more
captivating man asleep. That was when the
sheer beauty of his form could be appreciated
simply for itself.

His long, thick lashes made a dark crescent on
his high cheekbones. The straight, even nose
and perfectly chiseled lips were the ideal foil for

that beguiling dimple. . . . *Dimple? He must be dreaming of something very pleasing.*

As if to give credence to her evaluation, he growled softly in the back of his throat, exhaling steadily in his sleep. The small currents of his hot breath through the thin material of her T-shirt gave her goose bumps.

She shook herself. *No time for that; I have to work!* So she went back to staring into space.

Soon she was blithely typing away on her story while her mind wandered on to more arcane topics. What if Hippolito was, in fact, the only pet belonging to all those generations of Sparklings? It would make a great story. Idly she plotted the macabre tale in her head: The Quasimodo-like feline hangs on to the same family . . . and what? Lies there like a beached whale and demands to be fed tidbits generation after generation?

She giggled to herself. He did grow on you after a while, and he was kinda cute with that little pink tongue. She looked down at the screen and frowned. Her mind must have really been traveling, for her work was mistyped in several places. Letters that didn't belong popped up in the middle of several words.

Shrugging, she fixed the mistakes and went back to typing, looking off into space every now and then as she thought her article through.

When she glanced down again, she was horrified to see more of the same mistakes! She frowned. Something wasn't right here; she was an excellent typist.

She shifted her focus to her innocently sleeping husband. Hmmm. Pretending to type away at her article, furtively she peeped down from the corner of her eye.

A mischievous masculine finger snuck up over the edge of the laptop and hit a random key.

Aha! Caught in the act! The rogue.

"Tyber!"

He smiled into her midriff. "Whaaat?"

And here she'd thought he had been innocently sleeping away! She should have known better. Innocent and pirate didn't go together.

"Can't you just lie there? Like a normal person!"

He laughed into her skin. "Now, why would I want to do that, hmmm?"

An exasperated gust of air sailed past her lips. She had to watch him every second! There was no telling what he would do . . .

She stopped.

No, there was no telling what he would do.

Ever.

It was part of his very nature.

This man would never become mundane or repetitive or distant. Tyber lived life. He felt life.

Every second of every day. Why should her marriage to him be any different?

She inhaled a shaky breath. Was she losing the challenge? Secretly, she had hoped she would lose the bet. Secretly, she had used the bet to corner him into this investigation. Somehow, in some way, her eyes had been opened and in ways she had never imagined. *Who knew they were shut to some things?* The strange part of life's lessons was that you never knew how closed you had been until your eyes were opened. Once the truth was seen, there was no going back.

She paled as she gazed down at him.

Tyber instantly lost his smile, concerned that he had done something truly wrong. "What? I didn't mean to upset your work. I was just playing and knew you'd . . . *mpf*!"

Zanita had grabbed his gorgeous face between her hands and kissed him soundly on the mouth. Just because.

He blinked slowly when she released him. "What was that for? Not that I'm complaining." Like Hambone, he lifted his face, hoping for another serving.

"That was for being you." She planted a second helping, which was eagerly received. "I love you."

Tyber sucked in his breath. "Totally nonlinear, baby," he breathed. "Does this mean I should mess up some more of your . . . typing?" The expression he sent her was one of utter mischief, underscored with sexual innuendo.

Her lips twitched. "Try it and you'll think the flashlight incident was a stroll in the park."

"Ouch. The woman can wield a whip."

She just smiled.

"Hmmm . . ." He rubbed his jaw pondering *that* possibility.

Zanita placed her palm over his head and slam-dunked him back down to the quilt.

"Tonight the spirit speaks! He is close by, I can feel him!"

Tyber and Zanita watched Calendula obliquely. The woman was picking up something psychically. And she wasn't far off. The ghost *was* close by. Second floor of the closed wing, to be exact.

"What will the spirit say, do you think?" Zanita questioned Tyber in an aside.

"Eenie meenie chili beanie," he quipped.

Zanita elbowed him. "Shh! Someone might hear you. And you know, it feels a lot creepier in here knowing that there's an actual dead body in the house with us."

"Technically it's not a body anymore."

Zanita's tongue dropped out. "Eck. Don't remind me. That macabre scene was like something out of a Vincent Price movie."

"Dem bones, dem bones, dem dry bones," Tyber sang under his breath.

Zanita stifled a giggle. "I honestly don't think Todd knows his grandfather is upstairs in residence. Look at him; he's so sweet."

"If you say so, baby."

"On the other hand, Sasenfras must definitely know, if he—"

Tyber sat up straight. "You're right! He said he was in there once. He has to know. I wonder why he refuses to unseal the wing and why he hasn't told anyone about what's in there."

"Maybe he's afraid he'll be accused of the murder . . . or maybe he's afraid of something else . . . Something in that wing terrified him. It may not have been the corpse alone."

"Back to your ghost theory, huh, baby?"

"There are a lot of odd things going on in this house. You know, I'm not even sure about the Hippolito story."

He did a double take. "You actually think this inn has been haunted for decades by an enormously fat cat? You're killing me here."

"Pookah."

"Bless you."

"No, I said Pookah! Like in that movie *Harvey*. What if Hippolito is a Pookah? You have to admit he's strange."

Tyber gave her an odd look. "Compared to

what?" he asked cautiously. "An aunt with three hats or a pirate cat?"

"I just think it's a theory we shouldn't overlook."

"Uh-huh. Are you sure you're getting enough sleep?"

She ignored that.

"Look, baby, that cat is . . . well, I'm not sure what the cat is, but I know he's no 'Pookah.' "

She crossed her arms over her chest. "How do you know that?"

"For one thing, we can all *see* him. Real Pookahs can only be seen by Jimmy Stewart . . . and maybe Dr. Chumley—but only on the rare occasion."

She eyeballed him. "*That's* your counter explanation?"

"It's as good as yours."

A few seconds ticked by in silence. Then she waved a hand of pronouncement in the air. "I can see you are completely closed-minded to the paranormal."

"I don't know about that, baby." He grinned sexily. "What we did this morning seemed pretty paranormal to me. In fact, I still have several physical manifestations on my back from—"

She placed her hand over his mouth. "Someone will hear you!"

"*Amm norrr surr Sasenfraa wid iiii.*"

"What?"

He took her hand away from his mouth. "I'm not sure Sasenfras did it, but I do think he knows there's a body in there, which is why he has refused to sell to Todd or let him renovate."

"What if Todd knows, as well? Don't forget, he inherited the bulk of the estate. And he wants to buy out Sasenfras. Unfortunately, that still makes him a prime suspect."

"Not for murder. He was just a baby when Merville bit the, ah, dust."

"You're right. Property on the Vineyard wasn't that valuable then, either. Hard to believe, yet true."

"There are still several pieces to this that we're missing, baby."

"Savory bun?" Blooey stuck a plate of warm herb rolls right under their noses, ending that conversation. "Ain't these beauties?" He gestured with the plate, urging them to take one. "Wish I could get the recipe for these babies. Got a squash version I want to try."

Tyber groaned. *Not the squash torture again.*

Hambone looked up at the plate and smacked his lips. Blooey pulled the plate close to his chest. "Git off wit ye, ye scalawag! Ye already stole four of 'em!"

Blooey moved off with a determined Hambone dogging his steps.

Zanita shook her head. "Those two."

"I know." He bit into his bun. "Mmm, these are delicious."

Zanita took a nibble of hers. "Delicious? These are sensational!"

"Oh! It's savory buns!" Mark came into the room and literally clapped his hands in delight. "I just love Todd's buns!"

Tyber cleared his throat and tried not to look at Zanita, sure he would laugh this time.

"My wonders!" Auntie plopped into a chair next to Hubble. "These are richer than the ones they have at The Cellar in Macy's! Very chichi."

"And Todd said he's cooked up a special dinner for us tonight—steak au poivre with Delmonico potatoes." Calendula glowed with enthusiasm for the chef. "He is such a genius in the kitchen. Truly inspired."

"Yeah, but by what?" Tyber whispered to Zanita.

Zanita agreed with him. This adventure into ghost-busting had turned into a crime investigation. "After tonight's field work, let's go over what we have collected already, so we're in perfect synergy."

"I thought we were always in perfect synergy," he rejoined in a low tone. The suggestive look that followed made her blush. "Okay—meet you in the tub later."

"The tub?"

"Yes. Perfect place for a networking conference. Trust me." He raised his eyebrows up and down.

"You, Doc Evans, are trouble." She gave him a sidelong smile and turned to Auntie.

"Are you enjoying your stay, Auntie?"

"Mar-r-r-vellous!"

Tyber cringed and stuck his face behind the savory bun.

"I haven't seen anything weird today, though, dear, unless you count that ghastly rhododendron outside my window. You know, Todd, the lopsided one with those garish spiked branches?" She shook her head as if to say, "It doesn't do."

Todd shrugged. "That's one of the original bushes, Auntie. I think it's one of the few originals left, too. I'm sorry if its shape offends you, but it's a fixture around here."

"I suppose we all must sometimes *sacrifice* taste for heritage."

Tyber stared pointedly at her three hats. Now, there was a sacrifice if he ever saw one. Zanita kicked him under the table before he could say anything.

"Are you positively, absolutely sure she's your aunt?" he asked for the umpteenth time.

"Yes."

The deep groaning sigh of "relative realization" followed.

Todd mistook it for Hippolito's beg-call and tossed the unsuspecting cat a piece of steak. Never one to overlook a flying bit of food coming his way, Hippolito neatly opened his mouth—not unlike a Venus fly trap—and snapped it shut on the morsel. The brown eyes flared in momentary ecstasy before drifting closed once more.

"I don't know if I like that beast gaining from my pain," Tyber remarked drolly in her ear.

Zanita showed no sympathy. "Someone has to."

Tyber's mouth dropped in a theatrical pose of shock.

After a luxurious dinner laid out by Todd—with Sasenfras's help—Calendula suggested they all remain where they were seated. She intended to conduct a séance, and the old wood dining table was the perfect spot.

"Mark, go get the Ouija board from my room, would you, dear?"

"Sure." He got up and left.

"I hate Ouija boards," Zanita whispered to Tyber.

"Why?"

"They just have a tendency to be creepy, that's all."

"Baby, we're investigating a haunted house

with a murdered skeleton, flying kitchen gadgets, and a Pookah cat, and *now* you talk about creepy?"

She shrugged sheepishly.

Calendula instructed Todd to go into the kitchen and retrieve several of the objects that had been thrown about in the "amazing aerial display" of a few nights ago. He came back laden with the cherry pitter, nutmeg grater, vegetable peeler, marble mortar and pestle, and lemon reamer.

Calendula asked Mark to place each tool next to a person. "What is this supposed to prove?" Hubble demanded.

"These are the gadgets that the ghost seems to have a quarrel with. We need to find out why."

He harumphed.

"Isn't this exciting!" Auntie waggled her lemon reamer in the air.

"Now, why do I think that's the perfect tool for her," Tyber intoned dryly.

Zanita shushed him.

Calendula sat at the head of the table. "Mark, the cameras are on?"

He nodded yes.

"Good. Let's begin by joining hands."

Out of the corner of his eye, Tyber noticed Sasenfras preparing to leave for the day. He had already remained later than his usual time, having stayed for dinner at Todd's request. "Wait a minute, Sasenfras. I think we should *all* be present during this," Tyber said.

Sasenfras's shoulders hunched. "I don't go in for none o' this stuff here now."

"Too bad. Take a seat, my man. You're in," Tyber said. It seemed that the caretaker had suspended his three-word rule of communication for the occasion. *Interesting.*

Reluctantly, Sasenfras took a seat next to Auntie.

Calendula turned all the lights off except for three votive candles. The eerie glow in the room certainly added the right atmosphere.

"Everyone, place your fingers on the disc in the center and try not to concentrate on anything. Rather, simply let your mind go free."

"That should be easy for some of us," Tyber murmured in Zanita's ear.

She tried not to laugh. Tyber always did this to her when she was trying to keep a straight face.

For several minutes nothing happened. That was, if you didn't count Hippolito's steady snoring from under the table. In contrast, Hambone perched on the edge of the window seat and watched the proceedings with avid interest, his one eye gleaming in the candle light.

Sasenfras shifted in his seat.

Tyber's eyes narrowed. "What's the matter, Sasenfras?"

"At least we got cats in here," he grumbled. "Cats protect you, you know. From *things*."

"Relax." Auntie patted his shoulder, misinterpreting his remark. "They won't bother anything. They're after my hats. I swear Hambone thinks they're alive. He never takes his eyes off them."

Zanita surreptitiously glanced at Hambone. The cat wasn't paying the least attention to Auntie's moldy hats. He was focused on the doings at the table. She grinned to herself.

"What?" Tyber's breath teased against her throat. He took the opportunity to brush his lips over the soft skin in a light caress.

"Nothing." She smiled like a cat.

Suddenly the disc in the center of the board started to shake slightly.

"It wants to move," Calendula whispered to the room. "Don't press down too hard; let your fingers barely touch the plastic."

Hubble pshawed but complied.

"We have a question for the spirit in the house," Calendula called out in a clear voice. "Are you present?"

The disc wobbled, then suddenly swung to the *yes* side, dragging everyone's hands along with it.

"Why do you haunt this inn?" she asked. Which seemed forward enough to Zanita.

The disc was inert for a few seconds. Tyber glanced around the table. Auntie was beaming like a three-hatted idiot; Hubble was shaking his head in disgust at the event; Mark was enraptured; Calendula was concentrating; Todd was wide-eyed; and . . . Sasenfras was sweating. Very curious.

Then the disc slowly moved, and Auntie called out each letter as it passed. "S-t-o-l-e-w-h-a-t-i-s-m-i-n-e . . . Stole what is mine. I wonder what that means."

"Who stole from you?" Calendula asked.

The disc started to go to a letter, then stopped, spun around and stayed in the center of the board.

"That would have been too easy," Zanita whispered to Tyber.

He bent down to speak in her ear, low. "Or someone here prevented the disc from spelling out the name."

"You believe in this?" She was surprised.

"I think the subconscious acts on the disc."

Calendula tried a different track. "What was stolen from you?"

The disc vibrated and slowly moved again to the same letters. "W-h-a-t-w-a-s-m-i-n-e."

"Chatty fellow, isn't he?" Mark joked.

"Who says it's a he?" Todd gazed around the circle. "Could be a she."

"True." Blooey snitched the last savory bun.

Hubble let out a sigh indicating it was all shenanigans to him.

"I wonder why the spirit keeps saying that?" Zanita bit her lip.

"Can you tell us your name?" The disc slid over to the letter I, then went to A and M. *I am.*

"Yes? Go on!"

The disc wobbled over to the center of the alphabet.

Sasenfras suddenly stood and flung the board off the table. "I'll not stay here another minute with these devil's games! It's all right for you, Mr. Todd, playing about and trying to dig into things maybe better left alone!" He turned and faced the startled group. "And that goes for all of ya! It's not right to be playin' in the devil's work! Stay out of it if you know what's best for yourselves!"

With that, he stormed off.

"Well, that was some warning!" Auntie leaned back in her seat and crossed her legs. "I just hate it when I miss the denouement!"

Tyber choked on his wine.

"That almost sounded like a threat." Zanita wondered if anyone else had heard it that way.

"From Sasenfras?" Todd shook his head. "I admit he's a little balmy, but he wouldn't really harm anyone."

What about murder? Tyber wondered, watching the grisly caretaker through the window as he climbed nimbly up the back cliff.

Chapter Twelve

"So what do we have so far?"

"Ah, a sore spot in an unmentionable place and about half a bottle of shampoo on my head?"

"Noooo." Zanita floated closer to him in the tub, slinging her leg over his to get a better angle to wash his hair. As planned, they had met in the tub to discuss the case.

"Mmmm." Tyber let out a combined moan of pleasure, weariness, and resignation. The woman was determined to play with his hair.

"I meant, what do we have up to now on the case?" She dug her soapy hands into his silky mane while giving a slightly evil grin. She loved playing with Tyber's hair. She tried to conjure up something extra naughty to do with that froth of bubbles.

Tyber always thought it best to ignore *those* expressions of hers.

"It might help to go over what's transpired so far so we can see where we are." Her hands shaped an unmentionable body part with the soapy strands. It jutted out from the top of his head like an exclamation point.

"I know where we are—in the Jacuzzi. What the hell are you doing?"

"Um, nothing. Is it still sore here?' Her soapy hand snaked beneath the water line. Tyber sucked in his breath as she massaged him in a very special place with the touch of heaven.

"Ah, no," he answered truthfully before he realized what he was saying.

She removed her hand.

"I mean, yeah, it's very, very sore, baby."

"You poor thing." He tried his very best to look like "a poor thing." Her hand recommenced its massaging. Zanita's soothing touch was always magic.

"Tyber, I think we may have two things going on here . . ."

"You've got that right." He glanced down at the water.

"On the one hand, we have what I think is a genuine paranormal incident."

"That hasn't been proven. A little lower, baby." He guided her hand to where it "hurt" the most. Or best, depending on how one viewed it.

"On the other hand . . . what's this?" She pulled a round net sponge from the water and stared at it. Shrugging, she tossed it over her shoulder onto the tile floor, placing her hand immediately back under the water.

"What?" Tyber paled slightly. He had been mentally floating away under her ministrations. The quick find and toss were a wee bit too fast for his fogged faculties. All he registered was her hand in the water and a round thing sailing past his head. Both occurrences were too close to a certain part of his anatomy for comfort, even though logical told him there was no cause for concern. Males were funny that way.

"Nothing. It was just an extra sponge."

"Oh." He gingerly rested back, his color returning.

"Anyway, as I was saying, on the one hand . . ." She stopped. Her violet eyes opened wide. *"My god, what is in this water!"*

Tyber stared at her immobilized as her hand rapidly fished around in the tub, brushing him in several sensitive areas as she did so. Finally her hand seemed to grasp something solid, preparing to yank it up.

Tyber's mouth dropped open in horror. In a fluid motion he sat forward. *"Wait!"*

But Zanita got a good hold on something squirming and pulled it up fast.

Tyber went perfectly white and leaned back

against the rim. Closing his eyes, he waited to feel excruciating pain.

When none was forthcoming, he slowly opened one light blue eye. Zanita was holding a drenched Hambone over the water by the scruff of his neck. The pirate tabby had a glare of disgust on his face as he continued to drip into the water.

Tyber crossed his arms over his chest and raised an eyebrow. "Now, how did you get in here?"

"He probably came in to investigate the bubbles and fell in behind us," Zanita explained, remembering that her grandmother's cat used to do that. "I have never figured out the fascination cats have with humans in bathtubs. My grandmother's cat used to push the door open while you were soaking, walk up to you, and sniff at both you and the water with a cross-eyed look. Once she realized you were okay, she'd look at you like you were demented and leave. But she checked you every five minutes just to be sure."

Tyber chuckled. "Yep. They do have a repulsed yet fascinated interest in the bath."

She put Hambone down on the tile. He shook from head to tail, spraying them with water. Raising his tail in the air, the tabby tried to exit with what little dignity he had left.

Her hand went back to massaging Tyber. His came out to still her, moving it to his shoulder.

She gave him a questioning look.

"Three strikes and you're out. I'm not taking any chances."

"Huh? Anyway, we know that besides the paranormal activity happening here—and don't snort, that explanation you gave for the book suddenly appearing inside the cabinet was totally hokey and you know it."

"I'm still working on that one." He rubbed the back of his neck, his forehead furrowing as his hand encountered the exclamation point on the top of his head.

"Giving you some trouble?" she needled him, in the science.

He wagged his finger at her. "I'll get back to you on it later."

She raised her eyebrows. "So let's see what we have. The moving picture on the sideboard during dinner . . ."

"That one's easy. It was pulled by a thin fishing line to the floor. The line was then quickly retracted."

"I might buy that. Who do you think did it?"

"I have my suspicions, but I'm not saying yet."

"Okay. What about the poltergeist activity with the flying gadgets?"

"Someone just inside that secret panel at the top of the library stairs. And with a strong pitching arm, too." He grinned. "Maybe it was the ghost of Jerome 'Dizzy' Dean."

"Tyber! Be serious! I think all of us were present in the library."

He rolled toward her. "Not all of us."

She thought a minute. "Sasenfras. But why? To scare us from the house?"

"Or lure us to the passage."

"Which brings us to the message in chicken blood."

"Ah, the chicken blood. Puts one in a voodoo kinda mood."

"Voodoo?"

"You do."

"Do wh—don't start that!"

He laughed huskily. "The chicken-blood writing could have been done by anyone in the house."

"Including the ghost."

"Including the—" He stopped, realizing what he had almost said. "Anyone in the house."

She trickled water over his chest. "Then there is the matter of the Polaroid with my eyes wide open. I can't figure how any of this fits in."

"That's a dark horse, as far as I can tell. Let's put that aside for now, too."

She nodded agreement. "What about the Ouija board messages? Sasenfras seemed pretty upset."

"How can you tell?" he asked blandly.

"You're funny," she said, and went on, "Someone besides Todd is trying to get him to sell. And remember, he did speak fondly of Todd when we were at his house."

"Fondly?" he said incredulously. "We are speaking of Sasenfras for whom the wolves bay?"

"Well, fondly for him. Personally, I think it has to be someone else who's after him to sell."

"The question is, who would want only a wing of an inn? It's damn odd."

"Especially since said wing has a body in it."

They looked at each other.

"They might not know that," she said.

"They might," he said.

They were silent for a few minutes.

"You know, Sasenfras spoke rather strangely of Winnie, too. He doesn't really seem to blame her for her infidelity. His attitude seemed to be that she couldn't help herself."

Tyber rubbed his jaw and stretched his long legs over the rim of the tub. "That is strange. Especially for a *husband*." He gave her a side-long look. She ignored it.

"How do kitchen gadgets fit in? To scare off Todd, maybe? And why scare off Todd?"

"I suppose flying kitchen tools would really get under a chef's skin. You know how touchy they are about their equipment—just look at Blooey. As to how it fits in, that part is still at the ballpark, too, baby."

"Along with Dizzy Dean?" She wiggled her toe on his calf.

"Ahuh." He smiled.

"And then there was the ghost in my room."

"Ah . . ."

"Not a ghost?"

"Nope."

She put her hands on her hips, splashing the water. Tyber's gaze followed her motion with interest. "How do you know? I was there, and I'm telling you it was unearthly! The muted light, the book falling—"

"The book was pushed."

"*What?*" She splashed in the water. "How do you know that?"

He gave her a pure-science smirk. "Physics is the jewel of mystery."

"Quit the enlightened-guru routine and speak!"

He laughed. "Remember when I examined the place where you said the book hit the floor?"

She nodded.

"There was no marking, scratch, or groove in the wood floorboards. It was a heavy book, but still it might not have made a mark. I checked the empty slot in the bookcase which was directly above where you thought it had fallen. It seemed fine at first. But then you said that the book had fallen spine side up. The only way that could have happened was if it fell directly to the floor below. But when I examined the floor to the right, there were two nicks in the wood spaced precisely as I would expect from that kind of impact. I knew what I had to do then, but not in front of everybody in the room. I waited until I knew the room was empty later that night and came back up here. I drew an imaginary line from those nicks on the floor to the bookcase and found right at that slot . . . the book, *On the Road*."

"By Kerouac?" She was completely puzzled now.

"Yes, but I'll get back to that later. When I removed that book, voila! There was a small peephole in the back. Someone with a dowel could have easily knocked the book off the shelf and did."

"But what woke me up? I felt something brushing against my face!"

"I carefully examined the room and found another peephole under the desk. My guess is, whoever it was used a penlight and flashed it over your face several times to wake you up. A small fog machine, also made to filter through the other peephole by the books, created the wafting, unearthly look, along with the herbal-scented incense. To a half-dazed person just awakening from sleep, a spirit appeared."

"My god. But how did the slot that the book fell out of change places with the other one without my seeing?"

"In the time between when you came down

and when we all went back up, the perpetrator had moved the books over to hide the real slot."

"Who wasn't with you in the parlor when I was upstairs sleeping?"

He thought for a minute. "Everyone went in and out; it could have been anyone. There was plenty of time, and don't forget, whoever did it had it all set up ahead of time, so it wouldn't have taken them much time to do it."

"Why do you say that?"

"Because whoever did this is the same person who was in our room that first night. They planted that particular book in that slot."

"They wanted us to find it. Planned it. What do you suppose they are trying to lead us to?"

"More than the murder. There's something else underlying everything. I think the answer may be in that code."

"Any luck cracking it?"

He just smiled.

"Well?" She slapped him with the washcloth. "What does it say."

"I haven't completely broken it, but I'm very close." He stood up in the water, and rivulets of bubbles sluiced down his toned body. He offered her a hand up. "One thing I am positive of."

"What's that?" Her hands steadied herself on his slick, muscular shoulders. He lifted her out of the Jacuzzi.

"We have to go to Nantucket Island tomorrow.

Everything's been pointing us in that direction. I want to know why."

He walked over to the large glassed-in shower and turned on the taps.

"You want to see if you can find out anything about Sasenfras?"

"Yeah. And whatever else we can come up with. We can't keep this to ourselves much longer. There was a murder, albeit about thirty years ago. We're gonna have to call the cops in soon, baby." He tugged her under the spray with him to rinse off. Streamers of soap sheeted down his hair and golden chest. And her curls and legs.

"What was significant about that book by Keroac? The one that was placed in the original slot?"

"I opened it up, and you'll never guess whose name was on the inside of the jacket." The flats of his palms slid down her back and sides.

"Who?" She closed her eyes and let the warm water and him flow over her as she leaned closer, letting their lower bodies touch intimately.

"Our own flower child . . . Winifred Sasenfras. The plot thickens."

"Is that what this is? A plot? I had no idea it was called that." She grinned cheekily.

He laughed. "Wait till you see the pacing," he drawled wickedly.

There was no unnecessary conflict from her.
But then, he knew her outline word for word.

Tyber informed Todd that a sudden business
problem had cropped up and he needed to meet
with some colleagues in Boston right away but
that they would be back by the next afternoon.
He didn't want anyone knowing that they were
going to Nantucket. He also instructed Blooey to
hold down the ship in their absence and to keep
an eye on Auntie.

Zanita wanted to kiss him for that but knew
she would embarrass him.

"Aye, aye, Captain! Consider it done! Don't
you and Her Ladyship worry about nothing a-
tall. Me and Hambone will batten down the
hatches. Right, Hambone?"

The scruffy cat gave a whine and placed his
paw on Tyber's leg. Occasionally even a pirate
kitty gave in to embarrassing displays of affec-
tion.

Tyber got down on one knee and petted the
disheveled cat-head. "Sorry, pal, not this voyage."

Zanita furrowed her brow. How the tabby
knew they were taking a boat ride was beyond
her. Sometimes the Evans household was
beyond eccentric.

Auntie was not so easy to put off as Blooey,
who had a tendency to accept orders blindly

from his captain. She cornered Zanita in the foyer like a *force majeure*.

"What is this preposterous tale of your going to Boston!"

"Shh! Auntie, keep your voice down!" Zanita glanced anxiously around the hallway, looking for eavesdroppers. Not that her search would tell her anything; the house was riddled with peepholes!

"Well, where are you really going, darling? If it has anything to do with that delightful ghost, I want to go, too!"

Delightful? Thank goodness Tyber strolled into the foyer at that moment. The overnight bag they had hastily put together from their combined belongings was slung over his shoulder. "Auntie, you know we'd *never* ditch you," he drawled in a really believable tone. *Not*.

Auntie viewed him though slitted eyes.

"You know we just got married; we only wanted a night alone." He put his arm around Zanita's shoulders and said something under his breath that Zanita was sure Auntie wouldn't want to hear.

"Bull! You've managed very well up to this point, you mar–r–r–velously naughty boy, even to the point of dragging my poor niece under a bed!"

He winced at the reminder of her untimely intrusion. *Relatives*.

key. "The proprietor is sending up a pot of tea and some biscuits. Are you hungry?"

"Yes, a little." She followed him up the wooden staircase, noting the seascapes on the wall.

"We can go out as soon as we unpack. The innkeeper—"

"That would be . . . Mr. Crypt?"

"Ah . . . yes. He suggested his own restaurant, of course, which is famous, I think, but I told him we just wanted to go to a place where the locals would hang out. That way we can start doing some digging right away."

"Good idea. Where did he suggest?"

"The Den of Iniquity."

"Mr. Crypt suggested The Den of Iniquity?" She crossed her arms over her chest and gave him a patient look.

"Yep. He said all the locals hang out there—no tourists."

"I wonder why," she snorted. "It sounds like a vampire bar!"

He winked at her. "Not on Nantucket, baby. It's a chowder house."

"What kind of chowder?" she asked, leery. "I only like Manhattan."

"Manhattan clam chowder?" He gasped, horrified. "Isn't that the *red* kind?"

"You're not funny. You know vampires keep me up all night."

317

"No, no, I just won't respond to that. I'll be good."

"Ha!"

"I asked the innkeeper—"

"Mr. Crypt." She laced her hands behind her back. "Let's call it as it is."

"Mr. Crypt . . . if he knew of any Sasenfrases from the area. He said no."

"Hmmm . . . maybe he hasn't been here that long?"

"Since seventeen ninety-two."

Her mouth dropped open.

Tyber hastened to add, "His family, anyway."

"I'm not so sure about that. But maybe we'll have better luck at The Den of Iniquity."

Their room was charming.

A four-poster bed graced the center of the room. It was an antique, three-quarter-size tester, not too long and not too wide. The fit was going to be cozy, Zanita acknowledged; Tyber was a tall man who liked to sprawl unchecked in bed while hugging her securely in his arms. Definitely a snuggle night.

The bed was covered with lovely ecru linens heavily trimmed in Irish lace. The canopy was made entirely of lace; tiny handmade roses dotted the length of it. She sighed. Very romantic.

A large fireplace was to the right of the bed. Someone had already lit the fire—a nice, warm welcome for guests on such a cold evening.

Dancing shadows flickered across the hand-hewn beams on the ceiling.

Once again, Zanita felt as if she had stepped back in time. As her writer's imagination took flight, it was easy to envision herself in a room like this in the early eighteen hundreds . . . just waiting to have an illicit rendezvous with a pirate captain. Coincidentally, the rogue looked remarkably like Tyber. She would be waiting for him on the bed, sprawled out across the soft feather mattress, wearing nothing but—

"Earth to Curls!"

Zanita gave a startled jump. "What?"

"What are you daydreaming about, hmm?" He gave her that knowing male look that said, "You couldn't possibly be thinking of anything else but me and what I'm going to do to you in that bed later."

Zanita snapped out of it. "You don't know that for sure."

He viewed her through half-closed eyes. "Uh-huh."

"Oh, shush! I just got carried away by the romance of the room."

He glanced at the bed speculatively. "Lots of lace."

Zanita bit her lip. *What did that mean?* With a man like Tyber Evans, anything at all. She wondered how many ways a physicist could think of to torture someone with lace.

Dara Joy

Countless, she concluded apprehensively.

He was definitely ahead in their challenge so far. But he wouldn't gain any ground tonight if she let him know that she already had him figured out. She confronted him. "Get those ideas right out of your head!"

Tyber blinked, then he laughed. "What ideas?"

"Stop acting as if you don't know!"

He raised an eyebrow, waiting.

"The outrageous ones you are planning to torture me with later in the name of the unexpected!"

The rascal didn't even try to deny it. "You know you love to be tortured," he responded in a husky voice. "I'm just giving you what you expect, baby . . . *unexpectedly.*"

He calmly placed their bag down on a low table.

Zanita wasn't sure how to respond to that sexy salvo. The man was too tempting for her to deny it . . . at least with a straight face. In lieu of a comeback, she opted to unpack a few of her essentials as if she were too busy to be bothered to respond. As she headed off to the bathroom, his low, deep chuckle flirted with her.

"No answer?" he murmured provocatively.

She hunched her shoulders and kept going. She would counterattack when the timing was more favorable.

A knock sounded at the door. Mr. Crypt's assis-

320

tant, a tall, gaunt fellow, brought in a welcome tray laden with a cozy of hot tea and an assortment of biscuits.

Tyber took the tray from him. "Thanks, ah . . ."

"Cadarvah, sir," he sniffed in reply.

"Yeah . . . okay." He hastily tipped the assistant, hoping Zanita hadn't hear *that*. The man quickly pocketed his booty, giving Tyber a toothy grimace.

"Did he say *Cadaver*?" Zanita poked her head out of the bathroom.

Tyber hunched his shoulders. Now she had an answer. He conveniently turned away to pour the tea, knowing what was coming.

Zanita sauntered over and took a cup of fragrant Darjeeling. "How did you find this place, dearest? Was it in the booklet *Best Country Inns for the Undead*?"

He mumbled into his cup, "I heard it was very well known."

"From whom? The Zombie Union?"

He ducked his head and drank his tea.

Zanita gave a furtive little grin into her cup. She adored teasing him. The rogue looked so cute when he was chagrined. The Obadiah Crypt House! She almost laughed out loud. Only Tyber.

The Den of Iniquity was located in the middle of a dark cobblestone alley. A nondescript black wooden door flanked by a solid brick wall on each side gave no clue as to what was inside. The only way they knew they had the right place was that a small painted wooden sign of a pirate and a thief wrestling over a treasure chest hung above the lintel. Mr. Crypt had tipped them off to that.

"You're sure about the vampire thing?" Zanita asked Tyber warily.

"Relatively speaking." He gave her his physicist shrug.

"I was afraid you'd say that." She hesitated before going in. "Are you absolutely relative about that?"

"Positively."

"I see."

The interior was dark and smoky from numerous candles. Two massive fireplaces bookended the great room. Zanita could understand why the locals loved to congregate here. There was a definite old-world sea shanty atmosphere to the place. It was dank and mysterious and thoroughly captivating.

In one corner, a woman dressed in period clothes from Revolutionary days was singing an old maritime ballad. It wasn't until Zanita focused in on the lyrics that she realized exactly what the catchy tune was implying. The bawdy song was relating a crude tale of the goings on "in the riggin'."

And it rhymed, too.

"Oh my god." She blushed.

Tyber grinned.

They sidled up to the bar and soon learned that the fare, besides clam chowder, was a retro combination of burgers, syllabub, and mead.

"I notice that the chowder is New England style," she said pointedly to Tyber.

"And what else would it be?" The barkeep, a hearty woman in her fifties, had overheard her comment. "This is Nantucket, dearie." Smiling, she leaned over the bar to confide, "And if I were you, I wouldn't breathe a word about any other kind in here. To a New Englander, there is only one kind of chowder!"

"I agree," Tyber concurred wholeheartedly with a much too earnest expression. "What kind of kooky deviant would prefer, say, *red* chowder?"

Zanita stepped on his toe.

Chapter Thirteen

"I'll gladly pay you on Tuesday for a hamburger today!" Zanita said, imitating Whimpy.

The barkeeper gave her the Mysterious Face of Mars look. Obviously not a Popeye fan. "Sorry, we just take cash here." She pointed to the sign above the bar that said CASH ONLY.

Tyber rolled his eyes at Zanita. "That's fine. I'll have the chowder and some ale." The woman smiled brightly at the chowder order. He pulled out a twenty and paid her.

"Do you know where we might locate the Sasenfras family?"

"Sasenfras? Never heard of them, and that's not a name you're likely to be forgetting." She wiped the rim of a glass. "But I've only been on the island for about ten years. You might want to ask around the tavern. Someone is bound to know them. The local community is not so large and fairly close-knit."

They thanked her and went in search of a table. There weren't any available, so they ate their meal standing up by the bar. It wasn't long before they were joking with the regulars in the pub, especially those who were pressed up next to them, alternately swilling ale and chowder. Zanita grimaced at the combination.

"Bleck!" She shuddered. "How can they . . . *what are you doing?* Don't tell me you like that?"

"It's great! Try it, then swig some ale." He held up his bowl of chowder to her.

"No, thank you. I'll stick to my hamburger."

"You got to be more adventuresome, baby." He gave her a twinkling look from beneath his long lashes.

"That's not what you said the other night."

"True," he purred.

Unfortunately, no one knew any Sasenfrases on the island. "You know"—a man standing next to Tyber gestured with his ale—"you might want to talk to Junior Zaccheus Plante."

"Junior Zaccheus?"

"Yeah, Junior knows everyone who's ever been on this island, and all the locals know him."

"Sounds like the Bubba of Nantucket," Tyber

murmured to Zanita. "Where do we find him?" he asked the man.

"Why, he's sitting at that table in the far corner." He pointed out an ancient, grizzled seaman who looked as if he had stepped out of a Hemingway story.

"That's 'Junior,' hmmm?" The man was at least eighty if he was a day. Tyber briefly wondered how old "senior" was on this island.

"Yeah, that's him. If anyone knows, he will."

Tyber thanked the man, and taking Zanita's elbow, steered her through the thick crowd to the back corner table.

"Junior Zaccheus?" The old man squinted up at them. "I'm Tyberius Evans and this is my wife, Zanita."

"Humans and dolphins are the only two species that have sex for pleasure!" Junior barked, stone-faced.

Tyber, who had had plenty of experience with eccentric types, didn't even flicker an eyelash. "Ah, yes. I was wondering if we might have a word with you?"

"Have two words, if that's your pleasure, sonny. Talk is cheap." He cackled at his own amazing wit—inspired no doubt by the four empty tankards on the table. He invited them to sit down.

Zanita smiled prettily at the old tar. He was a

real character, and she had an affinity for characters. In fact, most of the ones she had met were members of her new family. She glanced sideways at her husband. And not just by marriage.

"Have a drink, boy." The old man turned and winked saucily at Zanita.

"Thanks, I just had one." Tyber showed him his empty mug.

"I ain't asking."

"Then . . . I'm drinking." He threw Zanita a look that said plenty and motioned to the waitress to bring them two tankards.

Junior pierced Tyber with a stern look. "Can you tie a square knot?"

"Yes."

"Hrrrrr." He scratched his scraggly beard. No one inquired as to what that sound meant.

"We were told you know just about everyone that's lived on this island." Tyber sipped methodically at his Guinness stout.

"Maybe I do," the old man answered shrewdly. He downed his tankard in four swallows and waited for Tyber to follow suit.

Tyber swiftly drank his ale and placed the empty on the table.

Junior signaled for another round.

The waitress, who seemed to be forever walking by with a full tray of tankards, slapped a pair on the table. Zanita wrinkled her nose at the potent brew and slid a tankard over to her husband. "Have you lived here all your life, Mr. Plante?"

"Yeah, lived here all my life—except for Double-u Double-u Two. I know most folks hereabouts. Who you looking for, little lady?"

Zanita was not partial to being called "little lady," but in view of this swabbie's curmudgeon status, she decided to let it go. "His name is Sasenfras."

He took a gulp of ale and wiped off his mouth with the back of his hand. "Which one?"

Tyber and Zanita glanced at each other.

"There's more than one" Tyber inquired dryly.

"Hell, yes. At least there was. Now, you probably are looking for Sasenfras, the Crier."

"Sasenfras, the Crier," Tyber echoed blandly. He took a deep, even breath. Sometimes life was a parabolic curve. At those times, he felt it was best to simply ride the swoop.

"Ya, he went on over to the Vineyard, last I heard."

"That's the one!" Zanita exclaimed excitedly.

"What can you tell us about him?"

"He was a strange duck. Proclaimed himself town crier one afternoon and after, that went up to the clock tower three times a day at seven a.m. noon, and nine p.m. That's when the clock strikes fifty-two times."

"Fifty-two times?" Zanita was fascinated by this local lore.

"Ya. Fifty-two times. Been a custom for a hundred and fifty years, though no one can say why."

"Wow."

"The Crier would climb the tower like a freakin' monkey." Junior Zaccheus chuckled at the memory. "Always was healthy as a horse. Looking for ships coming in and the harbor seals. I think he had too much of that whacky tobacky, if you know what I mean."

"Why did he look for seals?"

"Oh, that was due to his great love, Winnie. She claimed they spoke to her, told her tales of the sea. She was one of them hippie beatniks; quite a bit younger than him, but the crier was smitten with her."

Zanita was surprised at this new picture she was getting of a younger Sasenfras—the Crier, carefree, wild, in love. And slightly demented, by the sound of it.

"One time the Crier went to a town meeting and announced loudly that one day he would take the ferry off-island and go to France. Just like that! Everyone got a good laugh out of that one."

"Why France?" Tyber finished his ale and reluctantly started on the next one, which impressed Junior into ordering yet another round. Information never came cheap; Tyber sighed.

"He was always talking about going to some fancy French cooking school; the Crier loved to cook. Was good at it, too. Remember he made the best fish stew . . ."

"So he married Winnie instead and lost his chance?" Zanita gave her husband a concerned look as he swallowed some more brew. Why some men insisted on these macho competitions, she'd never know. It was clear Junior was measuring Tyber's worthiness for information by the amount of stout he guzzled.

"No, wasn't that way, Missus." She had graduated from "little lady" to "Mrs." Tyber must be doing pretty good, Zanita thought. "Winnie wanted him to go to France and was looking to go with him on some grand adventure. She always wanted to go to Europe and travel like an adventurer. That's what she said. Like an adventurer from Michener's book."

First Melville, then Hemingway, now Michener. Quite a writer's reunion we have going here, Zanita marveled. "What happened then?"

"Well, as I recall, he went to the Vineyard with her to make some seed money. Something about his brother helping him out. Don't know what happened after that."

Tyber set his tankard down with a clink. *"His brother?"*

"Yeah. Lived on the Vineyard in some fancy house, although the truth is, he was originally a bog worker who got airs when his wife inherited the place over there. Never liked him much. He was a hungry type, too, if you know what I mean."

"Yes . . . I think I do." Tyber had that look he always got when his mind was working out details. Zanita loved that look. His light blue eyes took on a mystical, searching expression; his well-shaped masculine lips came together and smoothed out, and one of his eyebrows lifted slightly above the level of the other as he captured and discarded ideas. She watched him, almost spellbound, for a full minute. He was an extraordinarily handsome man, but it was his mind that always fascinated her.

Still, Zanita was surprised at this new twist. "Can you tell us anything else about the brother?"

"Let's see . . . the Crier was real superstitious, I remember that. Heard the brother changed his name when his wife came into her inheritance."

"Do you recall to what?"

Junior scratched his beard again. "Twinkle or Glitter . . . something like that."

"*Sparkling*," Tyber and Zanita said together.

"That's it."

"What was his name before?"

Zanita was surprised by his answer. "Why, Sasenfras! Strange, too, for two brothers so alike. Sasenfras just went by plain Sasenfras, and Merville always hated the name and so was only called Merville to his face, even though he was really a Sasenfras."

"Merville," they both said together. Junior gave them an odd look, probably wondering why they were parroting him in unison.

"He never wanted anything to do with his own family, feeling they was beneath him. Was kind of surprised he offered the brother a job."

Yeah, as long as no one knew he was his brother. And he could steal the man's wife. Tyber slowly sipped his brew as almost everything fell into place.

There was only one thing that eluded him. He snagged a passing waitress and asked if he could borrow one of her pencils.

With it, he began writing on a napkin, letters and numbers tumbling across the length of paper.

"You got something?" Zanita whispered to him.

He stopped figuring and gave her a big grin. "Oh, yes. I got something."

He had broken the code and with it the final piece of the mystery

"I called Todd from the tavern and asked him to prepare a special formal dinner tomorrow night." Tyber flopped backwards and lay spread-eagled across the bed. Fully clothed, boots and all.

Zanita shook her head. Her husband had imbibed five stouts with Junior. For an investigator, information always had its dastardly price. She unlaced his boots. "Really, Tyber? Why?"

"It seems the right way to do it." He linked his hands behind his head and grinned.

"Do what?" She tugged first one boot off, then the other.

"Reveal all, of course. I think it's traditional in these cases." As she slipped his socks off, he sighed happily, wiggling his toes.

"Traditional, huh?" She tickled those toes.

"Yeppers. As investigators, we have a custom to uphold. Gather all the suspects together; get everyone nervous as hell until we point the finger at the guilty party. It'll be expected of us." He lifted his head an inch and squinted at the foot of the bed. "Are you tickling my toes?"

"No."

"Okay." His head flopped back down.

"By whom is it expected?" She bent over him, unbuttoned his jeans and unzipped them. This was a very wifely thing to do, she realized. At his feet, she grabbed the denim material at his ankles and began yanking his pants off.

Tyber obligingly lifted his hips to help her. Apparently, physicists were very sweet when sloshed.

"By everyone. It's called the climax." He wagged his eyebrows up and down suggestively.

"Ohhh, I see."

"Mmmm-hmmmm. So get your best bib and tucker ready. It's going to be a bumpy night."

"At the dinner?" She started undoing his shirt.

"Nope. Under the canopy." He suddenly wrapped her in his arms and quickly rolled over, pinning her beneath him.

"Tyber!" She placed her palms against his chest. "You're drunk!"

"Uh-uh." He winked lazily at her.

"*Ahuh*."

"You didn't think I'd forget about all this lace, did you, baby? Remember, there's always a climax to the story . . ."

She snorted. "You're being bad again."

"Can't help it; I'm a physicist."

"You mean a pirate! What am I going to do with you?" She blew out an exasperated breath as she released his hair from the band holding it back. The silky strands slid forward to tease her face. As always, it had the scent of moonlit nights; a unique Tyber scent.

He whispered in her ear exactly what *she* was going to do with him.

"You think so, huh?"

A dimple formed in his cheek. "Know so."

"And why is that?" She stretched against him and ran her fingers through his long hair.

He purred softly, liking the feel of it. "Because I'm going to give you reason to. . . ."

"What could you possibly do to entice me to do *that*?"

"I'm going to make you wild," he promised in a husky whisper. "All night long. Until you can't take it anymore . . ." His velvety lips skimmed hers in a bare, scalding prelude. "And you can have me . . . *any* way you want."

She drew in a quick, shaky breath. Yep, that would do it. The thought of this man making her wild was already making her wild. She grabbed his shirt collar in her hands and pulled it open, sending the buttons flying. "Go to it, Doc. Surprise me."

He growled, "Oh, I will."

Like every promise he had ever made her, his word was as good as gold. . . .

He took her shirt between his hands and ripped it open, as she had done to him. The buttons flew across the bed and onto the floor. Zanita didn't want to even think what Mr. Crypt was going to think about that when he came to clean the room. At least they weren't getting maple syrup all over the sheets as they did at the Marble Manor. Although from Tyber's piratical expression, anything was possible.

His index finger slipped between her breasts

and lifted the center of her bra. "Front or back?" he rasped.

In her dazed state, at first Zanita wasn't sure what he was asking; then she realized he wanted to know where the bra hooked. "Front," she croaked.

He raised an eyebrow and gently unclasped it. "Too bad," he murmured. "I would have liked to turn you over to do it."

She flushed slightly. "When has that ever stopped you?"

He chuckled low. "True. It might not even stop me now."

His long, nimble fingers went to her jeans and unzipped them. His large palms slid inside her pants and underwear, cupping her derriere. His fingers splayed against the round globes and squeezed the pliant flesh, bringing her up against his naked hardness.

"Tyber, you feel so good."

"Not as good as you do, baby."

He pushed the jeans down to just below her hips and left them there. She started to try to scoot out of them but he stopped her. "Uh-uh. I want them right there."

"Oh." She bit her lip, trying to think up the endless ways a talented man could torture a woman when she was bound up in her jeans. "Should I be worried?" She put her arms around his strong neck.

"Yes," he answered decisively.

"Oh." Her lips parted slightly.

He slipped inside the low opening of her pants where they gapped between her thighs and brushed his member back and forth against the tender inner skin.

She sucked in her breath.

"You weren't kidding, were you?"

He just smiled slightly, those infernal dimples of his popping into his face.

She instantly moistened for him. The dew covered him as he rubbed her making him slick and even harder. She moved her hips in and out on him, trying to get him to lose a little of his control.

A gust of air escaped his lips, but other than that he maintained his own direction.

"It's not going to be that easy tonight." He bit the tender spot under her ear and traced his mouth over her throat, sipping and suckling as he went, taking tiny pieces of her skin between his white teeth to deliver a series of sharp, erotic stings.

Her breath came out in a shaky stream.

Silken lips swept over her collarbone. He suckled at the skin between her breasts, causing her to rear up. "I'll never get enough of you." His words were wet and humid against the dampened skin.

He was going to erotically slay her tonight;

337

she knew it. She didn't even try to stop the sound of pleasure coming from deep within.

A hot, wet mouth covered the tip of her breast. The flat of his tongue swiped the hardened peak over and over. He drew on her sharply, strongly while the hands that were still cupping her bottom, half inside the jeans, lifted her tight to him.

"Oh-my-god." Zanita became breathless.

He kept toying with her, his mouth going from one breast to the other and stopping occasionally in between to press in the valley and draw on her. Bringing her to rapid simmer.

The peaks of her breasts were so extended that they were almost painful. Almost. It was an excruciating pleasure.

Her small hands pressed in on his shoulders, bringing her wild lover closer to her embrace. She wanted this man. Now. Forever.

There would never be another love for her like Tyberius Augustus Evans.

Deep down, she had known that from the day she met him. He had told her he had known it from the instant he set eyes on her. He called it an absolute force.

He was right—love was an absolute force. In a six-foot-plus package.

With eyes that made you feel the beauty in every second of life. Eyes you could watch for endless lifetimes.

"I love you so much, Tyber," she cried.

"Oh, baby." He fastened his mouth on hers to give her a soul-robbing kiss. "You know you aren't going anywhere without me, because I'm going to be right beside you forever. Tell me the challenge is off. Right now."

Her mouth parted. *Challenge?* Who had been thinking of the challenge? Tyber, that's who! Once a pirate, always a pirate! "You artful little maneuverer!" she snorted and tried to push him off.

It didn't work.

"Maneuverer? I don't think that's the right word, baby." He tsk-tsked as he grinned down at her, very much in the superior position. "And you being a journalist."

"I don't care if it's in Skunk and Blight! That is exactly what you are!"

"What did I do now?" he drawled languidly.

"You tried to use my infatuation with you to win your challenge!" Her chin nodded up.

"No, I didn't. I meant what I said, and you know it." Her eyes narrowed. "Well . . . perhaps there was a little strategy used—"

She guffawed.

"But you expected that from me. Tell the truth, Curls."

"That's it! Get out from between my legs!"

He could not help the huge grin that crossed his face. "Excuse me?"

"You heard me. Off!" She bucked her hips.

"No. And you know as well as I that this challenge is a phony, so quit the false outrage."

She stopped and stared at him. "A phony?" she squeaked in a tiny voice.

"Yep."

"Wh-what do you mean?"

"I mean you trumped up this ridiculous so-called challenge so that I would go merrily on your ghost investigation."

"Oh! How silly!" She wet her lips. "What could possibly make you think that?"

He slowly shook his head. "Zanita. Zanita. Zanita. Did you really think I'd believe for one minute that you didn't want to marry me because of some outlandish fear of us becoming Mr. and Mrs. John Q. Public?"

"Yes, that's what I thought."

He gazed down at her shrewdly. "What if I tell you we aren't really married?"

"What? What do you mean, we aren't married?"

He smiled like a shark. "You seem awfully upset for someone who was dragged into it kicking and screaming."

"Oh, shut up!" Her head flopped back on the pillow.

He laughed.

"Why do you have to be this smart anyway? It's not healthy for one person to have all those brains."

"You love them brains." He blinked. "What the hell am I saying?"

"It's a draw, then."

"No way."

"It is! You still haven't convinced me of the unexpected—*eeee*!"

One large hand pinned her wrists to the mattress over her head. "I haven't? I can remedy that right now."

"What are you going to do?" She watched him warily.

His other arm reached up to the lace canopy and dragged it right off the bed.

"Tyber!"

"I told you I liked this lace." He spread the lacy coverlet next to them and slowly dragged it over her, letting the intricate material scrape across her breasts.

"Oh, dear."

"Mmm-hmm."

His lips fastened on her right through the lace. The combination of his scalding tongue and the soft roughness of the material almost sent her over the top.

"I'm going to pay you back for this," she gasped, squirming on the bed.

"Good." He spoke around her nipple.

She tried to reach down on him, but he wouldn't release her hands.

"Later." He bit her through the cloth.

She screamed. Then belatedly croaked, "I hope Mr. Crypt's mausoleum is on the other side of the inn."

He grinned against her. "They heard you on the Vineyard with that one, baby."

"This is so undignified!" she burst out.

He roared with laughter. "Undignified? Hell, I'll show you undignified . . ."

He brushed the lace over her nether curls, his fingers twining in the material to work against the dewy folds.

Zanita squirmed. "I don't think you should do that."

"Why not?"

"Because I am going to scream louder if you continue—that material is very . . . provocative."

"I know," he whispered roguishly.

"You can't just use the canopy like this! It's not—"

"Don't worry. I'll purchase the canopy from Crypt. I have plans for it at our house."

She tried to wiggle away but couldn't. "Don't you dare bring that *thing* home!"

"Mmmmm-hmmm." He slid her jeans off and covered her whole body, including her face, with the lacy fabric. Tiny ecru roses dotted the netting, bathing her in a sea of flowers. "God, you look beautiful."

He kissed her through the cloth, leaning his entire naked weight on her.

He tasted so sweet. She trembled. "Let me loose so I can feel you," she groaned.

"You can feel me." His hips dipped into hers, pulling the material taut. She moaned.

She could feel the long, hard length of him draped in lace scraping against her thighs and lower belly.

"God, Tyber, please . . ."

"I am going to please you . . ." His voice was raw with his passion. "More and more . . ."

The fingers of his left hand strummed over her body, feeling every nuance of her through the lace. Every spot he touched hummed, alive with pleasure.

"Let me touch you!"

"No."

His teeth caught the fabric and tugged it over her curls. Soon his tongue replaced his fingers as he loved her with his mouth—lace and all. *Ground zero*. "Nuclear fusion reaction," she managed to mumble between gasping sighs.

"Uh-uh. This is pure fission, baby." He lapped her with his tongue. "Much higher intensity." Then he suckled on her lace-draped nether lips, causing scream number two to rattle the house.

Without giving her time to recuperate, he lifted just the material between her legs and entered her with a powerful thrust. Sinking deep.

Zanita sobbed his name as he quivered inside her, remaining motionless for a few moments.

He whispered, a hint of hot breath in her ear. He told her how she felt; how he felt; how he wanted to stay that way with her eternally, joined as one.

Then he began to move in her. Slow, even strokes that cascaded on and on. Still he held her hands above her head, enveloped in the folds of lace—as he was enveloped in her. He flexed inside her, rotating his hips, driving her wild yet again.

"Oh god, Tyber, release me!" she sobbed, totally undone by every sensation he was giving her.

"Not yet . . ." His mouth covered her lips again, robbing the moans from her.

His free hand squeezed her buttocks, then moved her hips in line with his. The rocking action penetrated his body, causing him to groan soul-deep in his throat. It was a sound he sometimes made in the throws of lovemaking and it always drove Zanita wild. It was the sound of the captor held captive.

Her cry of near-release resonated against his lips, into his mouth.

That was when he released her.

Her hands immediately went to his back, scratching down the length of it. She grabbed his buttocks and pressed him into her. Tyber growled, nipping at her lower lip. He grabbed the cloth and tugged it down off her head. His mouth seized hers and he thrust his tongue all the way into her mouth. The feel of that final contact of skin on skin undid both of them.

Scream/groan number three drowned out the honks of the Canada geese that happened to be flying overhead at that precise moment. It was a sure bet that they never had cause to make a sound that good.

Now, they really had something to bitch about.

Chapter Fourteen

"Come out from under that blanket, you miscreant."

"Me?" was the half-dead response. A slick, hot tongue teased the arch of her foot.

"Yes, *you*."

The blankets rustled. Tyber poked his head out from under the covers, his chestnut hair very tousled. "I think I have a headache."

"Perhaps it was the five stouts?"

"You think? I rather thought it was the tequila chasers."

"Tequila chasers? When did you have those?" She tried to sit up in the bed; he yanked her back down.

"No sudden movements, baby. When you went to the restroom, Junior put up the bet: How many could we down before you got back? He thought four, but, knowing you as well as I do, I said six. I won . . . or lost, whichever way you want to look at it."

"So that was what all that cheering was about?"

"Nnnn. . . ." His head dropped back onto the mattress.

"I can't believe you had six tequilas! You never even drink, except for wine and cognac." Her hand slapped down on the bed, bouncing the mattress.

Tyber winced. "It was worth it. Junior loosened up after the fourth one. Told me lots of interesting things." He rubbed his cheek against her leg in a silent plea for sympathy. And whatever else he could get.

She frowned down at him. "I'm not sure whether I should be giving you sympathy or not."

"I think you should." He nipped her calf.

She crossed her arms over her chest. Six tequilas! She glanced at him out of the corner of her eye. The man was a veritable *dynamo* on six tequilas. Of course, Tyber was always a . . . love force. Must be his knowledge of physics, she reasoned. "So what did Junior divulge?"

He wagged his finger at her. "Uh-uh. I'm keeping that to myself."

Her mouth fell open "Why?"

"Because you did not go through the initiation of the Brotherhood of the Worm." He tugged the pillow over his head.

She gasped. "You didn't, Tyber!"

"Hmf," came from under the pillow.

Zanita lifted the edge of the pillow; he squinted at her through bleary eyes. "Tell me you didn't."

"I didn't. But Junior did. Was rather surprised *he* didn't start seeing ghosts."

"And you won't tell me what he said?" She tried her pouting, "get Tyber" look.

"Nope." He grinned at her. "But you look awfully cute, Curls." He lifted his head and kissed her fast.

She blinked, then shoved him back down on the bed, ignoring the pain-wracked groan that followed. "You brat! I have a right to know!"

"I love driving you crazy." He smiled wanly as he rubbed his forehead.

She fumed down at him. "Tell me."

"Uh-uh."

Her violet eyes narrowed and a blast of exhalation flared her nostrils. "You're only doing this to torment me!"

"Of course. Why else would I do it?" Tyber snuggled back cozily into the pillows.

"You . . . !"

He opened his arms wide and whispered, *"C'mere."*

* * *

They arrived back at Todd's inn in the afternoon.

Sitting in the parlor, looking very nasty, was Zanita's best friend. "Mills! What are you doing here?"

Mills jerked her thumb in the direction of the kitchen. At that moment Gregor and Cody sauntered out with identical smirks on their identically handsome faces. "He is a golem, I swear! Tyber, please," she beseeched him. "Tell him to stop."

Tyber frowned. "What is he doing?"

"Well . . . nothing I can put my finger on. I think the two of them have something cooked up. Cody keeps showing up at my house and shop."

"You don't want Cody around?"

She hesitated. "I didn't say that exactly."

Zanita snorted. "You're crazy about that kid, admit it, Mills. You love when he bugs you."

Her shoulders slumped. "All right. I admit it. But then *he* shows up to get him."

"Well, he is his father." Tyber smiled. "I don't think you can have one without the other."

Mills turned and stared at the wall in a huff. Obviously, she wasn't buying Tyber's theory.

Zanita patted her hand. "Tyber will think of something. You'll see. He's very"—she noted the bit of lace sticking out of the overnight pack— "inventive."

Dara Joy

Gregor leaned against the wall, arms crossed over his chest.

"Hi, Gregor."

"Hi, Tyber."

"Whatcha doin here, bud?"

"Came to get Cody."

"Uh-huh."

The two of them exchanged a silent laugh.

Zanita rolled her eyes and motioned to Mills to follow her upstairs. "How did Cody get here?" she whispered.

"I don't know." Mills was stone-faced. "I turned around on the ferry and there he was. Of course, it was too late to send him back."

"That's called kidnapping, Mills," a laughing voice teased.

A purse sailed through the air in the direction of Gregor's dark head.

"Ah . . . I don't think she sees it that way, Gregor. And what was she doing on the ferry in the first place?"

He grinned sexily. "I'm creating an itch."

"A little advice. This is not the perfect way to woo a woman. Generally, when a woman indicates that she can't stand the very air you breathe, it's a pretty good indication that she doesn't want to be followed to Martha's Vineyard. Or scratch any itches."

"You think so?" Gregor pushed away from the wall. "Nothing wrong with making a woman feel

350

like she wants to . . . scratch." He winked at Tyber. "I thought I'd put some pepper in her salt."

"Somehow I don't think Mills is the spice type, Greg."

"You never know." He glanced up the stairs. "Cody adores her."

"How do you feel about her?"

He shrugged noncommittally yet continued to glance upstairs.

"Captain! There you are, ye rapscallion, ye!" Blooey came bustling into the room. *Here we go with the next chapter of lunacy*, Tyber surmised as he rubbed his forehead. Blooey was quickly followed by the aunt in three hats. *Ah, what a simple life I lead.*

"I helped Todd with that fancy dinner ye requested tonight. Made some of that squash soup ye love!"

Oh, joy. "Ah, thanks, Blooey."

The little pirate squinted his eye. "Are ye gonna put the slap on the ghost tonight, Captain?"

"Aye, sailor, that I am," he murmured.

"Mar-r-r-rvelous!" Auntie clapped her hands. "I can't wait to see you show them all what's what!"

Tyber viewed her askance.

"I just have to tell you," those locked jaws announced, "I really think it's a ghost from the Revolution! Or perhaps a Republican." She shrugged fatalistically.

"Ahuh." Tyber responded evenly.

Gregor coughed behind him.

"Why, hello, young man." Auntie viewed him cockeyed through her Elton-Marilyn glasses. "Aren't you the friend who has that brother?" She made poor Stan sound like the relative no one speaks of—not the theoretical physicist he was.

"Yes, ma'am."

"Well." She waved her hand, dismissing the topic.

Tyber massaged his temple to clear the static.

"That creep! I am going to kill him!" bellowed a feminine voice from upstairs.

Tyber turned to Gregor, saying blandly, "I think she is going to scratch the itch, pal, but not in the way you intended."

"She must have found that little gift I slipped in her coat pocket."

"Hey, Gregor, when do we eat?" Cody yanked on his dad's jeans. "Hi, Tyber! Where's Hambone? Can I play with him? Blooey says he's a scall-wag. What's that? Is that a type of cat? 'Cause I never heard of no scall-wag cat, have you? Gregor, when do we eat?"

Tyber shook his head in an attempt to retune the station. "You know, I believe Zanita needs me for . . . something." He started backing toward the stairs. Rapidly. "See you all at dinner. Remember, dress to the nines." He turned and mounted the stairs—three at a time.

"What's 'dress to the nines' mean?" Cody screwed up his face.

Gregor shrugged. "Damned if I know."

"Well, I think it means we all spruce up like they did on the *Titanic*!" Auntie beamed with excitement.

"That ship went down," Gregor pointed out.

They all assembled at the stroke of eight in the dining room for what was sure to be the strangest meal any of them had ever had.

Per instructions, everyone had donned the best of what they had brought with them, making an oddly dressed assemblage around the table, to say the least. Mark and Todd had lent out several of their jackets and ties. Blooey had wrapped his best kerchief around his head—to him, formal pirate regalia. Gregor and Cody had ties on over their T-shirts. Even Hambone looked spiffed up for the occasion; his usual motley fur was for once slicked down smooth. He grinned at Zanita, proudly showing her his several missing teeth.

Calendula, of course, looked lovely, as she always did. The other three ladies present had done very well dressing up their casual outfits.

Tyber, at the head, glanced over the table. All in all, he thought, we look like escapees from the nut factory trying to appear okay for the main event.

He had specifically arranged the seating place-

ments. Zanita was to his right, followed by Calendula, Auntie, Hubble, and Sasenfras, who
shocked everyone by appearing in actual black
tie, although the tux was moldy and moth-eaten.
Todd was at the other end of the table. Following the circle around, Cody was next, then Gregor, Mills, and rounding out with Mark on
Tyber's left side.

He had purposely seated the guests in this
fashion for the drama that was about to evolve.

Mills glanced over at Gregor, not at all happy
to be seated next to him. Especially after what he
had slipped into her pocket. She viewed him
askance and wondered not for the first time if
the Mazurskis had Gypsy/Rom blood. It wasn't
just his raven hair and green eyes, either. There
was a rawness to him just barely contained
beneath the thin veil of civility. No one knew
what he actually did, if anything. He always
seemed to be around, either helping Tyber with
his bike or pestering her.

She had no idea why he pestered her.

As far as she could tell, it made no sense. The
few outrageous snippets of information she was
able to glean about him did not bear thinking
about. He was a mystery, and in that regard
alone, her curiosity was slightly piqued.

A snore came from under the table.

Zanita peeked under the tablecloth. It was a
well placed Hippolito, in ecstasy, no doubt, from

being under all the food. He was stretched out in the center of the floor, feet stuck up in the air. The pink tongue was hanging out like kitty fly-paper. She chuckled.

Tyber took his seat, motioning to Todd to serve the first course.

"You know," Zanita whispered to him, "this reminds me of something . . ."

"Does it?" His lips curved slightly into a mysterious smile.

"Yes. I just can't think of what it is."

Tyber winked at her and addressed the group. "I gathered everyone here on this, our last night together, so that we could all see what, if anything, we have uncovered this weekend."

Everyone seemed interested in that statement.

Calendula was the first to offer an assessment of the investigation. "Well, from what Mark and I have seen, I believe this to be a genuine occurrence of paranormal activity."

Tyber placed his palms together, steepling his fingers. "Is that so?"

"Yes. The reading and impressions I received cannot be anything but genuine."

Hubble snorted from his place down the line.

Annoyed, Calendula turned to confront Hubble. "How can you possibly explain away all of the uncanny events we have witnessed?"

Before he could respond, Tyber answered for him. "He can't."

She smiled at him.

"But I can."

The smile died on her face.

"Are you sure you can?" Zanita whispered in an aside.

"I think so, baby. Bear with me." He addressed the group. "Let's take the jet-propelled kitchen gadgets first. If you recall, I remarked that they all seemed to follow the same trajectory."

"But you said you didn't find anything at the top of those stairs," Mark interjected.

"I misstated. I did find something; I just didn't want everyone to know about it."

"Is that fair? I don't think that's fair," Mark groused.

"What did you find, Tyber?" Calendula asked.

"A secret passageway at the top of the library staircase. I knew right away that was where the implements were coming from; they were being hurled from behind that hidden door."

"By whom?" several asked.

"I'll get to that. The next day, Zanita and I went into the passage and discovered our way almost blocked with webs. The natural assumption would be that the passage had not been traveled down for ages, and that whoever threw the gadgets could not have been down the tunnel, either, without breaking those webs. But that was not quite true."

"Why not, Captain?" Blooey leaned forward, already into the fetchingly lurid tale.

"Because the webs were from a spray can. Like the kind kids use at Halloween. They had been placed there on purpose."

"How do you know that?" Todd asked.

"We know that because when I went back to examine them the next day, they were conveniently gone. I believe it was you, Todd, who ordered that passageway cleaned."

Everyone stared at Todd.

Todd looked around nervously. "Yes, but only because you both looked so bedraggled when you came back into the house that day. I was embarrassed it was so dirty. Surely you don't think I did such a thing?"

Tyber didn't answer the question. "When we got through those phony webs, we traveled down an inside circular stairway to another passage. Hambone, our cat"—Tyber nodded at the kitty sitting by the table near Blooey, and Hambone sat up straighter, proud of his role in the story—"alerted us to the fact that he had been trapped in the passage after following someone else in. When we went back to get him, we noticed two things. There was another passage under that staircase, and the word 'Nan' had been newly written in what appeared to be blood on the wall."

"Way coool!" Cody shouted. "Yeah!"

"Mills, you should've taken an earlier ferry out so we wouldn't have missed all that fun and gore." Mills kicked Gregor under the table. "Any ideas who left the bloody trail?"

"There was someone that day who had ready access to blood."

"My gawd, this is getting rather nice and scary!" Auntie downed her bourbon in two swallows.

"Who had access to the blood, Tyber?" Todd asked, although he already seemed to know the answer.

"You. The chicken you prepared that night was free-range, and when I asked you if you had to clean the birds yourself, you confirmed it."

Everyone stared at him again.

He sighed. "Why would I sabotage my own inn?"

"Ah, but it's not *all* your inn, a fact we didn't know until later. But I'll get back to that. We had pretty much discovered that the passageway led to a trapdoor under the house, leading right to our veranda and easy outside access. Now, who would want outside access? I thought. If it's someone in the house, why not just do the mischief from the inside?"

"It was someone outside!" Cody piped up.

"That's right, Cody. Someone outside." He took a sip of Blooey's squash soup, grimaced, and laid down his spoon. "I'll get back to that later." Zanita wasn't sure if he meant the clue or the soup.

Todd got up to serve the second course, although his step was not as chipper. When he sat back down, Tyber went on.

"Then there was that curious Polariod photograph of Zanita which suddenly sprouted a set of eyes."

Cody gasped. "Awwwww-some!"

"I think we should blame Mills for our missing all this, Spike," Gregor stated baldly.

"*What?*" She turned to him, astonished. "I wasn't even here!"

He shrugged. "It's still all your fault. Right, Spike?"

Cody screwed up his eyes and gave her a beady look. "Yeah, Mills. You shoulda run away here sooner."

"Run away? He thinks I was running away?" She ground her toe into Gregor's boot under the table. He grunted.

Tyber ignored the interruption. "That photo was altered by someone with a lot of skill. At first I thought this solution too pat until I remembered something Einstein once said . . ." At the groan from his right, he paused.

". . . but I won't go into that. There is only one person here who has such a skill that I am aware of. It also happens to be the same person who pointed out the picture to us in the first place, drawing our attention to it so we would be sure to see it. And it was the same person who made sure it disappeared later so no one could examine it more closely." He stared at Mark. "You also have a rare 'skill' with Kirlian photography."

Calendula moaned. "Mark! You didn't!" His guilty silence said it all. "Don't you realize what you've done? You've compromised all our work!"

"I'm sorry, Calendula. I was just trying to help Todd. I didn't mean to hurt you."

"Help me?" Todd was confused. "How, Mark?"

"I thought if there was a chance the inn was haunted and we verified it for you, it would help your business. You know how some people love to stay at haunted inns. I'm sorry, Todd. I realized afterwards that I shouldn't have done it."

"That's it!" Hubble shouted down the table. "The experiment has been falsified! It's over!"

"Not quite. For you see, Hubble, Todd wasn't the only one to stir the pot, so to speak."

"What are you talking about, Evans?"

"Yes," Zanita whispered, "what *are* you talking about?" She paused. "This all seems so familiar . . ."

"It was you, Hubble, who slid the picture off the breakfront in the dining room that night Zanita was watching."

"Ridiculous!"

"Are you sure about this, Tyber?" Zanita mouthed to him.

"I'm guessing here; let's hope I'm right, baby," he whispered to her. "Not that ridiculous. You were perfectly placed at the table to do it with just a bit of fishing line. It was you who told me that most people see what they want to see because they *want* to believe. That's why it's so easy for charlatans to get away with so much. I think you counted on that fact. Once the picture fell, you quickly removed the line in the ensuing surprise and deftly pocketed it."

"Why would I do such a thing?" he sputtered. "I'm a skeptical observer! I want to debunk this place, not add to its ghostly legend!"

"Exactly. You have a new book coming out next year—I checked with your publisher. I think you needed one more debunking tale to add to your arsenal of remembered frauds, so you decided to create one yourself. When were you planing on discovering the fishing line. . . ? When you later came back and examined the area? Maybe it's in your pocket right now?"

Hubble reddened. Obviously, Tyber had guessed correctly. Hubble stood, throwing his cloth napkin down. "I will not hear any more! As far as I am concerned, this case is over, proven a hoax due to our friend Mark here. Good night, everyone." He stormed out, and Zanita had the uncomfortable feeling it was not the last they would see of him.

"Should we let him go, Captain?" Blooey was half out of his seat, ready to charge.

"Yes. He's finished. In more ways than one. I intend to report him to the psi-cogs. His investigative techniques will be called into question. Besides, he's going to just hate himself for missing this finale. It would make quite a book."

"Well done, Doc." Zanita smiled and winked up at him.

"Thanks, baby." He winked back.

"You mean there's more to this story? Mar–r–r–velous!" Auntie gulped her refreshed bourbon.

"Oh, yes, Auntie, there is much more. You remember the night that Zanita came running down here with the book? I've already shown her that the book was not sent her way by something supernatural, but rather by means of a peephole strategically placed behind the bookcase. I won't go over all the details now of how the effect was created except to say that there is another secret passage behind our bedroom." He faced Zanita. "And now I know exactly who it was, baby."

"Who, Tyber?"

"The same person who led us through all the passageways in the first place and the same person who wrote in blood."

"I didn't do it," Todd insisted.

"I never said you did." Tyber stared down the table at Sasenfras. "The night we went to visit you, you remarked as we were leaving that you had seen us"—Zanita pinched his arm, warning him to be careful—"ah . . . seen us. I was sure that view from the balcony was blocked by the tall end of the decorative hammock before it was moved. For those of you who haven't seen the hammock by our room, it's quite a fanciful design. The frame is custom carved and quite high, but I checked it again just to be sure. I was right; it definitely blocks that view. So the only way we could have been seen was from *inside* the room, or more precisely—the peephole." He turned to the caretaker. "As the old song goes, 'It had to be you.'"

"*Ewwww!*" Zanita cringed. Sasenfras had been watching them? *Yeck!*

"I don't think he could see too much from that angle, baby," Tyber murmured for her alone.

"But still . . ." She shivered.

Sasenfras grinned but not out of humor. "So you figured that out, boy, did you? Now, why would I want to lead you to the passages? Have you figured that out, too?"

"I think so. You have an accomplice, you see. And a very unlikely one, at that."

Everyone looked at everyone else at the table.

Tyber paused just the right amount of time to

build the suspense. His light blue eyes hunted out Calendula. "Mrs. Winifred Sasenfras, I presume?"

Several gasps rang out around the table.

"This one came as quite a surprise to me, and I have my lovely wife to thank for inadvertently helping me figure it out."

"I did?" Zanita cleared her throat and preened. "I mean, of course I did."

"Zanita mentioned in passing that Winnie was said to have a certain 'je ne sais quoi.' An old fisherman we met on Nantucket, Junior Zaccheus, told us she talked to seals. Now who does this describe? Our Ms. Brite is psychic in certain areas. At one time, she helped the police catch several criminals, but I suspect that work proved to be very disturbing to her ethereal nature. She decided to focus her talent in the investigative arena instead."

"I know this reminds me of something." Zanita blew a gust of air between her lips.

Calendula was quiet for a moment, then looked up. "Very good, Dr. Evans. How did you figure it out?"

"It was a combination of things. Zanita's ghostly visitation required two people to pull it off—one to flash the penlight and one to push the book off the shelf. The Keroac book was the dead giveaway, though. It belonged to you back then. The other perpetrator noticed it and placed it in the empty slot when he moved the books in our room. A sort of secret joke . . . and a secret clue."

"Why leave a clue?"

"Now, that is an interesting question, and it bothered me. Until I put the final piece together."

"Accomplice . . . why did he need an accomplice, Captain?" Even though Blooey thought himself on a pirate ship, the Arthur Bloomberg inside was still a very sharp man.

"Good point, Blooey. To answer that, I'll have to reveal what Zanita and I found in that sealed wing and why Sasenfras needed us to find it for him."

"What did you find, Tyber?" Gregor got into the tale.

"We found Merville. Dead as a doornail, if you'll forgive the cliché."

"*Grandfather?*" Todd was shocked. "But he was lost at sea!"

"No, it was only made to appear that way. They recovered his boat and he was reported missing, but his actual body was never found. That's because it's in this house."

"There's a body in this house? With us?" Mills paled.

"I'll protect you." Gregor tried to put his arm around her; she slapped it off.

"Go, Gregor!" Cody chirped.

"It appeared to be suicide at first. But what really bothered me was, why would Sasenfras want us and not Calendula to discover that body? What was he really after? And why did he then point us to Nantucket?"

"Yeah, what's the deal with that?" Gregor was now totally into the story. He and his son bent forward over the table, both of them black-haired and green-eyed and adorable.

"When we found the body, next to him was a paper with writing on it—in code. It wasn't until I was able to break the code that it all came together."

He reached into his pocket and pulled out the faded piece of paper, spreading it out on the table. "As you can see, the numbers threw me a bit because I needed to figure out where any commas came in. For instance, in this first line 52329625 could have been 52,329,62,5, but in the end it turned out to be more simple than that, which is usually the case."

"Eggheads," Zanita mumbled playfully.

Tyber chuckled and wiggled his foot against hers under the table. "The person who wrote this subtracted 3 from the 26 letters of the alphabet, then counted backwards starting at 23 for A toward 1 for W, starting at 26 again at X, ending with 24 for Z."

"That sounds so simple to figure out . . . not!" Zanita poked at him.

"So when you put it all together, you find out exactly what this is all about, and guess what? It's not dead bodies, ghosts, flying kitchen gadgets, secret passageways, changing photos, ex-hippies, or separately owned wings."

"What is it about, Tyber?" Cody put his chin in his hand, fascinated.

"What it's usually about, Cody. Greed."

Everyone looked nervously around the table, wondering who was going to get nailed next.

"The secret code reads: Savory Buns by Sasenfras. He is the real owner of the recipe, Todd. Not you. Sasenfras was very proud of that recipe. He loved Winnie and the savory buns he had created. Merville took them both. Merville stole the original recipe, recognizing its potential. Even then, buyers were interested in it. But Sasenfras had encrypted his prize recipe in code. When Merville realized this, he turned to Winnie."

"Winnie?"

"Yep. Winifred Sasenfras was able to recreate most of the recipe for Merville. She'd seen her husband make the buns hundreds of times. They were good, and yet there was a certain *je ne sais quois* missing. They were not *exactly* the same."

Todd was astonished. "You were after my buns all along!"

"*My* buns, sonny. And don't you forget it. Enough was stolen from me by you Sparklings."

He glanced at Calendula. "And this is the last of it!"

Todd felt uncomfortable. "But why did you torment me with the kitchen gadgets and implements? If I knew—"

"No! The proof of Merville's betrayal is that original recipe right there, and that's what I wanted! You're a wuss-butt, Todd, although I don't dislike you. I knew you'd call in some help if you got scared enough. And there was no way I was going into that place to look for it. Tried once and was scared silly by something I'd rather not talk about."

"All of this nonsense for a recipe for dinner rolls? Really!" Auntie's glasses slid down her nose.

"Not just any rolls, Auntie," Zanita said. "I remember when we first got here, someone said that a national concern was interested in buying the recipe. That could mean millions, right, Tyber?"

"Right, baby."

"I don't get it," Mark said quietly. "If Calendula was his partner, why get you involved?"

"Ah, well, because he didn't really trust her. You see, legally, Winnie is still married to Sasenfras, and therefore entitled to half the proceeds. She prompted Mark to invite her back here when she heard about what was going on and the fact that the recipe was for sale. It wasn't too hard to sweet-talk Sasenfras, who still has a soft spot for her—why else keep all that god-awful furniture around if not as a shrine? They made a deal; maybe not half the money, but some. Right, Calendula?"

"It's not what you think," she said quietly.

"I think it is," he said. "And I am sorry for this, Winnie, but the truth has to come out."

She nodded, looking down.

"You see, what the killer didn't know was that our victim was not dead yet from the poison when he left him. He managed to write a word in the dust of the table top."

"What did he write, Captain?"

"Dam."

Cody howled with laughter. Gregor belatedly covered his son's ears, grinning too. "Hell, I'd write that, too, if I'd been poisoned."

"I'll keep that in mind," Mills informed him.

He threw her a look.

"At least we thought that was what he trying to write. We even speculated that with his last breath he was cursing his murderer. It fit in perfectly with ghost lore in which the victim curses his killer, then comes back to haunt him. But that wasn't the case."

"How'd ya figure that one, Captain?" Blooey scratched his head.

Tyber continued, "When I decoded the note, I realized it contained the entire recipe. In that

369

recipe was a secret ingredient that only Sasenfras knew about—that was his legacy. You see,
the rolls are excellent without this ingredient,
but when added, it elevates the formula to
supreme culinary status, where Savory Buns
could take their place next to Hollandaise sauce,
Parker House rolls, and Toll House cookies."

"Now it makes sense!" Zanita was the first to
get it.

"Exactly. He was trying to write 'Damson' as a
clue, but he never got that far."

"What's Damson?" Mills asked.

"Damson is a type of small, purple plum. You
see, the only one who could possibly know that
item was in the coded recipe was Sasenfras." To
prove his point, Tyber asked Todd, "Do you use
finely chopped Damson plums in your savory
buns?"

Todd shook his head. "No. No, I don't . . . but
what a fabulous texture to add! It would give
them a whole different dimension."

"Where did you get the recipe for the buns,
Todd?"

"Why, it's been in my family since . . ." he
paused as he realized exactly how long it had
been in his family. "Since Grandfather's time. It
was handed down to me."

Tyber let that fact sink into everyone's
mind.

"So . . ." Zanita realized what it all meant before the rest of the guests.

"So . . . ladies and gentlemen, may I introduce you to Merville Sparkling—identical *twin* brother of the late, lamented Sasenfras."

"My god." Todd stared at his grandsire for the first time in utter horror.

"How did you find out they were twins?" Zanita marveled at her husband's acuity.

"Junior Zaccheus told me while you were in the ladies room—after the *sixth* tequila," he explained of the side of his mouth so only she could hear.

"You can't prove none of this, Evans. Merville committed suicide over guilt at what he had done to me!"

"Oh, I think I can. There were other disturbing signs. The medication for a heart condition, the painting of the cat turned to the wall . . . You see, the bottle of pills in the room was a giveaway, as well as the turned painting. The medication was made out to Merville; yet you have a heart condition which requires the same meds. Junior Zaccheus mentioned that Sasenfras was always healthy as a horse. True, he could have developed a heart condition, but taken with everything else . . ."

"Lies!"

"You tricked him into wearing your smoking

371

jacket and clothes, somehow getting him to drink the tea. I think you taunted Sasenfras at the end by placing the coded recipe on the table next to him, unlocking the box he kept it in. It wasn't long before the poison took effect."

"Ridiculous! I'm Sasenfras!"

"Merville liked cats, and so do you; you even made a comment about being glad they were in the room when we had the Ouija board out. Sasenfras must have disliked them. When he realized what you had done, as a last request, I believe he asked you to turn the painting of Megalito around so that it wouldn't be the last thing he had to look at—a cat. Personally, I think he wronged poor Megalito, but there's no accounting for taste. For some reason—perhaps a last shred of brotherly feeling—you complied."

"What motive would I have to kill my own brother?" Sasenfras scoffed. "You'd make a good fiction writer, Evans."

"You were driven by an irresistible compulsion to have everything that belonged to Sasenfras. Your ego never could bear the thought of being a twin. In the end, you had to have his life along with everything else."

"I did no such thing!"

"Yes, you did; and I knew it was you, *Merville*," Calendula said quietly. "Right from the moment I saw you again."

"Why didn't you just point him out to the authorities, my dear?" Auntie asked.

Calendula remained silent, head down.

"Should I answer, Calendula?" Tyber asked quietly.

She nodded.

"She was protecting someone."

"Who?" Zanita wondered.

"*Mark.*"

"Mark?"

"Me? Why?"

"Because you're her son, Mark. That's why she contacted you to work with her right from the beginning. She wanted to be near you."

Mark was staggered. "Is this true?"

Calendula nodded silently.

"You never told me . . . all this time . . . *how could you do that?*"

"I . . . I just felt it was better for you this way. . . . I wanted to tell you. So many times."

Mark seemed speechless until he and Todd suddenly looked at each other, horrified. "*We're related?*" They both wailed the question at the same time.

Calendula shook her head no.

They collapsed in relief.

"At the time, Merville and I . . . well, I was already pregnant. He assumed it was Sasenfras's, but it wasn't. In those days, I'm afraid I took the term 'free love' rather literally. I knew right away what Merville had done to Sasenfras. I ran away, but I was afraid for both of us. I thought he would kill you as well, Mark. He could never stand Sasenfras having anything. It was a sickness I didn't recognize until too late.

After you were born, I left you with the Kevins family who lived next door. I thought you would be safer if we were separated. I wasn't exactly thinking clearly at the time, I was young and scared and penniless. I knew Mary Kevins—she was a dear friend of mine and I trusted her and her husband to watch over you. I had read somewhere that people have a tendency to overlook what's right in front of them. It worked. Merville hounded me, but he never knew my son lived right next door. I—I checked on you all the time, Mark . . . when I could."

Everyone was silent at such a staggering confession. Except for Merville/Sasenfras.

"You're all nuts! I'm Sasenfras, I tell you! Merville killed himself!"

Tyber nodded to the police officers who were waiting behind the door in the kitchen. They came in and escorted a wildly protesting Merville away.

"He might get off on insanity," Tyber murmured. "He really does think he's Sasenfras part of the time. It would explain some of his actions, including why he left those clues. Initially, he willed himself the wing to protect himself. His other persona was even trying to get himself to sell the property to . . . himself. *He* was the other buyer, baby."

Zanita nodded sadly. "Imagine assuming your dead brother's identity for thirty-odd years—it would drive anyone nuts. Maybe he had a dual motive in bringing us to that wing; maybe a part of him *wanted* to be discovered."

"Guilt will do that to you. By the sound of it, he was always unstable. Probably psychotic. He believed he could get away with it and still one day reclaim all that was his, including his other 'half' in Sasenfras. In one sense, this was a genuine ghost investigation; Merville haunted himself."

"Does he actually own the inn now? Since it originally belonged to him and he's still alive?"

"That's a moot point. Todd is the direct heir. I'm sure the courts will declare Merville incompetent."

Mark approached Calendula. "I'll try to understand . . . mother . . . but it will take time."

"I know, Mark. And I'll give you that time. Remember that when I left, I had no proof. Who would have believed the rantings of a flower child when she claimed her husband was dead and his wealthy brother had assumed his identity? They would have thought I was either on hallucinogens or mad." She wiped the tears from her face. "We were both robbed."

He put his arms around her, giving her a brief hug.

Calendula spoke to Todd. "Todd, I want you to have my share of the recipe. You probably added your own touches to it. You're such a genius in the kitchen, you deserve it! I can't cook anyway." She smiled wanly.

"I won't hear of it!" Todd joined them. "We'll all be partners! The three of us! Calendula, you can do readings. Mark, it's time you stopped gallivanting around the globe searching for spirits when the best spirit is right here in your own backyard." He waggled his eyebrows at him.

Mark laughed. "All right—it's a deal, but you keep fifty percent, Todd. Otherwise Calendula and I might gang up on you."

Todd grinned. "Done! Say, what ideas do you have for decorating that musty wing . . ." They walked off into the parlor. These three friends had been through a lot; they would heal together.

"Another fine mystery solved, Captain!"

"Aye, Blooey!" Tyber sat back down and sipped his wine.

Zanita glanced at the doorway and saw a shadowy image of a white dog. He wagged his tail and barked happily at her, then disappeared. She blinked. *Asta*!

She snapped her fingers. *That's what this reminded me of!* Giggling, she picked up her drink and clinked it against her husband's glass. "To our favorite ghosts and the people who love them," she toasted.

He raised an eyebrow. "Well said, Mrs. Evans. To our beloved ghosts."

Chapter Fifteen

They returned to My Father's Mansion late that evening, choosing to let Todd and his new partners begin their bonding and healing in peace.

However, "peace" was not the operative word on the Evans front.

Mills and Gregor had bickered the entire way back on the late ferry, which turned into a freezing torture. Blooey sang "Sail Away, Joe" until they couldn't stand it anymore. Cody tested his "babe-o-meter" on the few hapless female passengers on board. And, as a finale, Hambone suddenly decided to slip his leash and lose himself on the boat right when it came time to depart.

Cats have an uncanny sense of the best time to aggravate a human. What's more, they always go for it.

Tyber spent a good thirty-five minutes hunting

the rascal down. He finally found him cuddled up to a dockside hussy-cat. "That's where the trouble starts . . . always. C'mere, you scalawag. I don't know how you got out of that leash, but I will discover the answer."

Hambone gave him a smarmy look, which was remarkably satisfied for a fixed cat.

"Hmmm." Tyber thought a minute, then shook his head. "Nah."

The drive back to Stockboro seemed especially long. Probably because they now were driving in a caravan of three cars—theirs, Mills's, and Gregor's. They split off just before town, with Gregor following Mills to make sure she got home safe.

When Tyber and Zanita finally went through the front doors, it was blessedly silent. "Ahhhhh." Zanita sagged against the portico. "I can't tell you how happy I am to be home."

"I agree wit ya, Mrs. Captain."

"Todd was a wonderful host, but that was a very intense weekend."

"Wasn't it?" Tyber winked at her as he carried in their bag on his outstretched arms. Hambone was curled up, sleeping, on top of the bag.

Zanita noted that Tyber looked as he always did: smart, awake, devilish, raring to go. She often wondered where he got his incredible energy from. It has to be a secret molecular spin-off, she decided.

She drooped wearily onto the bottom step of

the stairs. *I'm sure I look like something Hambone would drag into the house.* Nothing a little sleep wouldn't cure, though. Still, there was something she had to point out to Tyber before she shut the case.

"You know, you never really explained how the *Prominent Homes of Nantucket* went from the top of the end table to the enclosed shelf."

He viewed her through partially lowered lids. "Didn't I?"

"No. And I'm not accepting that wild Maxie's devil theorem, either. So don't try it."

He grinned. "I think it was more a postulate than a theorem, and it's Maxwell's demon, not Maxie's devil."

"Whatever; it doesn't wash."

He gently picked up Hambone and placed him in the middle of the comfy bench in the foyer. Without opening his eyes, the cat gave a short purr, stretched one paw out as far as it could go, and continued sleeping. Ghost-busting was tough work.

"I suppose you think it was the departed spirit of the real Sasenfras, helping us along by pointing in the direction of his murderer?"

"Actually, I do."

He viewed her askance, as if checking the motor to make sure all the parts were running.

That miffed her. "You know as well as I do that there was something odd going on there!

Merville saw *something* in that wing that scared him so badly he wouldn't return—despite knowing that the real recipe was still in there. I don't think it's impossible that a ghost was haunting the place. If ever a ghost had justifiable cause, it was poor Sasenfras."

There was silence for a few seconds. "It is a possibility," he finally acknowledged.

She blinked, shocked to her teeth. Was this Tyber speaking? "I'm stunned you're admitting that."

"I said possible, baby; I did not say *probable*."

She narrowed her eyes. "You just have to qualify, don't you?"

"It is my *raison d'etre*." He smiled, showing a hint of white teeth.

She rolled her eyes. "So what is probable to you? How *did* the book move like that?"

"My bet is that somehow Mark slipped it into the cabinet when no one was watching."

"Mark?"

"Yes. I think he was trying to help Todd again."

"Then why didn't he admit to it afterwards when you confronted him about the photo?"

"He was embarrassed enough by the photo trick, and with everything else going on at that dinner, I'm sure he was happy to just let it go by; hoping that we would, too. I'm sure he also played around with the readings from the instruments."

"It sounds good, Doc, but I don't think Mark was around the table to move the book."

"Actually, he was. No one noticed it, because he was untangling the equipment cords along the floor. I checked it out. We were standing on the other side of the room at the time. That table, from that angle, is behind the side of the couch. As we were talking, he was working his way along that wall behind the couch by the floor, untangling as he went. Our attention was fixed on the photo at the time, and all he needed was a moment to take advantage of the opportunity."

"Why didn't we see him?"

"Because he was kneeling; he was briefly out of sight behind the couch. By the time you discovered the book missing, he was already up and back where he'd started. Next to you. Which also took suspicion away from him."

She looked doubtful.

"Not convinced?"

Smugly, she reversed his words, giving them back to him. "Well, it's *probable* but not possible."

A furrow appeared between his brows. "How so?"

"You see, *I* checked it out as well, and the cables did not run all the way in that direction. The power cords wrapped on the other side of that couch, the one closest to us. I don't think he went anywhere near that book or side table."

That gave Tyber pause. "Hmmm."

"Uh-huh." She grinned like the Cheshire cat. Let Mr. Left Brain deal with *that*. Right now, she was completely beat. Besides, she loved having the last word. Her eyes started to close.

"Shall I light a fire down in the parlor, Captain?" Blooey came back in from the kitchen where he had placed the pies Todd had given them to take home. They had jokingly declined the savory buns.

Tyber observed Zanita stretched out across the step; she was already fast asleep. He had never met a woman who could fall asleep as fast as Zanita. "I don't think that will be necessary tonight. We are all ready for bed."

"Aye, Captain, me and Hambone are plumb tuckered out."

"Why don't you go off to bed. I'll see to Zanita."

"Sounds fine, Captain." He turned to leave, then stopped and turned back. "I was proud to serve with ye on this mission, Captain. It was a pure pleasure seeing you in operation again."

Tyber coughed a warning, glancing over at the steps. Luckily, Zanita was fast asleep.

"Aye. In any case, I'm sure Hambone feels the same. You're a right fine captain, Captain!"

"Thank you, Blooey. You both were"—he searched for diplomacy—"very helpful."

Blooey beamed. As he scooted off to his room, Hambone raised his head, watching him. Tyber crossed his arms and waited, knowing what to expect. Sure enough, the tabby jumped down from the bench, following the little pirate to bed. It wouldn't be long before they both had their nightcaps on. Literally.

Tyber fondly watched both of them leave. There was not a doubt in his mind that Blooey and Hambone would give their all to aid him if they thought he was in trouble. Of course, the resultant effect would probably be Stoogean— but at least their hearts were in the right place.

Slinging the travel bag over one shoulder, he bent down to get his wife. Scooping her up, he slung her over his other shoulder and headed up to their room. Zanita bounced on his back as he trod easily up the stairs. When his baby was out, she was out.

Entering their bedroom, he kicked the door closed and gently laid her down on top of the oyster-shell bed. Carefully he undressed her so as not to awaken her—even though that was highly unlikely. She was in the first stages of afterburn. He chuckled at his own pun while neatly pulling a thick flannel nightie over her head, poking her arms through, one at a time. The old house was still chilly from being empty and would take a while to warm up to its usual temperature.

He unpacked their stuff, then lit a fire in the fireplace, which was across the room from the bed. He always loved a fire in the bedroom. In more ways than one. The entire time, seven pairs of fish eyes watched him as if this were the most interesting thing they had ever seen. As usual, the little guys were lined up in a row, floating in the middle of the aquarium.

Task accomplished, he went into the adjoining sitting room, snapped on the TV, and settled back in a comfortable love seat that was mostly cushions.

Picking up the remote, he began flipping through stations until he found what he wanted. A "B" sci-fi movie from the fifties. His favorite kind.

Attack of the Killer Eggplant. Yeah. This promised to be quality entertainment. He put his stocking feet up on the wide hassock. The movie started off better than expected with the eggplant from outer space making wrap sandwiches out of several remote mountain villagers. Mountain villagers always got it first. More choice courses were sure to follow.

Tyber often wondered about the select minds that had come up with his great stuff. Surely they were the warped creative geniuses of our time. Neither begging excuses nor offering any. Tyber liked to call it *cinema confusé*.

The announcer came on and informed the late-night viewing audience (consisting of five individuals other than the M.I.T. dorms) that this was to be an all-night megamonsterhorrorathon.

Which was good, because for some reason, Tyber was not very tired.

This curious state had a name.

It was called unfinished business.

After the stellar eggplant film came *The Killer Pups*, followed by *The Woodstock Vampire Project* followed by *One Flew Over the Pterodactyl's Nest*. Zanita is going to be really disappointed she missed this, he thought.

Zanita.

The reason he was still awake. He did not like unfinished business, and as far as he could tell, their challenge had not been completed.

Curls needed to throw in that proverbial white towel. His masculine orneriness demanded it. Despite everything, he knew that a part of her was scared. His nonlinear love was not afraid of commitment; she was afraid of *uncommitment*. It made no logical sense, but this was Zanita; he had figured it out.

Sure, he more than suspected that she had set him up even while he was setting her up. That was one of the reasons he loved her so much. She always surprised him—

He stopped.

Just as she loved for him to surprise her. It couldn't have been too hard for her to come up with this fear-based challenge. But it was unfounded.

What she was afraid of would never happen.

The way they continually surprised and refreshed each other was part of their very makeup. It was intrinsic to who they were as individuals and as a couple.

The fact that they were always going to be different was never going to change.

Analyzing that statement boggled him for a moment. He was positive it was a paradox.

A beautiful paradox.

He watched the movie while one part of his mind worked on the problem that was no problem, and how to solve it. For a man like Tyber, who lived to solve the unsolvable, this was close to paradise. Being in his Zanita's embrace *was* paradise. He was not going to give up until the last T was crossed.

Finally, at three a.m., right in the middle of the pterodactyl nest, he had it.

A broad smile etched its way across his face, ear to ear.

Yes, that would do it, he acknowledged.

That would do it just fine.

He snapped the TV off and tugged on his boots.

Zanita felt something fiddling with her feet. Even in her sleepy state, she recognized those sensitive hands.

"Tyber, wha' are you doin' with my feet?" she mumbled groggily.

"Putting some heavy argyle socks on them."

387

" 'Kay." She started to fall back asleep, but the response nagged at her semi-unconscious mind. "Why are you doing that, Tyber?" She still hadn't opened her eyes.

"So your 'feets' won't get cold when we go outside."

"Oh."

Her eyes popped open. *"What do you mean, when we go outside? What are you doing?"*

His hands slid under her, lifting her up into his arms. "You'll see, baby," he promised.

"But it's freezing out there!" She squirmed in his arms. As he walked by the love seat in the sitting room, he grabbed a green chenille throw, draping it around her like a shawl.

Carrying her securely in his arms, he proceeded to descend the stairs. With a determined step, he negotiated his way through the halls and kitchen to the mud room in the back of the house, right out the door into the night.

"Where are we going?" She glared up at him.

"Shhhh."

His boots crunched through the snow as he hiked across the back fields. The land was rolling, with small hills and gullies. At one time, it had probably been used as pasture.

Forest surround the perimeter of the vast estate, making a black silhouette against the dark night sky. A full moon lit their way, causing moonbeams to dance on the glistening snow.

Their warm breaths made spiraling streamers of white mist in the cold air.

"Are we going to the woods?"

"Nope." He reached the center of the pasture and stopped. There, he inexplicably pivoted around on a boot heel. "Tell me what you see."

Zanita gave him a look that questioned his sanity, then observed the rear view of My Father's Mansion. The grand old Victorian was bathed in silvery light. Blooey had left a few night lights on. Illumination also came from their bedroom and sitting-room windows. Even from this distance, she could see the flickering shadows cast by the lit fireplace in the bedroom.

As always, the house filled her senses with warmth, calling out a silent welcome.

It was an extraordinary haven created by two very eccentric scientists.

"I see the house," she replied carefully, wondering what he was up to and why he had brought her out here in the middle of the wintry night, wrapped in a blanket.

"Look again, baby."

What was he seeking? She looked again. "All right. I see a *home*."

The corners of his lips curled slightly. "Better. Try once more."

She exhaled heavily. "I don't know what you—"

"Whose home?" he interjected.

At once she had an idea as to what he was

doing. She swallowed. "Well, Blooey's and Hambone's and yours, of course . . ."

"And yours," he said quietly, waiting.

"And mine," she agreed softly.

He cradled her to him. "I deeded over half the house to you, baby."

She gasped. "When did you do that?"

"Before we left for the Vineyard."

"Tyber, you shouldn't have! This house means so much to you. It's your dream."

"*You* are my dream. The house is simply a place where we can realize that dream. It's important to me that you understand that. It's important to me that you understand what you mean to me. Wherever we go, as long as we are together, that's the dream."

Her eyes filled with tears at his beautiful words of love. "Tyber . . . I just can't think of anything to say to follow that, except that I feel exactly the same way. I love you."

He kissed her. It was not an erotic kiss. It was a forever kiss of deep and abiding feeling. She felt it to her argyle-covered toes.

But what started out as pure love soon became pure passion. As heat flared between them, Tyber groaned against her lips, slipping his tongue inside her mouth. A small current of air, a combination of surprise and excitement, went from her mouth to his. A tingle breath.

A sweet tremor ran through him.

Zanita sighed against his warm lips. Surprising her, his hands suddenly splayed beneath her arms, lifting her up level with his face. His voice was raw against her throat and surely hot enough to melt all the snow in the field surrounding them. "Put your legs around my waist, baby."

"Like this?" Her legs went securely around him, tightening about his waist. The hard bulge under his zipper pressed tightly against her groin. The placement was highly intoxicating to both of them.

A sound of raw pleasure burst from him. "God, yes."

Zanita vocalized ardently against the folds of his ear. "I want you inside, Tyber . . . right now."

He groaned, deep and rough. "Are you trying to kill me?"

She nibbled on the curve of his sexy bottom lip. "Yes, with the little death, *la petite mort.* Right now, Tyber." Boldly her hand snaked down between her thighs and deftly unbuttoned his pants, releasing him.

"You're right, it is cold out here," he teased, tugging sharply on her earlobe.

She laughed, a happy sound in the night. "I'll make you warm," she promised.

"Oh, I know you will." Pirate lips pressed to the center of her chest, just above the scoop neckline of her nightgown. They were followed by a hot tongue dipping low under the edge of the fabric. He bit the tip of her breast gently over the flannel. "Remind me to bring you out here again in the spring."

"Why?" Her lips skimmed the top of his head; the supple chestnut strands shifted seductively against her mouth, chin, and throat.

"So I can wrap you in that lace we brought back." She felt his smile. "This flannel is too damn thick."

"You're spoiled." To show him how spoiled, her hand stroked his manhood, circling the thick length in a snug clasp. Her thighs drew closer around his hips at the same time.

A shiver traveled through him at her bold action. "You're right," he drawled hoarsely. "I'm spoiled for you." His hand reached under her gown to cup a warm buttock. "You know, baby, these make great winter hand-warmers." He playfully squeezed the round globes. "Come to think of it—year round."

"Stop that. I am not your personal human glove—" She stopped, her mouth forming an "O" as she realized what she had just inadvertently said.

He threw back his head and roared with laughter.

She turned beet red. "I didn't mean that the way it—*Oh!*"

He sank inside her, proving that she could be a very nice glove indeed. "Feels so nice, so warm . . ." he whispered against her lips before taking them in a scalding siege. He moved his hips in on her, gliding easily back and forth in the slick channel. "Like cashmere," he rasped.

"Oh god." Zanita was both abashed and excited by his intimate allusion.

Tyber kept moving inside her, steady, slow, with languid transitions. The rhythmic cadence reflected the aura of the night.

He was simply perfect.

For her.

"Look up, Zanita, at the stars." He moaned huskily, lost in the moment. In her.

She did as he instructed. All across the sky, streaking lights blazed across the heavens. "It's—it's so beautiful!" The presence of eternity was above and inside her. Transitory life fused to everlasting essence.

Love.

Her arms encircled his neck tighter.

He had known about the meteor shower. Her pirate-physicist had anticipated the event and carefully woven it into the fabric of their lives. A beautifully illustrated lesson on the nature of yin/yang, light/dark, man/woman.

The dual nature of all things came home to her.

In that moment, she truly understood the underlying principles of quantum theory; the bridge between Eastern mysticism and high-energy physics.

The moment of their ultimate release lasted forever; the moment was instantaneous.

Zanita rested her forehead against his; it was slightly damp. As they regained their breath, the cool, dry night evaporated the moisture from their skin. The scent of wood smoke tinged the air.

Tyber glanced over her shoulder. Then did a double take. He squinted, trying to focus on something in the distance.

"What is it?" Zanita turned slightly in his arms to see what it was that had caught his attention.

There, against the sky, on a hillock, twelve hogs marched. They snuffled gleefully across the landscape, illuminated by the moonlight. The Lenny Bruces of the hog world.

Zanita was shocked. Joe Sprit's hogs had busted loose again! In a dazzling display of individuality, they were stomping through the fields in the middle of the night.

"What are they doing all the way out here?"

"Apparently, there's only so much a feng shui master can do," Tyber commented drily. "Some of us"—he nodded to the Hogs, who were disappearing over the rise—"just need to be out and about every now and then to experience life."

She smiled, watching until the last squiggly tail was lost to sight. "So tell me, Tyber, are we actually married or not?"

An unholy light came into his pastel eyes. The left corner of that sensual mouth lifted in a sardonic grin. "I don't think I'm going to tell you."

Her mouth dropped open. "What do you mean, you're not going to tell me!"

He stared at her, waiting.

She bit her lower lip. If Tyber didn't tell her, then she would be forever wondering if they were or weren't. *Something sounded familiar about that.* It had a ring of duality to it . . .

Suddenly she broke into a huge smile and hugged him to her tightly.

Theoretically, like Schrödinger's infamous cat, as long as she didn't "lift that box," they would be . . . yet might not be.

It was the perfect cosmic solution.

She sighed happily.

And that was how Tyberius Augustus Evans, genius extraordinaire, won the challenge to solve their life together. He created a perpetual mystery machine.

Sometimes it was good to be a physicist.

HIGH ENERGY DARA JOY

Zanita Masterson knows nothing about physics, until a reporting job leads her to Tyberius Evans. The rogue scientist is six feet of piercing blue eyes, rock-hard muscles and maverick ideas—with his own masterful equation for sizzling ecstasy and high energy.

___4438-2 $4.99 US/$5.99 CAN

Dorchester Publishing Co., Inc.
P.O. Box 6640
Wayne, PA 19087-8640

Please add $1.75 for shipping and handling for the first book and $.50 for each book thereafter. NY, NYC, and PA residents, please add appropriate sales tax. No cash, stamps, or C.O.D.s. All orders shipped within 6 weeks via postal service book rate. Canadian orders require $2.00 extra postage and must be paid in U.S. dollars through a U.S. banking facility.

Name_____
Address_____
City_____ State_____ Zip_____
I have enclosed $_____ in payment for the checked book(s).
Payment <u>must</u> accompany all orders. ❏ Please send a free catalog.
    CHECK OUT OUR WEBSITE! www.dorchesterpub.com

Mine To Take

DARA JOY

He is full-blooded and untamable. A uniquely beautiful creature who can make himself irresistible to women. With his glittering green and gold eyes, silken hair, and purring voice, the stunning captive chained to the wall is exactly what Jenise needs. And he is hers to take . . . or so she believes.

___4446-3 $5.99 US/$6.99 CAN

Rejar

DARA JOY

Lord Byron thinks he's a scream, the fashionable matrons titter behind their fans at a glimpse of his hard form, and nobody knows where he came from. His startling eyes—one gold, one blue—promise a wicked passion, and his voice almost seems to purr. There is only one thing a woman thinks of when looking at a man like that. *Sex.* And there is only one woman he seems to want. *Lilac.* In her wildest dreams she never guesses that bringing a stray cat into her home will soon have her stroking the most wanted man in 1811 London....

_52178-4 $5.99 US/$6.99 CAN

Golden Man
Evelyn Rogers

Steven Marshall is the kind of guy who makes a woman think of satin sheets and steamy nights, of wild fantasies involving hot tubs and whipped cream—and then brass bands, waving flags, and Fourth of July parades. All-American terrific, that's what he is; tall and bronzed, with hair the color of the sun, thick-lashed blue eyes, and a killer grin slanted against a square jaw—a true Golden Man. He is even single. Unfortunately, he is also the President of the United States. So when average citizen Ginny Baxter finds herself his date for a diplomatic reception, she doesn't know if she is the luckiest woman in the country, or the victim of a practical joke. Either way, she is in for the ride of her life . . . and the man of her dreams.

___52295-0 $5.99 US/$6.99 CAN

Dorchester Publishing Co., Inc.
P.O. Box 6640
Wayne, PA 19087-8640

Please add $1.75 for shipping and handling for the first book and $.50 for each book thereafter. NY, NYC, and PA residents, please add appropriate sales tax. No cash, stamps, or C.O.D.s. All orders shipped within 6 weeks via postal service book rate. Canadian orders require $2.00 extra postage and must be paid in U.S. dollars through a U.S. banking facility.

Name_____
Address_____
City_____State_____Zip_____
I have enclosed $_____ in payment for the checked book(s).
Payment <u>must</u> accompany all orders. ❑ Please send a free catalog.
CHECK OUT OUR WEBSITE! www.dorchesterpub.com